SWORD *of* SARACH

SWORD *of* SARACH

A Fantasy of Family

Jo Ann Gilbert Stover

Library of Congress Control Number: 2021908734

HARDBACK: 978-1-955347-47-1
PAPERBACK: 978-1-955347-46-4
EBOOK: 978-1-955347-48-8

Ordering Information:

For orders and inquiries, please contact:
1-888-404-1388
www.goldtouchpress.com
book.orders@goldtouchpress.com

Printed in the United States of America

CONTENTS

DEDICATION

I dedicate this book to my husband, James, without whose love, ideas, and support I could never have written this story. A story that is our dream of our future life together in a new world

GLOSSARY OF TERMS

BAHURAJA	(Bah-who-ra-zhah)
SJHANARA	(Sha-hahn-a-rah)
AIALLRIIN	(Aahl-rin) Bahuraja's Mother
AKUNEM	(Ack-u-nem) Knowledge
AKUSHIEM	(Auku-sheem) Sorcery
ARAKS	Horned beasts with very long grey fur and pointed toed hooves
BALDRIC	Belt worn over one shoulder to support a sword or weaponry.
BHASHOMHOOK	(Bah-shahm A long dagger with a hooked point.
BHALOK	(Bah-lock) Short Sword
BOSRUA	(Bosh-rah) Pretty Eyes
BUTSUDAN	(Boot-sue-dan) Cabinet which is used to hold religious scroll - Gohonzon
CARPA	Saddlebag
CAWJA BIRD	Purple-headed bird that can't fly. Lays eggs anyplace.
CHAUSSES	A man's underwear
CHEENA	A cat-like animal about the size of a small tiger

CRANTIONS	Sea bird which builds nest in water. Has leather-like feathers.
DRESHER	Elven woman's clothing. Similar to a jumper with loose leggings. Has several pockets all around.
ECLOT	A small fat lizard
ESOGI EON	An indefinite length of time.
GAZABIRD	Bird without feathers - more lizard-like, yet flies
GHOLAC	(Go-lak) Mist of spirits
GHOLUMS	Mindless creatures which do the bidding of their masters. Can be in any form or material - Rock, wood, etc.
GORKA	A sleek horse-like animal with small scales and a head and tail like a lizard.
GORSKA	A stag-like animal hunted for it's tough hide and meat.
GURMON	A turtle-like creature which lived near and in the seas.
HADJII	(Haud-gee) The Ancient One's assistant
HAUBERK	Coat of armour, usually a type of chainmail
KAIBARA	(Kay-bara) Pet name of Bahuraja's gorka
LAMAISH	(Lama-eesh) Lover
MYAHAIEM	(My-ah-hay-eem) Peace
MJOHORA	(Mah-yo-hora) Father

MOANNA LEAVES	Thick spongy leaves which, when ground, become a pulpy mass. Used for healing cuts and bruises. Grow on a very small round bush.
MYAHAUM	(Meya-haum) Mother
MYU-SHOLAITOC	(Mao-sho-laee-tock) Swear-word meaning offspring of a female thoad.
ORRIS	Iris-like flower whose roots make potion for stomach ailments.
NAMU	(Namoo) Member of the graceful crane family; known for it sacrifice of self for its own; considered sacred by some sects.
NARA	New moon, by Elven reckoning.
SANSEI	Teacher
SESHU	Woman's garment with two wide straps of soft material crossing at neck, going down the front - covering the breasts - and attaching at the waist with a slim band. The skirt is two wide pieces of cloth at front and back and open at the sides.
SJOGAI	(Shogeye) Bahuraja's dragon-bodied alter ego created in his other life.
SURAHM	(Shur-aahm) Friend
SKELLERS	About 2 1/2 cents
THISKA	Small antelope with long curved and ridged horns.
THOAD	Mythical frog creature with claw feet and head of a lion.

SWORD OF SARACH
PROLOGUE

The mists were coming. Bahuraja sensed them even in his dream-sleep; the sleep before awakening. Panic gripped him and before he was fully awake, his hand had automatically reached for his sword. The dim light of pre-dawn touched his sweat-drenched face and his eyes slowly cleared. Awareness finally came upon him and he realized where he was.

Relaxing, his fingers left the hilt of the mighty sword, the Sword of Sarach, and he lay back upon his pillow of soft furs. A ragged sigh escaped his lips as he struggled to ease the tenseness in his body. He turned his head slightly to gaze upon the sleeping figure beside him. Sjhanara, his wife, lay quietly breathing in sleep. Her golden hair framed her face in soft ringlets and spread across her shoulders.

Bahuraja reached out and lightly touched one of the golden strands. His dream, temporarily forgotten, he felt the warmth of her body next to his. The blood began to course through his veins as he gazed upon his lovely wife.

As if she sensed his gaze, Sjhanara moved slightly, a soft sigh coming from her full red lips. As she moved, the coverlet exposed one of her breasts. Desire swept over Bahuraja as waves of the sea swept to the shores of his homeland. Bending over to kiss her eyelids, causing her to moan softly.

Rising to gaze once again once her face, Bahuraja saw her eyes open. Green eyes, flecked with gold specks sleepily caressed his face from beneath long dark lashes.

"So, my lord", her husky voice whispered, "me thinks passion becomes thy quest".

"Wife, with you beside me, can I ever think upon affairs of duty?" Sjhanara's reached up to pull her husband closer so she could seek his lips.

"Right now, my lamaish, this is your duty." Her lips brushed his and her body moved even closer to his.

Bahuraja could feel his wife's heart beating against his hard muscular chest as she raised her face for his lingering kiss.

Her lips and her eyes - oh, those eyes - so full of love and desire.

Later, their passion temporarily quenched, the couple lay wrapped in each other's arms for several moments languishing in the warmth of the aftermath of their lovemaking.

"You never cease to amaze me, wife", Bahuraja whispered as his lips brushed a damp tendril near her ear. "No matter when desire takes hold of me, you are always ready. You never refuse me. And it is always more exciting than the time before - even after all the years of our being together."

"It is not so difficult, my lord", the softness of her voice was like a caress. "I cannot imagine a better or more exciting lover than my mighty husband. Your mere presence can awaken my desire so I have no wish to refuse such pleasures."

"Ahh, spoken like a dutiful wife", chuckled the lord of the Manor Sarach. Pinching her backside, he evoked a squeal that culminated in a half-hearted tussle of tickling and laughter. Then, totally out of breath, the two lay back and relaxed for a while longer before the duties of the day commanded their attentions.

Bahuraja's mind involuntarily sought the outer reaches to explore and seek.

Sjhanara, her mind touching his, softly spoke. "My husband, what do you seek to find that is not here?"

He turned to her, a small frown playing across his rugged features. "In my dream-sleep I sensed something and seek to know if it was only a dream or if perchance there could be some reality to it."

"You are wise to do so, my lord, for you were not dreaming. I have known since moonrise that the Mists do come."

Bahuraja tensed as he watched his wife rise and leave their bed of love and begin to walk gracefully across the stone floor to the bathing room. Her naked body brought back the memory of the passion of just a few moments before, but his thoughts crowded out that memory as his mind went back to many years before when he first encountered the deadly Mists, or Gholacs, as the Ancient Ones called them.

The Mists were not exactly as the name implied - merely a mass of softly falling water droplets or dense fog as in other worlds. The Mists - Gholacs - of the world of Bahuraja Muebin Sarach were the energies of thousands of entities massed together to form a body; a body with no form, yet with a power of which no mere mortal could contend. It was as a young man that Bahuraja had first encountered the Mists. It was also this encounter that had brought Sjhanara to him.

These memories flooded into Sjhanara's mind too as she entered the bathing room of Castle Sarach. The steaming waters enveloped her still firm body as she stepped into the tile-encased pool.

"Ah, Destiny", her soft laugh echoed across the room. Light from the window casement made the water dance with a myriad of lights as Sjhanara arched her body into the scented aqua depths.

DESTINY REVISITED

The Ancient One carefully measured the exact amount of the green liquid into the now steaming cauldron. A putrid odor filled the darkened cave-like room, lit only by the fire on which the cauldron rested. Satisfied with the results, the wizened figure hobbled to a raised dais near the center of the room.

Kneeling, before an ornate cabinet, he opened the exquisitely carved doors. Selecting an aromatic stick of incense from one of the several jars, he placed one end into a holder. With a slight flick of one of his bony fingers, a flame leaped to the exposed end of the stick and the scented smoke spiraled upward to the roof of the room. Satisfied that all was in order, the old one closed his eyes, placed his palms together and began to chant the words to an incantation so old that even he had forgotten its origins.

As the words left his lips, the room began to shimmer and its contours lose shape. A shiver ran through the old one's frail frame, but his voice strengthened.

For hours the chanting droned on. Worlds - planets long extinct and yet to be formed – swirled around the bent figure. Faces and voices of spirits of every age, culture and universe joined to became one with his. His body floated above the now indistinguishable floor. Colors of every hue mixed and separated - created scenes in the air - then vanished nearly as soon as they formed.

Music, sometimes soft, sometimes so loud it would have deafened normal hearing, filled space and time. Its din was both beautiful and terrible - created by every instrument known to the ages.

After a time, the shimmering began to subside. The sounds and colors faded. Again the room resumed its normal shape and the ancient one ceased his incantations. As he creakingly arose from his kneeling position, joints protesting their long period of idleness, his red rimmed old eyes gazed upon the scroll in front of him. The ancient figures etched upon it seemed for a moment to have separated from the parchment and hung suspended in midair, and then, slowly settled back upon it.

Sighing, the old man reached forth gnarled, twisted fingers and closed the doors of the butsudan in which the scroll was housed. Satisfied with what he had witnessed, he returned once again to stir the cauldron at the fire.

He was tired, this old one. He could not remember his beginnings. It was as if he had always been. His thin parchment-like skin draped over crackling bones. Scraggly wisps of white hair clung desperately to the mottled head. His hands were thin and gnarled, with fingers like claws, the nails long and twisted. He wore a cloak of indescribable material, or color, that seemed to have a life of its own at times.

The most commanding part of this figure, however, was the head that rested upon this frail bony frame. Above the hawk-like beak of a nose and sliver of a mouth were eyes that held every secret of every universe. They were red-rimmed and overshadowed with heavy dark brows, but a fire emanated from them that belied age and space.

To gaze into them meant to fall into another dimension. These eyes had seen the creation of all things and the destruction of many. The wisdom contained within was the culmination of esoge eons of knowledge.

Passing his hand over these eyes, the Ancient One sighed. He was tired. The chanting had temporarily released him from the bonds of body and time, but now the rigors of age resumed their place and reminded their host of their presence.

Taking a wooden cup from a shelf near the fire, the old one dipped it into the boiling liquid. Raising the cup to his parched thin lips, he drank the contents noisily until there was nothing left.

Walking to a pallet covered with furs, he laid down to await the visitor he had seen in his vision. Once again, a sigh escaped his lips. "This time," he thought, "this time I know what I've missed before. I'm sure now that I have the right one to fulfill the prophesy." With this, he closed his eyes and drifted into a dreamless sleep.

What the Ancient One had missed had taken place more than an esoge eon before - in a distant place not even of this sphere. He was wise, this oracle of acumen, but even he had to search Time for the information that would bring forth his vision of prophesy.

He had not always been of this sphere. At its creation, the Keeper had sent him to record and supervise its histories. All universes, planets, elements, had to be kept track of and the peoples or inhabitants (if any) were recorded as meticulously as a cipher kept his books. So it was, this Ancient One, as was the name most called him, had witnessed, recorded, watched over, and occasionally, made alterations to the happenings of Acarda and its surrounding planetary bodies.

It was the only way continuous balance and harmony could be kept in the Universal Sea.

Throughout the eons, there occasionally occurred a phenomenon of notable consequence. The creation of Acarda was just such an occurrence. For this reason, the Ancient One had determined it was time for his divine intervention, as it were, in order for a slight error of history to be corrected.

Little did the young Bahuraja Muebin Sarach know that he was to be the instrument of that correction.

A NEW CREATION

When Acarda had been created, it was not the creation of normal consequence. No God, or Divine Creator had formed this sphere; it was the creation of an enlightened mind of one who had lived many eons before in a distant galaxy of this same universe.

This enlightened creator had possessed a physical body and had progressed through several lifetimes on a planet called Earth the third planet from its sun in the Milky Way galaxy.

His physical name on Earth was James. This name has no real significance here, but what is noteworthy, is that in one of his former lives in this plane, his name had been Bahuraja Muebin Sarach. It was this name that James had reclaimed in his later years.

As this entity progressed to its final stages, it had learned a great deal about life and the spirit. James came to realize that *Man*, as the mortals of his sphere were known, was the bearer of flaws that were capable of destroying itself.

Through enlightenment, attained after years of deep meditation and study of ancient laws, James learned of one of his names in one of several former lives. In that other, earlier life, Bahuraja Muebin Sarach had been a great warrior, statesman and humanitarian. Wanting to emulate these traits, James had searched for ways to help humankind, but found that the people either resented his ideas, or wanted him to do all things for them while they languished in apathy and self-pity.

Eventually, this Bahuraja retreated into himself and became a recluse. He came to realize that only through personal enlightenment could he attain the higher law of existence. Eventually he sought Nervana in order to leave this world for a higher plane.

James, through constant meditation and prayer, sought and tapped the essence of his former self. It was thus that the new Bahuraja Muebin Sarach came into existence and that James ceased to be.

After much trial and error, this Bahuraja also learned how to change the molecular structure of matter. With this knowledge, he could dismantle any object and put it back together again as it was, or by utilizing other matter along with it, create something else.

At first it had been a game to James, or Bahuraja, as he again began to call himself, but then he began using his skills to correct things in his world that he found in need, such as had the original self. He healed many of the sick and deformed, helped form better areas of living where *Man's* pollution had destroyed the waters and land.

His main source of interest, however, was the children. Having been an abused child in this lifetime as James, he desired to see the young have more so that they could perhaps help their world survive and help return it to its former beauty.

One would think that such a person would become revered by his society and bring great honor upon himself, but not the society in which this entity lived. The opposing factors that always exist in all creations for the sake of universal balance, banded together to destroy the only hope their world had for survival. They, as well as most of the other members of this society, could not understand how or why anyone would use such a power for the good of mankind instead of for his own self interests. If these opposing factions did not have this power to use as *they* saw fit, then they did not even want it to exist.

By the time the world leaders had collaborated and were actively seeking the means with which to destroy this master of molecular manipulation, Bahuraja had realized that his was a losing battle, despite all his good intentions and power. He could have destroyed the planet, but he actually loved all humankind in spite of their ignorance; to destroy the people was abhorrent to his nature. There had been enough killing and brutality and his endeavors had been to sow love and healing.

No, Bahuraja could not find it within himself to utilize his abilities in a destructive way. Therefore, after much meditation and planning, he brought forth all his energies to create a new planet on which he could formulate a better *PLAN* for life. Bahuraja sought permission, of course, of the Ultimate Creator and was granted that permission. This was quite unusual, of course, but Bahuraja was deemed worthy and was given that permission.

Mentally, he was allowed to go forth into the cosmos, select a desired location, gather together all the elements with which to create his new world. Then, he carefully selected the spirits of those individuals who had sought his tutelage and were totally in tune with him. Together, they would inhabit the newly created world and set up housekeeping. It didn't happen overnight, of course, but Bahuraja was given just a bit of assistance because his cause was just.

When Bahuraja was satisfied that his new world was as he wanted it, he assumed the form of a dragon, an alter ego he had also created, and took one last flight over the Earth. Tears flowed as he viewed *Man's* destruction of this planet that had once been so pure and beautiful.

Returning once again to his castle, Bahuraja spent time walking through the ornately carved and decorated rooms. How peaceful and beautiful was this place of his own design.

Bahuraja had created his castle on a remote island near the country of Japan. It was a tall and imposing structure of black obsidian with many spires and decorated with gargoyles and dragon heads.

The rooms were sparse in furnishings, but what did exist were rich in gold and other precious metals and fabrics. Richly embroidered tapestries hung from the walls and hand-painted porcelain vases stood as silent sentinels in corners.

The most imposing room held a giant Buhsudan. This Bahuraja had created by hand of the finest woods and lacquers. Having turned to an ancient philosophy of Buddhism in this life, Bahuraja had created this structure as the focal point of his deep meditation.

Ancient symbols were carefully carved on every side. A small table sat before it. Upon the table was a bowl of fresh fruit, a small porcelain container that contained a live bonsai tree, ornate holders for candles, and incense. All these represented life and the philosophy he had embraced. Enclosed behind the ornately hinged doors was a large parchment, or Gohonzon, with more ancient symbols written upon it. The words had been inscribed by an old Buddhist priest, a sensai, or teacher, according to the philosophy, and given to Bahuraja many years before.

It was to this room and this structure Bahuraja returned for the last time.

After donning a robe of the finest of silks and placing silk slippers upon his feet, Bahuraja entered the large room in which the Butsudan stood. He opened its ornately carved doors, lit incense and candles, and kneeled before the Gohonzon housed within. With prayer beads in hand, Bahuraja.

He was so tired. The words that normally brought peace and strength, had a finality about them. Raising his eyes to the inscriptions on the Gohonzon, he saw his former lives as well as his present one pass before him. He saw all those whom he had loved, some who had returned love, but many who had scorned him.

His had been a difficult life, but he had conquered it and now it was time to leave this sphere and return to the Life Force that had spawned him in the Beginning. Only from this force would this enlightened being be able to travel to the new world he had created.

The chanting and meditation completed, Bahuraja closed the doors of the Butsudan, but left one candle burning as a light to his passing. Placing one of the many finely hand-embroidered pillows beneath his head, he lay down before the Gohonzon. With hands folded across his chest, he closed his eyes and willed himself into his final sleep. Breathing and heart rate slowed until it finally ceased altogether.

If there had been an observer, one would have seen a wisp of vapor come forth from the body and hover for a few moments before rising and disappearing through the ceiling. A shudder passed through the castle walls and suddenly it and everything within began to glow with a strange blue light. Almost with a sigh, the whole island disappeared into nothingness. The memory and creations of Bahuraja Muebin Sarach and all he had been in this world were no more.

What happened to the old Earth? Well, the histories record that in a few years it nearly accomplished the total destruction of itself. However, the Keeper, in His infinite Wisdom, never allowed anything of possible future value to become totally destroyed. Upon Command, a former Savior, returned to this planet and restored order. But then, that is another story.

NEW BEGINNINGS -
BIRTH OF A CREATOR

The entity floated through the swirling mass of space. It was comfortable there; no pain or stress to inhibit progress through the eons of Time and Space. It could detect planetary bodies and cosmic debris as they passed by, but for the most part, this entity was alone in the void. Occasionally, it could detect the thoughts of other entities, but it did not try to discover their origins. If there had been the presence of feelings, the entity would have been said to have been totally at peace with its surroundings.

The flowing energy forces of the Universal Sea sustained this entity as it continued its journey. It really needed nothing else to exist. And yet, it seemed to be searching. It had a destination, as yet unfound. For time unmeasured it had roamed through this cosmic flow. Occasionally something would cause it to investigate a planet or group of planets within the galaxy, but after a closer look, the entity would retreat and continue on.

Eventually, the entity felt a drastic change in the flow of the sea. A ripple caused it to shudder and the entity felt itself drawn through the darkness of space into a bright cloud-like mass.

It struggled to free itself, but to no avail. This entity was not without intelligence or power, yet it had no control over this mass. It seemed that the more the entity struggled, the tighter the mass closed in upon it. After a time, the entity ceased its struggling and let the mass carry it. Another shudder revealed the mass changing into a tunnel formation. The entity was thrown through the center of this tunnel with a force that would have destroyed normal molecular formations.

This passage seemed to last for ages, yet in truth was only a fraction of time as we would measure it. An even brighter light began to form at the end of this tunnel. The entity could detect a slackening of its momentum.

As it neared the brighter light, a thickening of an atmosphere could be detected. There was an explosion as the entity passed through the light, then, nothingness. All awareness vanished. The opening to the Universal Sea closed, the mass dissipated, the bright light evaporated.

The entity was no longer a part of it. It was as if it had been spit out into another realm; as, indeed, it had been.

The fire lit room came alive with the gusty cry of the newly born infant. No slap on its blood-spattered behind was needed for it to fill its lungs and angrily vent its protests to this world it had jetted into just moments before.

The mid-wife carefully cleaned and wrapped the still protesting infant and then laid him to his mother's breast where his tiny bow of a mouth immediately began to suckle noisily.

A huge tower of a man entered the berthing room and knelt at the side of his wife. Pulling aside the wrapping, he examined his son from head to toe.

"You have honored me, dearest wife", his deep voice, filled with emotion, temporarily halted the feeding and startled the infant, but his mother guided her nipple once again to the tiny lips and the babe resumed suckling.

"I am happy to be the wife who brings such an honor to her husband", replied the woman.

"He is a beautifully formed child, is he not, my lord?"

"Indeed he is, my love, indeed he is, but not nearly as beautiful as his mother." Rising to place a kiss on the forehead of his wife, the Lord of Clan Sarach gazed down upon the mother and child. His love for both was clearly visible in his eyes.

"Rest now, Aiallriin. I will announce our child's birth to the rest of the clan and look in on you later. You and our young son will no doubt have many visitors on the morrow."

Kissing his wife one more time, the proud new father exited the room and went forth to appear before the crowd of people who had been gathering near the manor to await the birth of the child of their leader.

"It's a boy-child! Let the Clan rejoice! A boy-child is born to the mighty Clan Sarach!"

No sooner had the words been spoken than a cheer went up from the people. Someone began a jaunty tune on their flute and another began a dance. Flasks of wine were passed around and tipped in salute to their leader and to celebrate the birth of his son. A proud man was he who could boast that his first-born was a healthy boy. Hadn't the sages foretold that great things could be expected from this birth? All the heavenly signs and portents had foretold this event. Hadn't they always been proud to be a member of the mighty Clan of Sarach?

So intent on their celebration, the crowd did not notice the tiny gnome-like creature that had crept from the edges of the forest. Keeping to the shadows, he entered a back door of the manor and crept along the hallway until he came to the berthing room.

Making sure no one could see him, he entered and waddled to the cradle where the now sleeping infant lay. Carefully, so as not to disturb the child, or the resting mother, the creature lifted the blanket and searched until he found a mark on the buttocks of the babe.

It resembled the shape of the Namu bird, wings encircled above its head. The Namu was a sacred beautiful creature, noted for its sacrificial care of its young. The people considered it a good omen if a Namu nested nearby. They truly believed the Namu was a magical bird.

Nodding, the little elven carefully replaced the blanket and evaporated from the room and the house as quickly as he had come.

Far away, in a distant cave, a withered old sage stirred on his fur-covered pallet. A time clock seemed to swing its pendulum in his brain and announce an event in history that deserved recording. His assistant, Hadjii, the elven creature, would soon arrive and provide a full report. The Old One smiled, even in sleep, turned over and resumed snoring.

THE NAMING

Bahuraja Muebin Sarach was of noble birth. His father, Odjin, the Great, Lord and Clan leader of the Clan Sarach, had ruled this plane before his son. Odjin had earned the respect and leadership of his kinsmen by being a fair and just man. Many were the tales the young prince would hear at the knee of his father and many were the battles he would learn of from the other members of the Clan Sarach. Although a peaceful tribe for the most part, they could be a fierce foe in battle if ever their peace was threatened.

The battles for some time now, however, were contained in hunting the wild gorska or araks, the main source of meat and hides. Small hunting parties would set out every few weeks in search for the herds and after a successful foray, the men would sit around the fires and swap stories of the bravery or daring of this one or that one.

Bahuraja's father could hardly wait until his lusty son was old enough to begin instruction in the use of weaponry and go with him on his first hunt.

On the eighth day after a birth, it was the custom to present the newborn child for a naming ceremony. The whole clan was present because this child was the son of the king. The diverse colors of dress of the many visiting dignitaries from other nearby clans were also in attendance.

They knew that someday this child would be king and much depended on the continued good relations between clans.

The village priest was just about to bless the child when a commotion near the back of the crowd stopped him. The crowd was parting to allow the figure of a bent old mystic to approach the platform where the king, queen, and other participants of the naming ceremony were standing.

"Hold there, priest", the commanding voice of the Old One belied his fragile form.

The crowd gasped and began murmuring as to who this was to interrupt the naming of the clan king's child. The priest knew immediately, however, who this personage was. He waited patiently until the traveler had reached the dais, then, bowing, stepped to one side.

The Old One walked directly to the dais and stopped in front of the king. Looking intently into his eyes, he spoke.

"King Sarach", the voice carried to even the last and furthest person in the crowd, "This child is of special birth. It is I who will name him!"

The king stepped back in astonishment. The queen put her hands to her face and began to weep. What manner of person was this to interrupt the special naming ceremony and then take it over without question?

King Odjin was about to reach for his sword, when the mystic raised his right hand. A flash of blue light shot from his finger and the king's sword became a serpent. Immediately the king dropped it to the ground where it returned to its sword-shape.

"King Sarach, wouldst thou deny thy son the birthright that is his to command? I am here because the gods hast spoken to me through the prophesies. This child is the one spoken of in the ancient tomes. Bring him forth for his proper name!"

The priest did not hesitate, but took the child from its nurse's arms and stepped before the Old One. Without hesitation, the ancient mystic placed his hand upon the quiet infant's head. With eyes closed, he began to chant words unfamiliar to the crowd. The words were so ancient that even the priest did not have knowledge of them.

As the words left the Old One's mouth, they became colored shimmering images around the child. For a short time the babe and mage were nearly invisible. The king and everyone else stood rooted to the ground in awe of what their eyes could hardly believe.

"This child, from this day forward, shall be known as Bahuraja Muebin Sarach", the droning continued. "He hast come to this plane to be the ultimate ruler. Much will be said of him in the writings of the future. His family will be blessed by him. All will honor him and revere him. He will develop powers he knew before this life and this sphere. So said by the Ultimate Keeper of the Universe, Creator of all, so said by the ancient writings, so be it!"

No sound came from the tiny babe. His eyes were intent upon the face of the Ancient One. It was as if he knew what was and what was to be. As yet, he was as he appeared - a newborn babe still needing to suckle at its mother's breast and learn.

The final words of the blessing spoken, the mystic handed the child to its mother, who grasped it to her breast as if it were about to fly away.

"Thou doest not know what thee holds, woman", the sage spoke softly to her. "But thee are blessed above all the women of Acarda. In the years to come, thou wilt praise The Ultimate Keeper of the Universe for being the one to bring forth this child."

Turning to the king, he spoke again. "Thee, above all, King Odjin, wilt rejoice at thy son. Thy seed was selected to bring forth this special fruit to the loins of thy wife. But thy duty as parent will be tested. Pray that thy strength and knowledge be up to the days ahead for the training of this child until he comes into his own."

Without further ado, the Old One began walking back through the crowd of onlookers. As he neared the edge of the people, he turned once more to the king and queen. He raised one hand and suddenly was gone.

The people found their voices once again and for a few moments chaos reigned, but the king, raising his voice with authority, soon quelled their fears. He realized that this, indeed, had been even more of a special day than he had previously known. His son had been blessed by one of the sages of old. He had read the prophesies, but never had he believed one of them would ever be about him or his seed.

Although he did not know exactly what the meaning of all that had been said by the Old One, he now knew for certain his son was of special birth.

Bahuraja Muebin Sarach! The name was strong. It had substance. What was it the Old One had said? He had been sent from another time and plane? What did this all mean? Even his own shaman did not know.

Looking down at the face of the babe, King Odjin saw only the eyes of his firstborn son. A strong, lusty child with even now a grip of iron on the king's forefinger. Whatever the future held in store for the Clan Sarach, no one could have been more proud or humbled than the King.

THE YOUNG BAHURAJA

Nearly from birth, it became apparent that the young Sarach was gifted with special powers others did not possess. It sometimes caused his father and mother concern when they would suddenly see their young son rise from the floor or his bed and go flying around the room. Or, like the time as a mere babe, he lifted a table many times his size with mind power, then sitting on top of it, rode down one of the long stone hallways causing everyone walking within it to duck and dodge to keep from being hit.

Sometimes he would startle the kitchen staff by popping out of thin air, grabbing a tiny fistful of tasty treats and, if the mood struck him, chase the fat cook until she would nearly drop. Only when she threatened to leave the manor, did the lad stop this behavior. Her cookies, cakes and pies were too delicious to lose her.

If Bahuraja's father or mother tried to discipline him, he might suddenly disappear before their very eyes. He soon learned, however, that both parents had great patience where proper manners were concerned. Whenever he decided to reappear, usually at mealtime, an even more severe punishment might be applied. His bottom was still made of human flesh, and after all, he could not stay away forever!

Not every incident was so hair-raising. There was the time three-year old Bahuraja found a bird lying on the ground with a broken wing. He gently lifted the frightened fledgling and crooned a wordless tune to it as he carefully touched the wing with his chubby fingers.

In minutes the bird was perched on the toddler's finger, flapping its healed appendage. After giving a slight peck of gratitude to its newly found friend, it flew off to join other birds of the sky.

If this should have surprised the lad, it didn't appear to. He took the things he did in stride as if they were normal things he should be doing. Besides, it delighted him.

These and many other episodes showed his parents and those around him that the young prince was endowed with great, if sometimes exasperating, gifts. The sages consulted their texts and became even more positive that prophesy was being fulfilled.

So, with sighing looks to each other, Aiallriin and Odjin tried not to suppress their son's strange habits unless they threatened to cause havoc within the household or harm to anyone.

For the most part, Bahuraja was a loner. His strange habits and abilities made most other children leery of him. But Odj, the son of Korima, the cook, became his very best friend. The two growing boys could often be found either in the hayloft of the gorka barn or beneath a tall tarbo tree eating some of the small cakes they had snitched from the kitchens.

Bahuraja would make himself invisible, pop into the kitchen, grab a few of the cakes and pass them through the window to a waiting Odj. When he reappeared outside, the two would dash to one of their secret hiding places to enjoy their ill-gotten goods and laugh at the hollering from the kitchen as Korima tried putting the blame onto one of the cook's helpers.

As he grew into young manhood, however, the young prince began using his powers less and less. He did not like to be looked upon as different or odd by his peers. He began instruction in the arts of battle and the use of the weaponry of his forefathers - the lancebow, the bhashomhook, and the bhalok. Ah yes, the bhalok. That, above all others was the clansman's byword. Without the strong double-edged blade of finest steel gripped within his fingers, a clansman was naked, and never went too far from it at any time. Despite the lack of actual war, clansmen still kept their skills honed to a fine edge as they did their blades. One never knew when they might be needed.

It became a near obsession with the youth Bahuraja to be the best amongst his peers in the use of all weaponry. He could be seen in the training yard long after the others had tired or finished their lessons - improving his already nearly perfect skills.

He had a keen sense of fair play and wanted to be the best without using any power other than his natural physical strengths. In time, he had nearly forgotten those powers had ever been a part of him.

Young Bahuraja was very quick of mind and learned rapidly. He would plague his parents and teachers with questions, some of which were very in-depth and difficult to answer. Often the teachers felt they were the ones being taught.

When the time came for his "Test of the Zandorn", or the entering into adulthood, Bahuraja was quite sure he was ready.

The Test of the Zandorn was a ritual in which all Acardian youth participated. As the ancient ones - the holders of the akunem - had set down so many eons before, the young adult Acardian would gird himself, or herself, with armor and weapons and set forth toward the setting moons - Daton and Amire. They would enter strange lands and have many tests and adventures to experience before they would again return to their tribes. This experience was designed to mature the individuals and allow them to become valuable members of their clans and tribes.

Bahuraja had fashioned a shield of tough gorska hide. With a powder ground from the tarbo root, he made an amber stain with which he drew his talisman, the Namu, on the curved outer face.

A gift from his father was a daggerhook made from the finest steel. The handle was formed from the horn of a young thiska buck. Imbedded in the handle was a stone from the Mount of Gelenese, which was said give strength to the wielder.

None of the youths could own or wear the coveted bhalok, however, until he or she had successfully completed the Test and returned to their tribe. At the ceremony of Zandorn, each successful returning youth was presented with his own personalized bhalok. This coveted weapon would have been carefully fashioned by a smith constantly in prayer during the process and given a special blessing by the local priest. It was worn with pride for the remainder of the owner's life as it testified to the successful passage of youth into maturity.

Mounting his high-spirited gorka, Kaibara, whom he had raised and trained from birth, Bahuraja presented a handsome figure as he started out of the gates of Castle Sarach. His mother, Aiallriin, tried unsuccessfully to hide the tears that welled in her eyes. Odjin said his farewells with a voice much gruffer than usual. These parents knew that their son was no longer a babe and that when he returned, he would be a man full-grown. But for all their pride, a part of them longed to keep him close to their breasts as a little boy.

A TEST OF COURAGE -
A LESSON IN FEAR

Many weeks had passed with very little to create excitement or to offer challenge. In fact, riding the long hours on the back of Kaibara had created a tenderness all the riding Bahuraja had done before had never caused.

Each night when making camp, Bahuraja would rub a salve made from Moanna leaves on his tender buttocks and thighs. This helped ease and heal the rawness created by riding. The next day's riding, however would only create more soreness.

When he entered into the Valley of the Rains, even his long heavy hand-woven cloak of softened barbray fibers did little to keep out the dampness. It seemed as though only discomfort was to be his plight.

"*When is the adventure going to begin?*", he asked the blackened clouds. Was this miserable weather a part of the testing? The only answer was more driving rain and a cold wind to go with it.

Unconsciously, Bahuraja projected his mind to seek out anything that would challenge his skills as a warrior. All he found for his trouble was the fleeting tog lizard or wild herds of gorska, a thick-skinned, but tender-meated animal hunted by Acardians for food and hide.

As has been mentioned previously, there has to be a balance in all things, which is the Order of Truth, the substance of the Universal Sea. Paradise, or Eden on the planet Earth, was sacrificed because there was only one side of the coin - continuous Good. This, at first, sounds like an ideal thing, but it is not in harmony with the Order of Truth, a balance of both Good and Evil.

Therefore, despite the creator Bahuraja's well meaning intentions when he created Acardia, some evil nature had crept into the planet's matrix. Over the eons this evil reared its ugly head occasionally to create havoc, hence, the entrance of the deadly Gholac - the Mists.

One star-filled night as the two moons - Daton and Amire shined their lavender-hued light upon the scenes below, Bahuraja tied his gorka to a tatha bush near a rock outcropping and set up a small camp for the night. A fat, freshly caught eclot sizzled over a small fire, sending a delicious aroma to tempt the appetite of the already hungry prince.

Testing to see if his catch was done enough to eat, the youth sliced off a huge chunk and got down to the business of filling his loudly protesting stomach. After eating his fill, Bahuraja wrapped the leftover portions in a piece of hide and placed it in his carpa behind the saddle. It would be every bit as tasty for the morrow's breakfast.

Now that he had eaten, the day's traveling caught up with him. Kaibara was already dozing, one scaly leg slightly bent in rest position. Wrapping his cloak around him, Bahuraja yawned, stretched and laid his head upon one arm for a pillow. He soon drifted into a deep slumber.

Dreams began to edge into his mind; troubled dreams that caused Bahuraja to writhe in his sleep. Shapeless forms seemed to press near. Voices without words tormented him.

When it seemed as though he would be smothered, Bahuraja awoke, drenched in his own sweat.

Rising slightly onto one elbow, he sat up and looked about him. The night was quiet except for the occasional nightcall of the gazabird or the coughing of the cheena. A feeling of foreboding caused the warrior to come to his feet with all senses alert. Something from the darkness without probed his mind, something that caused him to shudder. Whatever it was, it was more horrible than anything he had ever before encountered.

His mind withdrew hastily from this unseen thing, yet still Bahuraja somehow felt unclean. It was as if something had tried to soil his very soul with thought.

Shivering from more than just the night's chill, Bahuraja considered putting more branches onto the fire. Changing his mind, however, he began to clear the camp. He would leave this place now, tonight, and not wait until the dawn. Even Kaibara, his gorka, was stamping about, pulling on the strong anchorstrap that had kept him from wandering while Bahuraja slept. His eyes were wild with fear and his nostrils flared.

"I feel it too, my faithful Kaibara", the nervous youth admitted. Hastily gathering the last of his belongings and strapping them to the back of the gorka, Bahuraja turned to cover the still burning embers of the fire.

Suddenly all was darkness! The gorka screamed and could be heard thrashing about, but try as he could, Bahuraja could see nothing! A terrible weight seemed to be descending upon him; he could barely breathe! There was a humming sound that was becoming louder and louder. It was as if a thousand voices were all vying to be heard and none of them being understood.

Fighting to keep control of his senses, Bahuraja drew his bhashomhook and turned in place to protect himself from an anything that might try to surprise him in this engulfing darkness.

Fear walked up his spine and tickled at the roots of his hair. Gasping for every breath and struggling to keep from being pushed to the ground from the overwhelming weight of this unseen foe, the youth strained to see or be able to strike at something - anything!

The humming became a deafening roar. All his training had never prepared the young warrior for anything like this. Breath coming in ragged, short gasps, he yelled at the darkness. "Show yourself, you coward of the universe!

"What devil has spawned you, you accursed myu-sholaitoc of the outer reaches! Show yourself, I say!"

Heart pounding, as if it would jump from his chest, the youth staggered and reeled under the now ear-splitting noise.

Unable to keep his balance any longer in the total blackness, Bahuraja fell to the ground, covering his ears with shaking hands. *Am I to die before I can even prove myself in my first test?"* The gasping prince thought through the clanging clamor in his head.

He could barely hear the screams of his trusted gorka anymore. There was only that terrible humming, the crushing pressure of darkness, the tearing within his mind that seemed to be literally ripping his very soul from within. He could feel himself weakening. His struggles were becoming slower. There was no sense of direction - of up or down - only a black void.

It was as if the darkness had swallowed up the air and space, leaving only emptiness. It was impossible for Bahuraja to utilize any of his powers now. He knew he was dying.

With what strength he had left, he prayed. "Oh mighty Namu", he gasped, "Enfold me in your wings and carry my entity home to the breast of the Ultimate Keeper. If I am to die thus, may the gods know that I tried to die in honor."

Bahuraja felt his life forces ebbing. Consciousness was nearly gone. His last thoughts were of his parents and his home.

A HEALING ENCOUNTER

"Awaken, Warrior", a voice from a far distance seemed to beckon. "I command you to get up!" more demanding now. Bahuraja struggled to find consciousness. This was not at all like he had thought coming home to the gods would be like. His body did not want to respond to his mind. There was something cool being placed upon his brow. Then, in his mind, came a soothing chant.

"Amah, Anet, Yono, Kama. Amah, Anet, Yono, Kama." Over and over the words droned in a sweet feminine voice - definitely not his own. Strength surged through Bahuraja's veins and sinews. His mind began to clear and the heaviness lifted from his chest.

At last Bahuraja returned to full consciousness and opened his eyes. It was still dark, but a paleness near the horizon indicated dawn was approaching.

Above him, a vision framed in golden hair gazed upon him. Concern etched the beautiful features of a young woman seemingly clad in very little but a filmy seshu. Her full firm breasts lightly brushed against his chest as she leaned over him.

His senses fully returning, Bahuraja reached up to touch her hand, to see if she were real or only a figment of his imagination, a being from the beyond.

"I am real", the words formed in his mind. "The Gholac had nearly consumed you. Had I not read of your presence by the searching of your thoughts, the Mists would have absorbed you into their mass".

The woman spoke in the tongue of the people of the Monnaryu region of the Northern clans. She spoke softly, but her voice was husky and held strength.

"But, but how did you dispel them, when with all my strength and power I could not?" Bahuraja choked the words through a still tightened throat.

"My people have dealt with the Gholac before", the words were verbally spoken this time. "The Gholac dwell in a dimension of time outside of ours. Only during the flaring of our sun - when we are in the Year of Conjunction of the planets - do the Mists enter into our realm. It consumes the entities of those who cannot overcome it.

"Only those with great strength and of the Gifts of Zandorn can truly overcome it." Her manner was bold and brash.

Bahuraja recalled his youth and some of the strange powers he alone seemed to have and had not used for some time. "I was blessed at birth with gifts that no one could explain to me and yet none of them worked against that horrible apparition!"

"Yes, I sensed as much", by this time the woman had moved away from the still reclining prince and had begun putting more pieces of tasha branches on the now brightly blazing campfire.

The light from the fire danced over her scantily clad body. She was not very tall, as Bahuraja could determine even from his position on the ground. Her breasts were full and her hips showed the promise of being able to bear many children with ease. She moved with grace and yet there was a strength of purpose and determination in every movement.

This was no mere myahaum-lamaish, a woman only useful for bedding and bearing children. There was something more. He felt he should know her.

Rising to a sitting position, Bahuraja checked himself to make sure he was clear-headed enough to stand.

"There is no reason for concern, now", she spoke without turning. "You have all your facilities. I checked you over as you slept".

This was slightly disturbing. "I appreciate your intervention in my behalf", he voiced, trying not to be embarrassed. "But I still do not understand why I could not fight this, this thing with my own powers."

"Do not feel ashamed, Warrior. You could not fight the Mists entirely alone. Your powers are strong, but not yet fully proven. By your own admission, you had nearly forgotten most of them.

"By the time I could come close enough to blend my powers with yours, you were nearly gone, but even as you were losing consciousness, our powers merged and we were together able to fight the Mists back into their own dimension."

She came near again and sat down next him. "We blended perfectly and were able to control the Mists and send them back to the plane of their origin. Does it bother you that a woman helped you in your first test of the Zandorn?" The question was almost in the form of a challenge.

"How did you know that this is my ...?"

"I have searched your mind and know much about you, Prince of Sarach. Even do I know that you have a small mark upon thy hip in the shape of NAMU that was there at birth. That is why you have chosen NAMU as your talisman."

"How dare you!" Jumping up, Bahuraja presented the picture of an enraged buck gorska. "I gave you no permission to search my body or mind!"

Her laugh was full and gusty. "Ah, my surahm, you do resent me, then. Should I have left you to your own destruction? In order to help you, I had need to enter and merge with your own powers to fight the Mists. It takes more than one mind to fight them. Can I help it if all your dark secrets were a part of the bargain?

"If you would but use those powers you possess, you would also know of me. Do you not wish to thank me for helping you? No? Then shall I leave you." Still smiling, she rose.

"No, please, forgive me for the fool." Bahuraja reached out and touched her on the arm. The skin was soft and as his eyes met with hers, a strange warmth overtook him. Yes, now thoughts began to rush into his mind.

"You - your name is ... Sjhanara." Her eyes were so beautiful. He felt as though he were swimming in them. "It's funny, I almost think I should know you."

"Yes, my lord", she answered in a soft voice, "Sjhanara Yagenta Hajatnii. My homeland is many leagues from here and I, too, prepare myself in the Test of the Zandorn. But I don't think I've met you until now.

"It was chance that I was here in this valley when the Gholac attacked you. And yet, I sense that it was not chance at all. I have known many warriors, but your thoughts reached me from afar and I feel I was drawn here."

Still looking into her eyes, Bahuraja felt the magnetism drawing him as a moth to a flame. This young woman was not even up to his shoulder, and yet she vibrated strength and beauty.

"I am beyond myself", he exclaimed apologetically. "You are right. I could not have beaten the Mists alone. Please forgive me for being so ungrateful, my little bosrua. I would have been consumed had you not merged your powers with mine. I guess I was too puffed up with my own pride to admit that I needed your help."

"All is forgiven and forgotten, prince. Now I think you should see to your gorka. He lives, but is frightened beyond my ability to get close enough to heal him. Fortunately, the Gholac dos not contend itself with the lesser mind or you would be afoot."

Being reminded of Kaibara, Bahuraja pulled his eyes away from the lovely young girl and hurried to where he had tethered his gorka. The beast lay on the ground, eyes wide with fright. A wide path had been torn where its tail had thrashed in its frenzy to escape the awful darkness. A wide gash along its flank oozed greenish-tinged blood, and it was plain to see it had been caused by one of the large thorns of the tatha bush. The anchorstrap was twisted tightly around its neck, causing the poor beast to have difficulty in breathing.

Oh, Kaibara, my friend, what devils have caused you to suffer so!" Softly crooning to his gorka, Bahuraja carefully cut the anchorstrap and held Kaibara's muzzle between shaking fingers as he tried to calm the beast's fears. He then ran his hand to the spot where the gash ran its ragged path.

Searching his mind, he recalled his childhood and his strange ability to heal small animals of their injuries. It had been such a long time since he had utilized many of these talents. Would it work for him now?

Carefully placing a finger at each end of the wound, Bahuraja closed his eyes and tried mentally to picture each damaged cell. Concentrating on first one end of the gash and moving slowly to the other, his healing powers began to take effect.

Bahuraja felt Kaibara's thick skin quiver as the knitting of tissue slowly closed the gash. Soon only a long faintly green scar marred the animal's flank.

Sjhanara had by this time also moved to where the beast lay. "You truly have the power of healing, my lord. The Ultimate Keeper has gifted you greatly." Sjhanara was kneeling beside him and true admiration bathed her face.

A frown crossed the prince's brow. "This is the first time I have ever had to use this power on such a great friend. May the gods bless me with never having to use it thus again."

"Have you no other friend than this lowly gorka, then, warrior?" The words were spoken softly.

Bahuraja again looked into those disturbing eyes. "I have other friends, yes, in fact, one very close friend that I grew up with, but none so faithful as my Kaibara. I raised him from a young gorka folt whose mother died giving him birth, but even more, I cannot stand to see anything suffer - especially an animal who has served me so well."

"You are a man of complexities, Bahuraja. You are not only blessed with great powers of The Ultimate Keeper, but with compassion as well. Me thinks your life will go well."

Sjhanara turned and walked over to where her weapons lay on the ground near the fire.

"I will leave you now, oh mighty warrior. I must continue on with my own Test. My people have need of me. I have a great deal of ground to cover and much to learn before I am ready. May the gods protect you and..." her eyes lowered and a blush slightly tinged her cheeks, "may we meet again one day under much better circumstances."

Sjhanara then looked deeply into Bahuraja's eyes and for one fleeting moment their thoughts merged. Turning away quickly, she strode into the dawning day, her seshu billowing slightly away from her hips.

Bahuraja stood transfixed and watched as the vision of Sjhanara disappeared from his view. A deep longing wrenched at his chest and an emptiness never before experienced overcame him. *"What akushiem is this, that a mere woman can claim more from me than I have ever known before existed?"*

Shaking his head to clear his mind from the pictures the thought-blending had placed there, he saddled his now healed and calmed gorka and then, he, too, left the camp.

SJHANARA

Similar disturbing thoughts assailed the mind of Sjhanara as she walked along her newly chosen direction from the camp. She was not unused to the world of men, having been raised with seven brothers and no sisters, but this Bahuraja was somehow different. So easily did their thoughts merge during their brief encounter. She had felt both comfortable and ill-at-ease during the time she had been in his presence.

She had always been able to hold her own with her brothers and the other young men of her native country of Monguu. In the wild harsh forests of the northern lands, her father, Janor, had taught her the same as her brothers, much to the dismay of her mother, Sjyenti. She soon had come to hold her own in the mock battles she and her brothers participated in.

Sjhanara had not taken as easily to the world of women. Those daily feminine tasks were boring to her. Giver her a bhashomhook instead of a hearth brush any day. Her delight was in the hunt of the mighty gorska and arak, not the preparation of them for the evening meal.

Yet this handsome stranger had stirred feelings of feminine desires Sjhanara had never experienced before. She almost could picture herself at a cooking fire, preparing the evening meal for this handsome prince - Bahuraja.

The images of little ones playing near their feet gave vent to other images of the ways of man and woman. Her heart began to beat rapidly, bringing a rosy glow to her cheeks.

Sjhanara knew of these things, yet had always shied away from the advances of the young men of her village. She was not going to end up as her sisters of the tribe, a drudge to husband, children and the cooking fires. Not Sjhanara! She was going to be a mighty warrior - just like her father!

She was already his favorite of all the Hajatnii children, but that was not enough for Sjhanara. As a young child, she had toddled over near the hand-carved seat of her father, Janor, and tried to lift his double-edged sword. It represented to her Janor's great strength and power. She had seen him lovingly hone its blade to a fine sharp edge. In the firelight, it glinted brightly, seeming to have a life of its own.

Sjhanara vowed that one day she, too, would own just such a blade, maybe even this very one - her father's. She had even persuaded one of her older brothers to carve her a sword from the branch of a tawn tree - complete with some of the ancient letters of their tribe etched into the hilt.

The young girl had amused her parents and brothers with imaginary battles with the family pets until even her father's constant hunting companion and pet, Tome, would run, whimpering, to hide beneath a tasha bush to escape her.

"Little warrior of the cradle", her brothers had nicknamed her.

Sjyenti tolerated her daughter's actions, thinking that she would someday outgrow them and become interested in the ways of the women of the tribe.

She soon discovered, however, this was not going to be. All her attempts to teach her daughter the ways to prepare food, to stitch gorska hides into the clothing they wore, to clean, to weave, all such tasks were quickly rejected. As soon as her mother's back was turned, Sjhanara would escape those hated tasks and once outside, pursue her real love, the training as a warrior.

Sjhanara learned only enough domestic skills to get by, but cared nothing for the refining of those skills. Why, should she learn these stupid tasks, the girl would argue, when she, the mighty Sjhanara, would become the greatest warrior of their tribe?

Finally, her mother gave up even trying. The only real interest Sjhanara took in her mother's knowledge, was the preparation of potions and the uses of herbs for healing. This, the young girl learned with great enthusiasm. This Sjhanara knew could come in handy during a hunt if she or someone became injured or ill. Even the young men learned the importance of this knowledge.

Hoping that this, at least, would be of value to her daughter, Sjyenti fashioned a beautiful payka from softened gorska hide. Several pockets lined the inside of the payka and a wide bead-embroidered flap folded over to cover the opening.

An assortment of healing herbs, each wrapped separately in bags made from the intestines of araks, were placed into these pockets. A carved arak horn, pushed through a leather loop, held the flap in place. This bag became one of Sjhanara's treasured possessions.

Sjhanara had also displayed talents of mind-blending. This was an unusual ability that caused even more concern to her parents and siblings. This was not known to exist in other members of the tribe. Her brothers learned quickly that they must shield their minds from their young sister, or she would embarrass them at the evening table.

Once Sjhanara had innocently described, in detail, her brother Olan's exploits with a woman of a nearby village.

Olan had choked on his food and overturned his chair trying to grab Sjhanara's neck across the table.

Their mother had turned her eyes to the ceiling and placed her hands over her face in an attempt to hide her embarrassment, but Janor had roared with laughter until all were soon laughing with him. His great laugh was as catching as the swamp fever of the marshes, and no one could stay angry long when he gave vent to his mirth.

Later, however, he admonished Sjhanara in private to be more careful with her 'talent' and to keep her mental findings to herself.

Olan eventually forgave his little sister, but was very careful from then on that she could never see into his thoughts.

As Sjhanara blossomed into adulthood, her body took on the familiar curves and softness of beauty. Her long flowing air was as spun gold and her eyes a rare green with flecks of gold that danced when she smiled.

The young men of her tribe began to take notice of the young woman and many appeared before Sjhanara's father for permission to pay her court, as was the custom. But the young Sjhanara would have none of this.

"These infantile fuzzy-faced thoads should stay suckling at their mothers' breasts where they belong", she would announce. "I care not for their posturing and feeble show of strength. My path is not to the cooking fire and slavery to a man's bed. I will train for the Test of Zandorn and best all of them!"

To her dismay, Sjhanara did not grow very tall. The top of her head of golden curls only reached the lower flank of a half-grown gorka and she had difficulty manipulating some of the full-sized weaponry of the tribe.

Finally, after much badgering, Janor had his weapon-maker fashion a scaled-down metal version of the bhashomhook that

Sjhanara learned to wield with expertise. She also cajoled Gagnon, the armor maker, into creating a lightweight chest armor that allowed room for her budding breasts.

It was no small feat for him to take measurements without touching the girl. It would not do for Janor to have the armor maker's hands cut off for being too fresh. Sjhanara only laughed at the poor man's discomfort.

The result, however, was a beautifully molded piece that had two small curves in the chest plate within which Sjhanara's breasts fit quite comfortably.

The armholes were softened with leather edge bindings to lessen chaffing. As a finishing touch, Gagnon had chiseled the clan symbol - an arak head - onto the front breastplate.

Sjyenti would wail in despair and plead with her daughter to consider her father's position and the honor it would be to become the wife of one the fine young men who sought to court her, but Sjhanara turned deaf ears. In her new armor and wielding her scaled-down weaponry, she was a force to be reckoned with and no man would take this from her! After awhile, the young men who at one time had found Sjhanara desirable as a possible mate, ceased their interest. Who wanted to marry a woman who might put a blade to their throat if she became vexed over some small matter or other?

Her father finally ceased his chuckling and whenever he gazed upon his beautiful daughter, his face put on a frown of concern.

In the spring of the Year of the Nopshu, or Awakening, Sjhanara approached her father. "Myahaiem, Mjohora", she stated proudly and formally as she stood before Janor, "I come before you in full armor and skilled in the weapons and arts of our tribe and desire to venture forth to the Test of Zandorn!"

Janor looked at his beloved daughter from beneath craggy brows. The love he felt for her was evident. He saw the small budding breasts, so ripe for the tender touch of a husband. His gaze followed over the contours of her hips and thighs - now girded in the light seshu - so capable for bearing children. But as he looked upwards into Sjhanara's eyes, he saw a firm, strong, steady resolve. Her look of strength of purpose melted any objections he could have raised to her request.

"I can deny you nothing, my daughter. You have prepared yourself well for the Test of Zandorn. I can only give you a Father's Blessing." His usually gruff voice cracked a little. Then, clearing his throat, Janor indicated a place at his feet. "Kneel before me, Sjhanara."

As Sjhanara kneeled and bowed her head before her father, Janor released his bhalok from its scabbard and placed the blade upon her right shoulder. The weight of it nearly pushed her to the floor, but she concentrated on her strengths until the sword's weight became controlled.

"Sjhanara Yagenta, daughter of the Clan Hajatnii, you have the blessing of your father and clan leader to go forth to your quest. May the Ultimate Keeper's gifts be ever a part of you. Use them well and you shall reach your Destiny. Arise now, Sjhanara, and stand before me."

A trembling Sjhanara again looked into her father's eyes. "Thank you, oh mighty Janor", her voice tried to sound firm, but a quaver betrayed her. "May I always bring honor to the Clan Hajatnii and return victorious to the house of my father."

Thus stated, she betrayed the little girl still within and rushed forward to wrap her arms around Janor's neck. An observer would have seen a tiny tear course down one cheek and fall silently onto Janor's broad shoulder, but when she again stood before her father, a smile lightened her face.

"I go now to ready for the journey." Turning, she could scarcely contain herself with excitement and had difficulty keeping herself from dancing from the room instead of walking in the way of a would-be warrior.

It was well she had left hurriedly, for Janor was having difficulty in stemming a flow from his own eyes.

The very next day, Sjhanara had set out on her journey full of enthusiasm and sense of adventure. She, Sjhanara, would be brave and strong. She would fight many battles and bring even more honor to her tribe and father! As she left the encampment of her clan, Sjhanara's step was brisk and light. Her parents watched their daughter leave with mixed emotions upon their faces. Janor, proud to have a brave daughter such as Sjhanara, and Aiallriin with tear filled eyes and a fear in her heart that her only daughter would never fulfill her role as a wife and mother.

As mile after weary mile passed beneath her feet, however, and nothing of any significance occurred, Sjhanara became irritable. Even the beauty of the strange new lands she was entering did not appeal to her any more. She wondered if anything would happen where she could test her skills.

She began using her telepathic powers to reach out into the distance - searching. She had no idea what she was searching for until, one afternoon, something touched her mind that caused her to shudder. She knew immediately what it was that seemed to cause her mind to feel sullied. Then, she also detected faintly the distressed thoughts of another mind!

It was then that Sjhanara found Bahuraja and helped him fight the dreaded Gholac, or Mists.

PROGRESSION OVERSEEN

The Old One chuckled as the scene faded and the brew resumed its thick bubbling in the huge caldron. Looking very pleased with himself, the frail ancient began searching through the many vials and crocks lining the stone walls of the room. Taking a sip of this, and a pinch or two of that, he added it to the caldron and began to hum a strange tuneless melody.

"All goes well, Master?" Hadjii had popped into the room unnoticed and his unannounced entrance startled the old man.

He dropped one of the vials he held and it fell with a crash to the stone floor, spilling its smelly contents. "Hadjii, when wilt thee ever learn not to sneak up on me?" He tried to be harsh with this small misshapen dwarf, but in his own way, Hadjii had been a valuable assistant and had helped to pass some of the long eons of time.

The elven waddled over to take a peek into the caldron and watch the scenes that formed in the brew. "Does the Master not see all and know all before it happens, therefore knowing of my arrival?" The voice had the tone of groveling servility, but the Old One knew Hadjii was teasing with him.

"One of these eons, my friend, I will turn thee into one of those mushroots thee often hide under, dare thee to mock me!"

"Aheeee, not that, Master! Do I not serve you well?"

The joking and chiding continued until the two strange beings could contain their mirth no longer and the cavern was filled with their cackles and laughter.

Drying his rheumy laughter-tear filled eyes with a corner of his sleeve, the Old One gasped air into his thin chest and looked with fondness upon his little misshapen assistant. "Ah, Hadjii, what wouldst I do without thee? By the by, all is going quite well. Bahuraja hast just had his first encounter with the beautiful Sjhanara."

"Ahya", was the pleased reply. "And do I take it that they found each other pleasing to the eye?"

"Yes, Hadjii, I doest believe I detected some stirring of the emotional juices within the blood of both. They also worked together to survive the first of the many tests they will encounter, the dreaded Gholac. They go separate ways for the time being, but no doubt Fate will bring their paths together again by and by." Again, a light cackle escaped the wizened old lips. Fate was another one of the Ancient One's tools he often used to his advantage.

"What do you see in their near future, oh Wise One?" Hadjii had many capabilities, but seeing into the future was not one of them. He sometimes envied his mentor this ability.

"We'll just let the future take its course for the time being, Hadjii. But I doest have some instructions for thee. Bring yonder stool and come sit by the fire near me. My bones ache from the dampness and the fire warmeth my thin old blood."

Hadjii picked up the tiny wooden stool and placed it near the large chair of the Old One. Two heads bent together, the larger whispering words of instruction, the other nodding occasionally as it absorbed what was to be.

Firelight flickered on the blackened walls of the cavern long into the night, casting strange shadows. If an occasional groan or squeak or fluttering emitted from these shadows, neither of the two beings paid any attention. Nothing was strange or stranger within these walls, or beyond the power of the Old One to control.

EARTH QUAKE

As the days passed, Bahuraja noted a change in the countryside he had entered. The grasses, what there was of it, grew in thick clumps and was dry and brittle. Kaibara nibbled at it when Bahuraja stopped to make camp for the night, but wasn't too enthusiastic about it.

There were not many trees in the area, but what few there were, were twisted and bent as if some giant hand had molded them. Water was scarce and so was game. The young prince had to search far and wide to find even the smallest of animals for his evening cooking fire. The dried gorska meat in his pack was fast diminishing and Bahuraja hoped he would be able to replenish it before it was gone entirely.

It seemed odd, too, that he had come to no villages. In fact, he met no one, even though he was following what appeared to be a well-worn path. Since it was obviously going somewhere, however, Bahuraja chose to continue along its course. It had to lead to something or somewhere, didn't it?

The youth was carefully on the lookout for any movement or object that might indicate habitation or possible game.

Since leaving his home, Bahuraja had traveled a more or less lonely road. The few villages surrounding his homeland had been passed in a very short time at the beginning and the young man had soon entered a wilderness area. The only person he had encountered was the beautiful girl, Sjhanara.

Just the thought of her name brought a flush to his cheeks and an ache to his groin. He wondered what it would be like to possess such a vision.

Not that Bahuraja had never known the flesh of a woman. Both he and his friend Odj had been tempted by the wiles of some of the girls of the tribe. The loft above the gorka stalls had given a soft bed of sweet scented hay where on occasion one or the other of the boys discovered the mysteries of the opposite sex.

For the most part, however, Bahuraja could not bring himself to dally in this sport often. When most of the other young men of the tribe gave pursuit on a regular basis, Bahuraja kept more to himself. He had too much respect for womankind to just use them in his own lusty pastimes, no matter how willing they might have been.

He saw the great love which existed between his father and mother, even after all their years together. In his heart, he wanted such a love, not just some cheap temporary rolling in the hay. In fact, just about the only time the fluttering eyelashes and sweet smiles of a lass would tempt him, was if he was in dire need. Sometimes he would look at himself in disgust and wonder at its control over his body.

Odj would shake his head at his close friend and laugh whenever Bahuraja rejected one of the flirting girls' advances.

"BahBah", he would chide, using his pet nickname of his friend, "you break the hearts of all the girls and show no remorse for it. Are you too good for them?"

Bahuraja would only smile at Odj, knowing that many a lass had known Odj's hand upon her thigh. "Odj, you are the heartbreaker, not I. Besides, if I am to be ready for the Test of the Zandorn, I must preserve my strengths as much as possible."

This would cause Odj to snigger, knowing full well that his friend could outlast him in bed or battlefield and still have strength to spare. But he also knew of Bahuraja's respect of women and wished that he, too, had such high moral standards.

Bahuraja's reverie was brought to an end by Kaibara's sudden halt and nervous stamping. The gorka's nostrils flared and his eyes rolled; obviously something had caused alarm in the beast.

"What is it, Kaibara?" Bahuraja was immediately on the alert. His heart began to pound, as the young man began to remember the horrid Gholac.

No sooner had he asked the question, than the ground began to rumble and shake. Bahuraja feared the return of the deadly Mists, but the sky had not darkened as before, nor was he feeling the despair and heaviness of before.

Kaibara reared and jerked as the ground continued its quaking. Dust rose from the sparse landscape and what trees there were bent and twisted and shook as if alive.

Bahuraja had difficulty keeping his seat as Kaibara tried desperately to escape whatever was causing the ground to writhe and quake. Cracks began to appear as the ground heaved and sunk in areas where it had been level just moments before.

The youth made a decision. Kicking the flanks of his gorka, he yelled for it to run. Needing very little encouragement, Kaibara stretched forth his thick legs and began to race across the heaving landscape. Bahuraja guided him over the suddenly appearing cracks and around newly formed rises. The cracks began to widen. Trees and earth fell into the crevices. What other animals had been hidden in this wasted land could be seen scurrying or leaping all around the man and his beast.

Some became victims of the yawning gaps of ground and their pitiful cries would end just as suddenly when the gaps came together again.

One such crevice opened right in front of the frantic youth and his steed. With a gigantic effort, Kaibara, needing no urging from his master, gathered all his strength and leaped over the yawning cavern and landed heavily on the other side. The jolt nearly unsaddled the rider, but the beast gathered its legs together again and resumed its dash from the horrible quake.

Dust choked the lungs of both beast and rider and the effort of running caused the breath to come in short ragged gasps. Sweat poured from man and animal alike as fear and exertion drove them onward.

Exhaustion began to tell on Kaibara, but fear would not allow him to slow his pace. Bahuraja knew that if they did not escape this holocaust soon, there would be no escape. Neither man nor beast could last much longer.

Suddenly the earth gave a tremendous lurch and a huge crevasse opened right in front of the pair. It was too wide to jump over, even if Kaibara had had the strength. Bahuraja tried to turn the frightened beast to the right, but momentum carried them forward. There just wasn't room enough for the turn.

For an instant it appeared that the gorka was racing over the air itself. Then with a scream of fright, Kaibara began to fall. Over and over, downward into the abyss went man and beast. Bahuraja lost hold of the saddle and reins and only had time for one last thought of parents and home and a quick prayer for his soul before being lost in unconsciousness. Suddenly the shaking ceased. A low rumble sounded from deep within the bowels of earth and then silence reigned.

THE GOHONZON

The young man awakened slowly. He had difficulty clearing his mind. There was still a feeling of falling and of being tossed and thrown about in an abyss of darkness. He couldn't collect his thoughts; it was as if something had jumbled everything together.

Finally, opening his eyes, he gasped as he looked into the grinning face of... of what?

Sitting up, his head reeled, and he had to place both hands on it to keep from passing out again.

"Having a hard time getting used to the atmosphere, eh?" A voice spoke in a strange accent that the youth could not place the origin of.

"I..I..where am I, anyway?" his mind clearing a little more, the man again tried opening his eyes and looking at his surroundings.

"Hee, hee, hee", chuckled the gnome-like figure standing near him. "You mean you can't even recognize your own creation?"

"My...own...what?" Slowly, the fog began to clear from the Bahurja's brain and with shaking legs, he stood, using the tree trunk beneath of which he had been lying to support himself.

"Yes, yes, yes, your new world, your new life, do you not remember?" This time, the elven's voice seemed edged with impatience. "Hurry up, now, pull yourself together, we have work to do.

We have been waiting a long time for you to get here. Now that you are here, there is much to do. We have a journey to make."

Glancing about, the elven sighed", You just couldn't find it in yourself to appear closer to the Ancient One's cave, could you? Ah, well, so be it! Come on, come on! Those legs of yours can walk, I presume."

With a slight hop, the creature turned and with the aid of his short gnarled staff, started a wobbly-hobbly gait down a small path.

"Wait", quickly catching up to the creature who was, at most, only two feet tall, Bahuraja reached down and grabbed it by a topknot of hair sticking out from its otherwise bald head. "I'm not going anywhere until I get some real answers. Something isn't quite right. Who are you, anyway, and how did I get here? I can only remember.... falling from...from.... oh, by the Ultimate Keeper! "

As the pair rounded a curve in the path, a huge rock formation slightly resembling a castle appeared in the distance before them. It was bathed in a thick shimmering light from which an occasional bolt of lightening would either enter from or emanate outward into the atmosphere. The sight of this edifice welded the young man to the path as if his feet had been nailed there.

"Well, at least you have knowledge of deity", again the grating voice. "If you will just follow me as I ask, all your questions will be given an answer, but hurry, we must not keep the Ancient One waiting a moment more than is necessary."

Poking Bahuraja in the leg with his staff to get him moving again, the creature hobbled toward the looming structure before them. As they neared the base, an opening appeared where moments before there had been solid rock. The stone just seemed to melt away and an opening take its place. Passing through this opening, the youth saw that the walls were smooth as glass and although no lanterns could be seen, a light seemed to emanate from the very walls themselves.

"What is this place?" questioned the youth. "Where are you taking me?"

"Questions, all you do is ask questions!" came the grating answer. "I am not the one to ask, young one. If you would just move along, you will find out soon enough!"

After a few curves in the passageway, the pair reached another wall. Raising his staff, the elven spoke something in a language totally alien to Bahuraja. Another doorway melted into view and revealed a narrow shaft that reached upward.

As soon as the pair had stepped onto a platform within the shaft, the doorway disappeared to became a wall again and the platform began to move upwards. There was nothing to hold onto and Bahuraja thought the velocity with which the platform was moving would crush him into it, but he soon became accustomed to the speed and ventured a look upwards to see where they were going. Only a narrow speck in the distance betrayed an opening and gave the viewer knowledge that there really was and end to this crushing ride.

As the shaft neared this opening, the platform slowed down and then halted. Bahuraja found himself and his companion in the middle of a huge room that in some ways resembled a cave, and yet it seemed as if the sky made up the ceiling.

Planets and other heavenly bodies glittered and moved overhead to curve out of sight as the sides of the room came into view.

All manner of things lined the walls. Vials and containers of all shapes and sizes rested in carved out niches. Various herbs hung seemingly in midair, their aromas pungent. Also prevalent was the dry, dusty smell of age.

A huge black cauldron rested upon an ornate grating above a brightly burning fire near the center of the room. The smell of its contents was indistinguishable and the young man wasn't too sure he even wanted to know what was cooking there. A greenish colored smoke rose and curled as whatever vile smelling liquid was cooking boiled and bubbled within.

Looking down as he stepped from the platform, he saw it melt into flooring. There were no lines to show that there had ever been a shaft where moments before the two had just ascended.

"Wait here", the elven ordered, "And don't become too curious before I return. It could have disastrous results!"

As if he had any desire to touch anything, the youth thought to himself. His mind was already reeling with questions and confusion. Vague pictures tried their best to present themselves from the recesses of his memory, but he just could not get a grip on anything tangible.

Spying a fur-covered chair near the fire, he gingerly sat down to await whatever or whomever was coming next. From this vantage point, he could examine the room in more detail.

He looked more closely at some of the containers with strange contents that rested in niches within the walls. Some of them contained essences which shimmered. Some contained things that moved. Bahuraja decided his curiosity was best kept in check. He had no real desire to deal with whatever those containers might reveal.

After his senses began to relax a little, the youth became aware of a sort of melodic rhythm of sound. It was very faint, yet soothing. He began to relax even more, the rhythm wrapping him in a warm cocoon of sound. His eyelids became heavy despite his fight to keep awake. Soon he slept.

"Are you sure this is he?" the voice came from far away.

"Most certainly", another voice, somehow familiar.

"Well, only you would know, Master", the first voice seemed closer now. "But he does not appear to be knowledgeable of his real position in this world."

"It is as it should be", again the second voice. "The veil has erased his previous knowledge for a time. He must establish himself if he is to fulfill his Destiny here."

Placing one gnarled bony finger on the sleeping youth's forehead, the Ancient One canted words to some timeless spell.

"Arise, Bahuraja Muebin Sarach! Awaken to thy Destiny!"

The words shot through the youth like a bolt of lightening. His eyes popped open and he fell backwards from the chair as he focused on the imposing figure standing before him. Scrambling to his feet and once again gaining some balance, he tried to calm his frantically beating heart.

"There is no need to fear, Bahuraja", the old man smiled.

""Hadjii here tells me thee hast a few questions thou needeth answered. If thou wilt relax and calm thy mind, I wilt give thee what thou needst to know at this time."

"I, I, you know my name", stammered the young man, suddenly remembering it himself.

"Yes, I called thee by the name thou wast given at birth in this plane and have been known by in other ages, give or take a few. Thou wilt remember more in due time, but for now, it is enough to know that thy name is Bahuraja Muebin Sarach. This is thy world, created by and for thee and those thou didst select in thy past life and world to share this with thee.

"Thee fashioned all things within this realm, or at least set the molecular structures in motion from which things can be formed. Thou doest not remember all this, of course - that is why I am here. Thou canst only remember thy present childhood, although it is in a different phase of this world.

"I will be thy sansei, or teacher, for a time until thou doest remember all things. Thee already hast all the knowledge contained within thee, but it is not the nature of things to come into a new existence all knowledgeable at first. This is to give thy new form time to adapt."

The ancient one droned on and on, filling Bahuraja's mind with information, yet with each piece he received, the youth found there were even more questions.

What did this old man mean - *'new existence', 'his creation',*? Where was he, what had happened to his parents, what had happened to bring him to this *'phase'* as it was called?

His mind was a jumble of confusion, yet somehow he did not fear the ancient old wizard or his misshapen dwarf. His natural curiosity made him pay attention to every detail and word in hopes that some logic would soon come to him.

He had no concept of time passing, so insatiable was his need for knowledge. When finally the voice of the teacher slowed to a stop, Bahuraja discovered that several days had passed. During this time, he had eaten nothing or slept, yet he was neither hungry nor tired.

For several moments he just sat there absorbing what he had heard, trying to sort everything into proper perspective. He didn't feel like he was special, but this old one had informed him that, in a way, he was like a god. He was not invincible, however, he had a physical body that could feel pain, suffer, find joy, know extremes of all senses, and yes, eventually, death's sting. In Bahuraja's case, however, it had yet to be determined just how long a life he would enjoy.

He would, in time, rediscover powers that could be used for good or evil, but that he should concentrate on cultivating wisdom before experimenting on the use of those powers. These powers were different from the ones he had always known about - his so-called Gifts of the Ultimate Keeper. It was all confusing and exciting at the same time.

"Well, young Bahuraja", the wizard had risen from his chair and stretched his aching old joints. "Thou hast absorbed enough for a time. I suggest thee again go forth into the land and continue to seek thy destiny in this world thou art now a part of. Just remember, develop thy senses, be always alert, challenge all things. When a question seems to have no answer, there will be a way placed for thee to discover one."

"How will I know that I have found this *way*, as you put it?"

"Thou wilt just know. That is all I wilt say. As I have told thee, thou already contain the keys to all knowledge deep within thee. It is up to thee to bring it forth through meditation and awareness. I will teach thee how to do this. Before thou leavest this place, I have one more thing to present to thee."

The ancient one moved toward a large ornately carved cabinet resting on a raised dais at one end of the room. Raising his hand, the doors of the cabinet opened, revealing an old, weathered parchment on which strange symbols and figures were written.

"Come, Bahuraja, kneel with me before the Gohonzon." Bahuraja did as he was bidden, his eyes drawn like a magnet to the scroll. From deep within he felt a slight stirring - as if a door was opening within his soul.

With a few instructions from his sansei, Bahuraja concentrated upon the writings of the scroll. The ancient voice began to chant. Over and over the words rolled forth from the thin old lips, the voice becoming stronger and stronger.

Bahuraja could hear the words with both ears and soul. His own lips began to mouth the strange dialect and yet it seemed vaguely familiar.

As he stared at the scroll, the words began to lift from the parchment and take on a life of their own. Bahuraja could feel his spirit gravitate toward those words. It was as if it wanted to burst forth from his physical body and return to some other place. He became one with the words, the chanting, and the old one. He could feel himself rising from the floor of the cave-like room. He was afraid and content at the same time. Time had no meaning, space had no barriers and all things were made clear. He could see the walls disappear, he felt whisked away on clouds of awareness. There was no weight to his body, he seemed to be able to go at will to beyond the beyond.

As the Ancient One changed from one mode of his incantations to another, the formations also changed. Slowly, the room began to once again reappear and the words that hung suspended before the scroll shimmered before the young man's eyes for only an instant more before returning to their resting place on the parchment.

Not wanting to give up one precious moment of what he had just experienced, Bahuraja did not move from his kneeling position even after the Old One rose. He just wanted to savor the sensations over and over again and hold them within his breast. It was as if that was all the food and sustenance he would need for life.

"Yes, my son, in a way, that is all the food thou doest need", the voice was uttered within his mind, not out loud. *"But thy physical body will require more of thee."* This time the words were spoken out loud. "Arise, Bahuraja, and receive this gift."

Bahuraja reluctantly rose from the floor and turned to his teacher.

"Hold out thy hands." Doing as he was bid, he found a rolled parchment placed into his grasp as well as a string of ornately carved wooden beads.

"This scroll is thy own personal Gohonzon, Bahuraja. Hold it sacred as the writings upon it hold the meaning to all things. Thou knewest of it in thy past lives and it will be thy guide in this one also. Just as we have chanted before the other one in this temple, so thou art to chant before the one I have given thee. Never allow it to become profaned. When thou hast taken possession of a home, enshrine it as I have enshrined mine.

"Listen to thy entity when thou doest pray before it and thou wilt develop thy strengths and knowledge."

"I don't know what to say, Master", choked the youth. "I have no words to express my feelings. Everything has happened so quickly and I have yet so many questions, but I will do as you bid me."

"Go with the Spirit, young Bahuraja. I will be here for a time to make sure all goes well with thee. Remember, continue to seek thy destiny wisely and all that thou art will come forth and thou wilt inherit all that which thyself created in a time before thee ever came here."

The last words had barely faded from the Ancient One's lips when the room and all of its contents suddenly disappeared.

NEW PHASE

Bahuraja found himself standing on a grassy plain, a group of hills in the far distance and the light of the bright red sun bearing down upon him. Slowly he turned one way and then another, a shocked look of disbelief etched upon his face.

Had he really experienced all those things, been with a strange old mage, an elven, or had it all been just a dream? Where was he now? What had happened to the ancient one who had taught him? Where was the cave? The only proof of anything was the rolled-up scroll and string of prayer beads he still held tightly within his left hand.

Then a shocking revelation overtook him. Where was his gorka, Kaibara! He was no where about! In fact, the tree where the dwarf elven had found him after the terrible earthquake was nowhere to be seen.

A whole world seemed to have vanished and another taken its place.

Bahuraja's mind was suddenly flooded with thoughts of home, parents, of his beginning the Test of the Zandorn.

"Oh, by the gods!" he agonized aloud, "What has happened to me?"

The basic function of a growling, empty stomach finally brought the youth to his senses.

During his sojourn in the cave, food had not seemed necessary. Now, however, reality bared its ugly head and Bahuraja realized that he was in a strange place, hungry, and no weaponry to provide Him with food. In fact, he was totally without clothing as well! His only possession was the Gohonzon the ancient wizard had given him.

"Got yourself a bit of dilemma, eh, fogwort?" There, sitting on a huge mushroom-like growth, was the ugliest creature Bahuraja could have ever imagined. It was not much more than a blob of protoplasm with protuberances emanating from the top of what might be called a head. These protuberances appeared to be its eyes because they rotated as they examined the naked youth before it.

When the creature spoke, a mouth of sorts would appear from its gelatine-like mass and with each word, yellow-green slobber drooled from the opening. The mouth disappeared when the speaking stopped. The creature didn't smell very good either. In fact, one could even say the odor wafting from this creature was gagging.

If Bahuraja's stomach hadn't been so empty, he would probably have vomited, but as it was, all he could do was cover his nose and mouth enough to filter in only enough air to breathe.

"Well, well, aren't we sensitive! A real priss, no doubt. I ask you again, fogwort, are you finding yourself in need?"

"Slightly", gagged the youth. "You see, I somehow have found myself without..."

"Yes, yes, yes, I know all about it", came the exasperated reply, "Now, would you like some help, or do we just stand there making a complete idiot of ourselves? How anyone could think of you as a creator is beyond me, but if your '*Majesty*' would collect himself enough to allow this lowly subject of his realm to assist, I could perhaps assuage your hunger at least."

Wondering what kind of *'sustenance'* this horribly ugly and odorous creature would come up with, Bahuraja finally had to admit to himself that, for the present, he had no alternatives.

"I guess my predicament is up for suggestions", he managed to choke out.

With a sound that could have passed for a sigh, the creature unraveled itself from its perch and fell with a *'plop'* to the ground. "If you will sit down, and close your eyes", it slobbered, "I will see to it that you are provided sustenance".

Bahuraja did as he was bid. For a second, his mind was blank, but another grumble from his midsection caused images of steamed vegetables and roasted meats and cool beverages to march through his mind.

"Not so fast, not so fast, fogwort", the blob croaked, "You're new here, remember? These things take time. Now, open your eyes and fill up!"

Slowing opening his eyes, Bahuraja beheld an array of delicacies spread out before him. Steamed vegetables covered with creamy sauces, a platter of tender sliced meats, a variety of sweet juicy fruits and a huge tankard filled with a thirst-quenching liquid that caused the gastric juices to flow.

Not quite trusting the vision before him, Bahuraja looked toward the blob-like creature.

"Don't look at me, fogwort, you created this disgusting looking mess", the blob mouthed as it extended a finger-like probe to touch one of the fruits, "I'm only the translator. Things take a bit of time in this plane, and until you get the hang of this atmosphere, you may need a little help from time to time.

"Now are you going to eat all this, or just stare at it?" The fruit the blob had been poking was drawn into the glob-like mass. "Ummm, not too bad at that!" With this one last parting remark, the blob suddenly disappeared.

For a moment, Bahuraja was startled, but another protest from his stomach brought his focus back to the mouth-watering display before him.

"Oh well, I guess one doesn't look a gift-blob in the mouth", thought the youth. Shuddering at *that* thought, he began to dig into the delicious repast before him.

It was only after his stomach was quite sufficiently filled and his thirst quenched that Bahuraja began an overview of his recent experiences. He recalled the visions he had witnessed during the long chanting and meditation session in the cave.

He had been a part of all that existed and yet somehow separate at the same time. He also recalled being aware that he was special in some way - not of the ordinary. The Old One had said that he had created this world and all that was in it. At that thought, he shuddered, wondering that he could have created that horrible smelling blob of a short time ago. Then he remembered the ancient sage stating that his creation also held a matrix of the elements to form creatures or situations that were necessary for the continuation of this world.

"But if I have created all this, and I have come here from another life to inhabit my creation, then why can I not remember all things now, instead of having to wait?" These questions and more racked his mind as the young man sat in the warm sunlight.

After a time, however, the warmth, combined with a filled stomach, caused the youth to become drowsy and seek refuge from his confusion in a nap. His one last thought as he drifted into a fretful sleep was that he had apparently accomplished something very unique and, therefore, was the only one of his kind in this world - except for the Old One - and he didn't count.

Even in sleep, images coursed through Bahuraja's mind; vague images that, no matter how hard he tried, Bahuraja could not quite grasp into consciousness. Voices seemed to be speaking and yet he could not decipher the words. Sometimes he envisioned another entity who seemed so familiar as to be like himself, but in another time and place. Faces that he felt he should recognize marched before him; smiling faces, concerned faces, entreating faces; who were they?

Then the sleeping youth became aware of the soothing sound of chanting. The rhythmic droning melted away the confusion, the panic, the nightmare of thoughts unfathomable.

He became immersed with the sound and floated in its soothing blanket until he finally fell into a deeper, dreamless slumber.

After several hours, Bahuraja awoke refreshed. For a few moments, he lay on his back allowing himself to languor until the last few cobwebs of sleep dissipated. Raising himself to one elbow, his eyes fell upon a neatly stacked pile of clothing nearby. Curiosity brought the youth to his feet.

Closer examination revealed a fur-trimmed jerkin and trousers of soft tan leather, a finely woven chausses of the softest of materials, a pair of fur-topped soft leather foot-hugging boots with fine beading on the instep and soles of a tougher nature. A fine bhashomhook and baldric completed the ensemble.

It was with some embarrassment that Bahuraja remembered he was totally naked! Another mystery. What had happened to his other clothing? When he put on the new garments, he discovered that each piece fit perfectly.

"*Well, whoever fashioned these for me, certainly knew my size*", he thought.

Then, the young man remembered the words of the blob. It had said that the food had been created by Bahuraja himself! The blob had told him that it was only a conduit of sorts.

Did this mean that all he had to do was *think* of an object and it would appear? Didn't the Old One say that all knowledge was contained within himself and that in time he would know how to use this knowledge?

Slowly, from the recesses of memory, pictures of molecular structures dissipating and reforming came forth. "Have I done this before?" he voiced the question aloud. "Do I have the knowledge and ability to make anything happen? Is all I have to do is wish for it?"

"Not quite as simple as that, but close!" The voice startled Bahuraja and he spun around to see the elven Hadjii who had led him to the cave of the Old One emerging from behind a nearby bush. "You have the ability to create things from matter, but this gift must be used wisely. You can't just go around zapping things into being willy-nilly!"

"I wish to the gods you creatures would quit popping out from behind every nook and cranny every time you took a notion. I'm having enough trouble grasping my situation without all this interference. If, as I've been led to believe, I am the creator of this sphere, then how did you and some smelly blob of a creature I've recently come in contact with, come into being? I can't imagine in my wildest dreams, and I've had some pretty good ones lately, that I would create the likes of you."

"You not only have the manners of a myu-sholaitoc thoad, you have a bad temper too! If your Lordship would quit hopping about like an eclot on a hot rock, I will help you in the next step of your education! I'll add that your temper isn't going to make me feel any better about it either."

"I'm sorry", was the youth's calmer reply, "It's just that I seemed to be possessed with thoughts and dreams I cannot fathom and here I am in a world filled with strange happenings and creatures supposedly created by my own hand during another lifetime on some planet in another galaxy!

"I only now remember that I left my home and parents on a simple quest of manhood and here I am, stranded in a different 'phase' of my own world. I've lost my faithful mount and friend Kaibara and have no clue as to what happened to him. For all I know, he's dead and wild creatures are feeding upon his carcass."

"In other words, you are frightened out of your wits and could use a bit of assistance. All of which is why I, and others are in existence. For the time we are required for your reeducation, we will appear and guide you. I, Hadjii, have been assigned by the Ancient One to be your chief guide and instructor. From the sound of things, I had best stay with you for a time until you get better acquainted with things. Agreed?"

A more docile Bahuraja replied. "I'm sorry, Hadjii, I would appreciate your help."

"That's more like it, my lord. Come, follow me. We will journey for a time while the sun still graces us with its light."

Again, assuming that hobbly, wobbly gait, Hadjii turned and headed eastward toward the sun. "We just might be able to make it to yonder forest before Zol sets. It is not wise to be out here in the open spaces during the hours of night."

"Why should we be afraid of the dark, Hadjii?"

"There are forces unseen that sometimes roam these open spaces at night and all decent creatures do not venture forth until Zol again pokes its head above the horizon."

"Forces? What forces?"

"Oh, I'm sure one as curious as you will encounter some of them one of these days - or nights as the case may more properly be", was the reply followed by a grating cackle.

Bahuraja suddenly remembered the deadly Mists and it caused him to shudder inwardly. It must be just such a phenomena that Hadjii referred to.

ELVEN ENCOUNTER

Sjhanara's feet were tired, her back ached, she hadn't eaten all day, and her water bag was nearly empty. If she didn't spy something soon, she was sure she'd starve. At least that was how she felt. If only she had a fine animal to ride, she thought as she trudged along. Her envy for Bahuraja's steed, Kaibara, reminded her of the handsome young man.

"A lot of good it does me to think about him!" she hissed through dry, cracking lips. She shielded her eyes with her hand and checked the position of the sun. As near as she could guess, it was late afternoon. Night would soon be upon her and still no game in sight.

A sudden fit of anger caused her to kick at a stone lying in the path. Pain stabbed through her, foot to ankle.

"Owwwch!" hopping on one foot, she tried to rub the offended appendage. Stopping for a moment to examine it, she saw that the stone had caused a rather large bruise to form. The toe was also beginning to swell.

"Intelligent girl, Sjhanara", she mumbled to herself. "Make yourself lame and *then* how will you get yourself about?"

Sjhanara limped on, becoming more and more irritable with each painful step. Her foot was really throbbing now and she knew she was going to have to stop awhile and rest.

In the distance, she could just barely make out a small stand of trees. Perhaps, if she made it that far, she not only could rest, but there might even be an eclot or a nest of bird eggs that would stem her hunger. With greater resolve, she pushed herself forward until she reached the grove.

Easing the pack from her aching shoulders, she found a nice shaded spot beneath the hanging branches of one of the trees. As she sat down, leaning against the trunk of the tree, her attention was immediately drawn to her throbbing toe. It was turning quite an angry purple now and was quite painful.

Drawing her pack closer, she rummaged through its contents until she found the small, folded leather pouch her mother had made for her. Untying the thong holding it closed, she unfolded the pouch, revealing several small pockets in which various herbs used in healing nested.

Selecting a few of the Moanna leaves from one of the pockets, Sjhanara crushed them into her drinking cup and added a few drops from her nearly empty water flask to make a thick paste. The poultice was then carefully spread upon her toe.

Tearing a small strip from one of her headbands, she wrapped the toe and tied it with a soft knot. The cool poultice began working almost immediately and Sjhanara felt that by morning, if she kept off of her foot for the night, she should be able to walk fairly well.

"I'll just have to be more careful about my temper!" her voice echoed her thoughts. "It was a stupid act, to kick yon pebble. It surely was not the cause of my discomfort."

Sjhanara continued chastising herself as she put away the packet of herbs and surveyed the nearby area for something edible.

Only a few feet away, a small bush caught her eye. Bright bluish red berries hung in clusters from nearly every branch. Perhaps they would be good to eat, she hoped.

Using her walking staff as a sort of crutch, she hobbled over to the bush. Picking one of the larger of the juicy looking fruits, she took a small nibble and held it on her tongue. If it burned, or tasted bitter, then she knew it was probably poisonous. When nothing happened, she ate the rest of the berry and waited a few more minutes to see if her stomach would react to it. There was no adverse reaction except for her stomach demanding more than just a tiny tidbit.

Filling the front of her seshu with several handfuls of the sweet tasting berries, Sjhanara hobbled back to the tree and sat down. The berries were quite filling and also quenched her dust-parched throat. "It would have been nice to add a roasted eclot or some toasted tasha root to this meal, but this will just have to do", the now yawning girl told herself.

Her eyes were beginning to get heavy. She had traveled far this day. That, plus the stress of hurting her foot, was cause enough for rest. She should build a small fire, she told herself as she pulled her cloak around her shoulders. A fire would keep away the chill of the night and dissuade any creatures who might possibly harm her. She was so tired, though...soooo tired...

"She's quite ugly."

"Yes, quite."

"Do you still think she'd be suitable?"

"Oh, yes."

"I agree. There's only one problem."

"Problem?"

"Yes, Her length. She must be - hmmm - at least 10 tail points long."

"MMmm, yes. At least 10. Perhaps even longer."

Two elvens rested on their haunches in front of the sleeping girl. They had discovered her as they took their evening foraging walk through the grove. Each elven was only about two and a half feet tall. They wore jerkins of small softened dragon scales and pantaloons of scraped leather gorska hide. A top-knot of hair sprung at the center of their otherwise bald broad heads. Their ears were sharply pointed and each sported a bulbous nose and slightly slanted eyes. Their feet were almost too large for their short bodies and no shoes or sandals adorned them.

The pair had never seen mortals in this part of their world before. They knew they existed, but for the most part, none had ever traveled into this section.

The elvens' main function was to forage for food for the local dragon - Sjogai. It slept most of the time, but whenever it awoke, it was quite hungry. In order to keep the dragon appeased, the elvens provided a generous supply of food at the entrance to his cave. In this way, Sjogai was happy, and in return, the dragon provided protection to the elven community.

The appearance of a mortal in this vicinity, however, was quite abnormal. The pair of elvens immediately realized the importance of their find. It went without saying that Sjogai would also be interested in this discovery.

As the two elvens pondered over the size of their find and how they were going to transport the sleeping girl to Sjogai's cave, Sjhanara decided to awaken.

She began to stir and in doing so, accidently hit her injured toe against the trunk of the tree she had slept under. "Ouch!" The explosive exclamation startled the elvens to immobility.

Sjhanara sat up suddenly and began rubbing her sore appendage. "By the hairy thoads of Acarda!" she swore.

Such language from such a beautiful mouth! It was then that she noticed the two small creatures huddled together in fear close by.

"Well, what are you staring at? Haven't you ever hurt yourself before?" It didn't dawn on her at first that she had never seen the likes of these two diminutive creatures before. All she was aware of was abruptly coming out of a wonderful sleep due to extreme pain in her stupid toe!

The elvens finally reacted. One turned to run, the other also turned, but because they had turned in opposite directions, all they accomplished was to run into each other. They crashed to the ground, squealing in fear and exasperation, each trying to get back up. With each hurried attempt, however, all they succeeded in doing was to get entangled with each other again.

The scene was so comical, Sjhanara temporarily forgot her throbbing injury and began to laugh.

Again, the elvens tried to gather themselves together for an escape, but only succeeded in tripping over Sjhanara's pack.

"Get off of me, you gutsnipe!" the one on the bottom yelled as he tried to get up.

"You've got your arm caught in my jerkin, you frogdropping!" exclaimed the other, who was having no better luck righting himself.

"Now, now, now!" Sjhanara reached over and grabbed the pair by their waist belts and pulled them apart. "What do we have here? Why, it's two little mushkeys. Aren't we cute?"

"Let go of us!" the frightened pair cried in unison.

"Oh, I'll let go of you, after you tell me who and what you are." Sjhanara was having fun with this game.

"Now you've done it, Othorn!" the bigger of the two was still trying to twist his way to freedom.

"It was all your fault, Othux", sobbed the other. "You just had to play the big leader. You were the one who thought this giant a suitable prize for Sjogai. Oh me, oh my! Now we may be the meal instead of her!"

"Prize for Sjogai? What or who is this Sjogai! And what do you mean – meal?" the girl held tightly even though this new revelation caused her alarm.

"It's none of your business, who Sjogai is!" Othorn had quit struggling temporarily. He had suddenly thought of an answer to his original problem.

"Well, I'm making it my business, small one!" was the girl's reply. "I'm not releasing you two until you tell me what I wish to know." She could be very stubborn when she wanted to be.

"Please, Othux, just tell her what she wants to know. Maybe she'll have pity on us and let us go! Please, oh please, don't harm us" Othorn squealed. He could just picture himself being spitted over a hot fire as dinner for this mortal creature.

"Shut up, scab breath!" Othux expounded trying to stretch close enough to box Othorn's pointed ears. "Please, gentle lady," he began to plead, "You are a mortal female, are you not? Release me and I'll tell you anything you desire."

"Only if you promise not to run away. I have need for food and drink. Perhaps you can help me locate some."

Now Othorn really started sobbing in earnest. He could already feel the hot breath of the cooking fire.

"Would you stop your caterwauling, you offox! What is the matter with you, anyway?" Othux was now in full command of the situation or at least thought he was.

"Can't you see?" wailed Othorn, "*We* are going to be the breakfast! You just had to awaken her. We'll never see our homes again. I'll never see my Meekin or Budji! Oh, woe, oh woe!"

Sjhanara's heart went out to the cute little elvens. She hadn't realized that her size would have scared these creatures so. "I have no intention of eating either of you", she soothed.

Immediately, Othorn ceased his crying and raised his pudgy, tear-stained face. "You aren't going to eat us?" there was still a sniff or two left in his bulbous little nose.

"Of course not!" the girl replied. "It's plain to see that you are intelligent beings. I was only in hopes that such as you could help me, a stranger to this land, find sustenance."

All this time, Othux had been appraising the girl. The old ones had prophesied that there would one day come into their lands, a mortal of special content. Could this wisp of a girl be the one foretold? It did not seem possible, however there was no doubt that she was quite different from anything he had ever seen before. He knew that if he could just get her to Sjogai, that possibly the mystery could be revealed.

Sjogai was the protector of great wisdom. Yes, Othux decided, somehow, the girl would have to be brought to Sjogai, but not as a meal.

"Ahem!", Othux assumed what he imagined was a very authoritative pose. Sjhanara turned her green-eyed gaze to this creature who was the obvious leader.

"I assume that you have a name?" continued Othux.

"I do. My name is Sjhanara Yagenta Hajatnii. I am the daughter of...."

"I care not of your parentage", came Othux' reply. "I believe we can best answer your questions if you will but follow us for a short distance. We can take you to a place where wisdom resides."

What a strange way of putting things, Sjhanara thought; however it was obvious that these two diminutive creatures would not satisfy her curiosity. Just possibly they could take her to someone who would! Would this be the Sjogai they spoke of?

The trio made preparation to depart; Sjhanara shouldered her traveling packs while the two elvens argued on who was going to lead.

Othux won, much to Othorn's disgust, and after testing the position of the sun, he set as fast a pace to the west as his short pudgy legs could waddle.

Sjhanara followed and Othorn trailed behind - his face puckered into a sour frown.

Although Sjhanara's toe was much better after the poultice and rest, it was still bothersome and caused her to limp. Seeing her discomfort, Othorn forgot about his own problems long enough to offer his walking staff to the girl as an aid. It was a little short for her to use, but the top had a natural rounded end that fit nicely into her palm. Using it more as a cane than a crutch and her own longer staff as balance, the elven staff relieved the weight on her foot a great deal.

Her wide smile of thanks and a quick kiss on the top of his bald head caused a blush to push upwards from Othorn's neck to the very roots of his topknot. He thought she had a very beautiful smile even if he did think mortals were ugly.

By the time the three travelers entered the barren area Othux had called the Valley of Sjogai, Sjhanara was beginning to wonder about the wisdom of having come with these two small creatures. As she gazed about her, she could see that nothing seemed to live in this valley. There were no bird calls; no small game grazing or skittering across the sandy soil; no bushes or trees or even grasses growing! As they neared an outcropping of rock, Othux motioned for them to stop.

Sjhanara was thankful for a chance to sit down and rest her aching body and ease her throbbing foot, but as she watched Othux as he waddled towards the outcropping, she became a little fearful.

Turning towards Othorn, who had been left to guard the girl, she queried, "Where is it that Othux goes that we must abide out here?"

Othorn, feeling braver without Othux to cut him down, ventured to tell the girl that Othux had gone to announce their presence to Sjogai.

"Who is this..this mysterious Sjogai that you keep speaking of?" Sjhanara's question caused a frown to appear on the wide little brow of her companion.

"I dare not explain Sjogai, mistress", was Othorn's reply. "He will explain himself when it suits him. Much depends on his mood, me thinks."

The elven nervously drew lines in the sand with his large big toe and refused to look directly into the girl's eyes.

Sjogai's moods could definitely make a difference on whether he held a conversation with his audience or made a meal of it! Othorn did not want to cause any more fear in this mortal than she already displayed. He was becoming just a little enamored with her and was already beginning to think her not as ugly as he originally had.

SJOGAI

As time passed and Othux did not return, Sjhanara became more and more anxious. She realized that this small elven, Othorn, could not keep her from leaving if she chose to do so. She stood several hands taller than he, even as short as she was. She also had her bhashomhook tucked in its sheath beneath her seshu. What if this Sjogai was some ogre with an ill temper. What would she gain by staying when it could possibly cause her harm? Was this a test of the Zandorn, or was it a trap?

She had just about decided she was going to make a run for it, when Othux reappeared at the entrance to the outcropping and waved for the two to join him.

Othorn stood up and waited while Sjhanara picked up her pack and weaponry. She gave him a small nervous smile then assumed what she hoped would pass as the demeanor of strength and courage of a warrior.

Upon entering the entrance to the cave, Sjhanara gasped as she withheld a huge cavern just below the ledge where she and her two diminutive companions stood. Othux lead the way down, seemingly unaware of the beauty surrounding him.

Light flashed from many different colored crystals protruding from the cavern walls. Long stalactites grew downwards from the high domed ceiling, dripping multicolored liquid minerals that created swirled patterns on the cavern floor. Here and there some large broken spires lay creating the illusion of fallen temple columns.

The center of the cavern, however, appeared swept clean of any large debris. There were a few scattered bones and some large almost circular pieces that did not look to be part of the stony landscape. Curiosity caused Sjhanara to ask what they were.

"Sjogai's scales", was Othux's reply.

"Scales?" Sjhanara's shaky voice betrayed her increasing nervousness.

"Yes, scales. Sjogai sheds his outer layer once every hundred years or so. He does not do this here, however. These are just a few that scraped off during a scratching. Sjogai comes here to scratch from time to time because the points of the long spires can relieve him. Sometimes, one or two of his scales will scrape off. That is what you see here."

Othux's explanation was given in a tone as of parent to ignorant child - as if Sjhanara should have already known why and had forgotten.

Sjhanara decided this Sjogai, whatever or whoever he was, was not a mortal, as she had perceived and from the size of some of the scales, he was quite large. Her brave front was fast becoming overtaken by a quivering fear.

Finally, the trio reached the floor of the cavern and began to cross over to a large opening at the other side. The cavern was immense! Sjhanara felt dwarfed as they crossed its center. They skirted pools of liquid color shimmering in the light.

How beautiful this all was, thought the girl. A king's palace could not contain more riches or a temple to the gods be wrought that held more majesty. Sjhanara almost forgot her fear as she beheld the beauty of this place.

As they neared the entrance to the next large opening of the cavern, Othux halted and turned to face Sjhanara. "You are now to enter Sjogai's sanctuary. He is expecting you. I would advise you to show the proper respect and pray he finds you worthy to be in his presence. Speak only when he requires it of you. To do otherwise could be fatal. Do you understand?"

Sjhanara nodded, not confident of her ability to speak at all after the admonition just given.

As Sjhanara passed beneath the high arch of the sanctuary, she could only gaze at the scene in extreme wonder and awe. The entire room was shimmering crystal. The walls were nearly smooth, but not quite. They seemed to be faceted columns of brilliant crystalline light that changed colors constantly. A faint, musical chiming, much like thousands of tiny bells, created a backdrop of soothing sound.

In the center of this huge room, a raised platform held a dragon of immense proportions reclined on a huge red silken pillow-like bed. His head arched upwards towards the ceiling of the room above a body of pale green scales that shimmered with gold highlights. The hind legs, folded and resting upon the bed, were each endowed with three large clawed toes in the front and one claw in the back. Two shorter front legs were crossed upon the dragon's chest.

It took no intelligence to see that these claws could totally rip anything to shreds with one swipe of one of the huge feet.

Large leathery wings lay folded across each side of the beast; the tips curved in hooked claw-like form. Sweeping back from the top of the head clear down the entire center of the dragon's back was a ridge of elongated bony scales that stood upright, ending with a spear-like tip at the end of a very long tail.

The tail was curved around the hind legs of the dragon as it lay in its reclined position, but the girl could see that it, too, could be a very damaging appendage if used as a whip.

It was the head, however, that really commanded the frightened girl's attention. As Sjhanara and the two elvens stepped to a platform near the base of the dragon's bed, the huge head descended so as to be better able to view the visitors.

Two flared nostrils rested at the tip of a tapered nose. The mouth was closed, but the wide line curving from just beneath the eyes testified to its great maw. Two large incisors curved from beneath the lips on either side of the front of the mouth, giving an even greater indication of damaging strength.

Highly arched eye ridges curved over the deeply set eyes and swept backward on the long, rather narrow head. Beneath these ridges, the eyes were as two beacons of fire - seeming to mesmerize all they surveyed, yet, after a few seconds of staring into these eyes, Sjhanara suddenly realized she was no longer afraid. A calming peace seemed to take over her body and she felt a warmth as her tense muscles relaxed.

"So, Sjhanara Yagenta, you finally grace our presence!" the giant beast's words hissed as they reached the girl's mind, but the words did not come from the dragon's mouth.

It had spoken! What was more, it knew her name! The shock of that realization nearly caused Sjhanara to faint. This huge apparition actually had the ability to speak with intelligence, even if it had been in her mind. "I, I am here", was all Sjhanara could utter.

At her words, Othux and Othorn started, because they had not been privy to the dragon's mental message. Sjogai turned his gaze to the two tiny elvens and its maw curved into what could almost be considered a smile.

"Do not be alarmed, my two little friends, you have done the right thing by bringing the girl to me."

Othux drew himself up to his full two feet of height and stuck out his small chest with importance. "It was I who made the decision to bring her to you, oh Mighty Sjogai!"

"Now wait just a minute!" argued Othorn. "I, too, helped to bring the girl here. Was it not I who found her sleeping beneath yon tree? Was it not I who guarded her - at great risk to myself, I might add - while you gained audience with Sjogai?"

"See here, you mealy-mouthed eclot brain!" Othux began, but Sjogai was not about to let the two elvens continue.

"Enough!" Sjogai's hissing command echoed from wall to wall causing a clamor like a hundred gongs and causing the shimmering crystal to turn brilliant reds and oranges.

Immediately Othux and Othorn fell to their faces at the dragon's feet. Their small shivering forms quaked with fear at the anger their arguing had caused.

"We beg your forgiveness, oh Mighty Sjogai", they wailed. "We forgot ourselves!"

The pair presented such a comical scene to Sjhanara despite the omnipresence of the dragon that she couldn't help a slight snicker from escaping her lips, but as Sjogai's fiery eyes turned towards her, she tried to suppress herself.

Heavy lids covered Sjogai's eyes for a moment and when he again opened them, there was only amusement.

"What am I going to do with you two?" Sjogai hissed. "Pray get up from the floor and stand before me with dignity or I swear I will banish the two of you to the very presence of The Ultimate Keeper!"

Othux and Othorn quickly jumped to their feet and stood before Sjogai with eyes downcast.

"I would speak with the girl alone", Sjogai continued. "You two are forgiven - again. However, if you don't learn to contain your arguing, I may have to cast a spell on the two of you and turn you into - now let's see - what would be a proper punishment?" One of the large front talons raised to Sjogai's maw and picked at one of his fangs.

"Oh master, we will be good, honest!" the pair wailed in unison.

"Just you see, oh Mighty Sjogai!" offered Othux.

"Besides, who would bring you your meals and the delicacies from without, if not your two willing servants?" Othorn's quavering voice added.

All the time the two elvens spoke, they were backing away from the room. As soon as they were out of the doorway, they turned and scurried to a nearby tunnel, one of many that channeled into the main cavern.

When they thought they were quite far from the burning eyes of the dragon, Othux turned and boxed the pointed ears of his companion. "You just had to start it all, didn't you? We might have gotten a reward instead of nearly ending up as dinner, but nooooo, you just had to stick your fat bulbous nose into the conversation. I've a thought to..."

At that moment the tunnel lit up with a bright blue light. The face of Sjogai appeared before Othux and Othorn from within the light. "I warned you two! Now, until I need you again, I think you both could do with a good lesson. Both of you are banished to serve in the nursery of dragons! Let's see how much time you have to argue there!"

In a flash of light, the two elvens found themselves several miles away from the Sjogai's cave. They were in a different cavern beneath the earth, but this time not nearly as pleasant. Several dragon eggs in various stages of development lay in neat rows along the edges of the walls. In the midst of this, several squawking, fledgling young dragons thrashed about.

It was to Othux and Othorn that they now looked to for food and care.

The elvens would also be required to keep the nursery clean of dragon-droppings - a mean task in itself. And since the previous nursemaid had been given a vacation just prior to the elvens' arrival, Othux and Othorn had to begin immediately.

As Sjogai had warned, there was little time for arguing here.

"Now, Sjhanara", Sjogai shifted slightly on his volumous silken bed, "Where was I? Oh, by the way, would you care to sit down?"

Immediately, several large pillows covered with delicately wrought and intricate designed fabrics appeared before her. "Are you perhaps hungry?"

When Sjhanara looked as if she might nod to the affirmative, a table laden with all manner of fruits and sweetmeats plus a carafe of mellow wine appeared in front of the pillows.

The girl looked up at Sjogai as she sat before the tempting fare with a questioning awe upon her beautiful face.

"Oh, I really don't need Othux and Othorn to bring me anything", was Sjogai's reply to the question in Sjhanara's mind. "You see, I am able to provide quite adequately for myself. However, I do allow some of the elvens to come to me with their gifts because they always provide information of the outside world as well. As long as they believe they are necessary to me, they serve me well, but these two do try my patience at times.

"Now eat, Sjhanara. I know you are filled with questions as to your being here. I will attempt to answer them while you partake from my table."

Sjhanara's hunger overrode her caution and awe. She took a small morsel and tasted it. It was delicious! She selected what appeared to be a slice of yellow fruit. It, too, was sweet and tasty. In no time, several other of the large selection of meats and fruits found there way to the girl's hungry lips.

Sjogai waited until Sjhanara seemed to be nearing an end to her eating before he spoke. "Did you find my humble offering to your liking?"

"Oh, yes, thank you", the girl replied breathlessly as she looked around for something with which to wipe her mouth and hands. Immediately a napkin of a delicate gauze-like material appeared near her platter as well as a small crystal bowl of clear water in which Sjhanara could dip her fingers.

"Yes, I can read minds and anticipate needs almost before one thinks them." Sjogai tried to put the girl at ease. "But I rarely get a chance to entertain one so lovely as you, Sjhanara."

Sjhanara felt a slight blush rising at the compliment. "I do thank you for the meal...Sjogai? Is that your name? I must admit I was more hungry than I imagined under the circumstances."

"But now you wish to be informed as to why you are here? Of course!" Sjogai raised one of the mighty talons and the table immediately disappeared from sight. "If you need anything more to eat later, my dear, I will bring it forth.

"Now", the dragon continued, "you seek your destiny on your Test of the Zandorn. Am I correct?"

The girl nodded.

"Have you had anyone ever tell you what the Test was really about?"

"Well, I only know that one must go forth into the wilderness and meet the challenges and prove one's self worthy. If one returns to the home clan valiant, then a place of honor is created within the clan and that person is considered an adult."

"And how does one prove that he, or she, has been valiant?" questioned Sjogai, his large eyes narrowing. "What's to stop one from just going forth, idling away some time and then returning home with a claim of bravery, therefore avoiding any danger to self. Could not this be done without anyone from the home clan being any the wiser?"

"Oh, no!" was Sjhanara's vehement reply. "The clan priest questions all those who return. One is honor-bound to be truthful in their answers. Any who try to be otherwise is immediately cast out of the tribe and it brings dishonor to the entire family. It would be unthinkable to do such a thing! Besides, I intend to be very valiant so that I may stand beside my father one day as able as my brothers to defend our clan if need arises."

Sjogai had difficulty suppressing the amusement this slip of a girl's remarks created within him. However, this old dragon was very knowledgeable. He knew of her bravery and courage. She was very special - although she had no knowledge of just how special - yet!

"So, little one, you desire to be a mighty warrior for your clan; perhaps even step into your father's boots one day as leader. Does not the hearth fire and being a good wife and mother tempt you then?" Sjogai's eyes seemed to drill into the girl's very heart as he awaited her reply.

Sjhanara squirmed a little under the scrutinizing gaze of the dragon. How should she answer? What if she gave the wrong answer? Was he testing her? He had even seen into her mind the desire to be clan leader someday. Was this all a part of the Test of the Zandorn?

She looked up into Sjogai's piercing eyes and again felt the calming warmth of his gaze. He was not the fierce destructive force one would first suppose when in this mood. She felt almost as if he was a great friend.

"I suppose that someday I might marry", came her soft hesitant reply. "But I have not yet met the one whom I find worthy or who meets my standards to be my husband."

"Have you not?" Sjogai's question startled the girl.

"There have been many who have thought himself worthy and have asked my father for my hand, but I would have none of them. They were, ...they were..." the girl's voice trailed off as she suddenly remembered a tall handsome stranger in the wilderness whose gaze had caused her to blush and whose voice had made her heart beat slightly faster than normal.

She could still feel the warmth their mind-merging had caused within her and the strange sensations being near him created in her body. Even now, just the thought of this stranger - Bahuraja, he had called himself - brought a flush of pink to her cheeks.

"So, you do have one possible contestant?" Sjogai pressed.

"I wouldn't say a contestant, exactly. I met a stranger at the beginning of my journey. We fought the Gholac together. I know very little of him."

"That will be rectified in due time, little bosrua", came Sjogai's disturbing reply.

Little bosrua, that is what the young man Bahuraja had called her. The name meant '*bright eyes*', yet was not a term used in her home territory.

A change in the tone of the chiming caused Sjogai to lift his head. He seemed to listen for a moment before returning his attention to Sjhanara.

"Sjhanara Yagenta, I'm afraid my presence is required elsewhere for a short time. I will make everything available for your comfort during my absence, however I do require your staying for a while. Will you do me the honor of being my guest?" Sjogai's manner was of the utmost graciousness, yet Sjhanara had the feeling her leaving would not be looked upon as acceptable until he had finished with her.

"I..., I would consider it an honor to be your guest .... for a time", she replied, "But you do understand that I must be on my way soon to continue my quest." She wasn't going to let even such an apparition as this huge dragon deter her from seeking her destiny!

"So, shall it be." Sjogai blinked one of his slit-pupiled eyes and immediately a door appeared within the crystal walls of the room. A diminutive elven woman stood at the opening.

"If you will be so kind as to follow Elvandora, she will show you to accommodations of which I pray you will find comfortable until my return."

Sjhanara thanked Sjogai and turned to follow the tiny elven woman. She couldn't help looking back over her shoulder, however, at the dragon's preparation for departure. He had uncurled himself and now stood upon the huge pillow-like bed in full height.

Sjhanara gasped at how large he was. She could barely see the huge head that only moments before had been at her eye level. How majestic he was. The girl felt no fear, only awe.

Sjogai extended his folded wings and stretched them to full length. From wingtip to wingtip he measured a good one hundred forty feet; from head to the end of his tail he measured at least seventy-three feet.

His size alone would have commanded respect, but Sjogai was not your usual everyday kind of dragon. His basic body color was a pale green with a rustic tinge to the mantle on his head and the rigid upright spines that ran the full length of his backbone. In certain light, the broad scales covering his body glowed with the dull sheen of gold.

Now, stretched to full glory, Sjogai raised his head toward an opening that suddenly appeared at the very top of the huge crystal room. As his wings began to lift him, the room chimed loudly from the vibration. Slowly, he began to rise, then faster and faster as he gained momentum. As he neared the opened ceiling, he stretched his tail and used it as a rudder to clear the edges. As soon as his full body was outside, Sjogai took a bearing by a quick look to the east. The huge wings carried him gracefully through the air with great speed.

It was in the air that Sjogai was in his true magnificence. The light from the sun shone down upon his scales creating a brilliance to nearly outshine the orb itself. The wind created by the flapping of his wings made trees bend and grasses flatten. His sharp gaze missed nothing as he sped through the skies.

There was no small detail he did not see, no animal, no sea, no creature-form. Sjogai loved the air. Here he was truly free and could claim dominion.

Sjhanara sighed as she watched the dragon's exit from the large crystal room. As she turned to follow Elvandora, she tried to imagine what new adventure was before her and what part the huge reptile Sjogai was to play in her life.

AGNOR'S WINE

As Hadjii and Bahuraja trod on, Bahuraja surveyed the passing countryside and tried to imagine his creating each blade of grass, each flower, each bush; it all was quite overwhelming. Why couldn't he remember doing all of this, he kept asking himself. Why did he have to relearn things he should already know how to do? What cruel joke had been played that put him into this position?

The Old One had told him that in time he would know the answers to all his questions. His was a very unique situation. In his former life, he had gained great wisdom. Before leaving that life, he had decided to create, not only a new world and the inhabitants therein, but also a challenge for his own entity.

He would enter into the world as any child, but he had set *'keys'* that would trigger the possibility of his regaining that knowledge of his former self. It was a test as to whether knowledge did pass on with the spirit; that not all things were a *'learned'* response.

As Bahuraja progressed in this life, certain trials and situations would supposedly come forth from his inner being, bringing the enlightenment of past experiences and lives.

If this was all true, then Bahuraja had created his own life's game, so to speak. It was enough to make the youth's head spin. Too much in such a short bit of time for him to fathom the depth of it all, he decided, shaking his head.

In a very short time, it seemed, the pair neared a forest of strange looking trees that also brought a cooling cover from the hot waning sun. Their thick, heavily barked trunks lifted twisted branches of wide-needled foliage heavenward, creating a canopy that nearly blocked out the light.

Bahuraja realized, with some surprise, that for such a short-legged creature, Hadjii could cover a great distance with ease and speed. By the time they had traveled well into the midst of the forest, the little man did not seem at all tired, while Bahuraja, young as he was, felt shaky and winded.

"You will gain strength as you get used to the atmosphere", Hadjii seemed to read his mind. "It's a wee bit thinner in this phase of your world than that where you were born."

"What kind of trees are these anyway, Hadjii?" queried the youth.

"They are called pinefir", was the elven's reply. "We elvens call this forest home, for the most part. The trunks of the pinefir grow quite large and offer us a place to tunnel and hide, when need be."

Halting at the base of one huge, gnarled old tree, Hadjii raised his staff and knocked twice on one of its protruding roots. A tiny door in the trunk of the tree creaked partially open and a bulbous nose accompanied by one questioning eye appeared.

"Who disturbs me?" queried a gravelly voice.

"Get thee hence, Agnor, you old gorka-breath!" Hadjii growled, "You have visitors who require lodging for the night. Now open up quickly before I crack your head open with this staff!"

The eye and nose were followed by the other eye and the rest of a face. Only then did the door fully open. "Why didn't you say who you were, Hadjii", Agnor whined, "Ahhee, and who is this giant-one who accompanies you?"

"Do you not recognize your own creator, oh filthy slime-infested glutsnipe?" Hadjii slammed beneath the entrance-way and was about to add a few more bumps to the already warty-complected Agnor, but Bahuraja's booming laugh stopped him in his tracks.

Turning, Hadjii viewed his lord sitting on a stump outside, holding his sides as his laughter over the haggling of these two silly-looking elvens shook his whole being.

"Stop it, you two", gasped the youth, "I just wish you could see yourselves. And the language! Tell me, are you friends or enemies?" Another spasm of laughter took over at this point until it seemed he would collapse from lack of breath.

"Well, well", remarked Hadjii, "you also possess a keen sense of humor it seems. Ridiculous we may seem to you, but when dealing with this old fogwort, one must take the upper hand at the getgo, or possibly suffer consequences!"

"Consequences, indeed!" replied Agnor, "My brother, Hadjii is puffed up with his position in life. I, Agnor, must remind him from time to time that he is not the only one of importance on this planet. Welcome, Prince Bahuraja, I knew of your coming and have a place prepared for you for the night. You are quite large, however, and may find the lodgings a bit cramped."

Putting a ragged, thickly woven shawl around his humped shoulders, Agnor pushed past his brother Hadjii and exited from the still open doorway. Placing his hands on his hips, he measured the tall lad with his eyes.

"Yet, methinks, upon second look, that my accommodations may be suitable enough. Come, follow me!"

By this time, the sun had begun receding behind nearby hills and darkness was fast swallowing any daylight filtering through the tall trees of the forest. Hadjii and Agnor seemed to have no trouble seeing the tiny path through the brush, but Bahuraja had to bend over and squint in the waning light so as not to lose the pair as they led him along.

Pushing aside brush and branch, the trio soon came to a small clearing. Nestled in the midst was a small cottage, Firelight streaming from one of the windows.

"There", Agnor voiced, "Try the door and enter. You will find plenty of food, a warm fire and bed for the night. I even included a bottle of my finest brew to quench your thirst, however, I warn you, drink it slowly and not too much. It packs a kick!"

This remark caused a cheery cackle to come forth from Agnor's lips and he gave Hadjii a knowing look and slap on the shoulder.

"And you, brother, would you like to come sup with me and share a bit of the brew before turning for the night? I have much news to impart and I would like to hear whatever news you have as well."

"Delighted to share your table, you old thoad-warted sot!", replied Hadjii.

Turning towards Bahuraja, he said, "I will look in on you before I sleep, my young lord. Sorry your size prohibits your joining us, but I'm sure my brother has left you a well-stocked table and I would advise going to rest early. We leave as soon as Zol makes his presence known on the morrow."

As soon as the pair of elvens left, Bahuraja took inventory of the tiny cramped room of the cottage. A fireplace took up nearly one whole wall with a cheery warmth eminating from its depths. The crackling of the burning logs lent a peaceful note to the interesting room.

A roughly hewn wooden table and a couple of chairs occupied the center of the room. A pallet covered with aromatic pinefir boughs hugged the far wall. A fur-covered pillow and a folded fur hide blanket lay in a neat pile at the foot. It didn't take much of a look to note the bed would be much too short for Bahuraja's length, but for one night it would do for the tired lad.

Crossing the floor to the table, Bahuraja spied a plate of meat and a bowl of fruit as well as the bottle of brew Agnor had warned him about. There were no plates except for the one the meat laid upon and no utensils to eat with or cup to drink from.

"Hmm, these inhabitants must eat quite simply", the youth noted.

Picking up a haunch of the meat, Bahuraja turned one of the chairs towards the warm cheery fire and began to eat. Washing his food down with an occasional sip from the bottle, the day's events again began to sort their way through the youth's mind.

There were still more questions than answers, much to the aggravation of the boy; it caused a burning fire consuming him from within. The more he learned, the more he wanted to know.

The terms *creator* and *destiny*, haunted him. Half remembered images floated just beyond his reach, tantalizing him to a near frenzy of impatience. But patience was what he needed most, his sansei had cautioned. He needed to practice patience and learn one thing at a time. *Or relearn.* Was that possible?

Was he really awake now, or only dreaming all of this? Had he already dreamed this in another life and was now living it? Was there solidity in anything or was all matter only as tangible as your dreams and thoughts created it to be? If he ceased to imagine or think, would everything he saw and felt disappear?

This very food and drink in his hands - was it really filling his body because he desired to be filled or was it all just imaginary?

Frustrated and angry, Bahuraja tipped the flask of wine to his lips, drained it, then threw the flask into the fire. As the pottery broke, spilling the small remaining contents onto the burning logs, the flames exploded into the room, scorching the leather covering his legs.

The foolhardiness of his act, brought the young man to his senses, or to be truthful, to the lack of them. He had consumed quite a bit of the brew and when he had tried to jump away from the flames, found his body did not respond very well.

He knocked over the chair, and fell over the table, scattering what was left of the food onto the floor. When he tried to stand up, his body would only allow him to rise to his knees. Bright balls of light swirled inside of his head prohibiting him from focusing his eyes clearly.

Crawling across the floor to where he knew the bed should be all he was able to accomplish before collapsing was to pull a few of the pinefir boughs on top of himself.

It was this scene that greeted Hadjii when he peeked in before he, too, retired for the night.

"Ah, my lord Bahuraja, thy throne evades thee", the elven chuckled as he spread the fur coverlet over the sprawled figure lying on the floor. "Rest well. I pray your head will allow your body to carry it on the morrow." He then tiptoed from the room and quietly closed the cottage door, knowing full well that the now loudly snoring figure on the floor probably would have not awakened if a tree had fallen on him.

The youth's sleep, however, was not undisturbed. Strange visions coursed in and out of the fog. Faces and words could be seen and heard, yet Bahuraja could not recognize or understand. He would reach out at something only to have it disappear. Bahuraja could feel himself being pulled toward a destination, but where?

The image of a beautiful sword appeared; a weapon of strange design and much larger than those of his present knowledge. It seemed to speak to him, to call him. What did this mean? What was it that he was supposed to do?

All during the night dreams came and went, sometimes causing tears to form and run down the young man's cheeks, sometimes his fists would flex in anger, sometimes a smile would lightly touch his lips, giving a softness to his dream-tortured face.

Towards dawn, the dreams faded and allowed Bahuraja to drift into a deep, soothing sleep.

Awakening slowly, Bahuraja became aware of the shuffling of feet and the sounds of a fire being laid on the hearth. There seemed to be bells ringing - or was that within his head? He tried to move slightly, but his body was sore and stiff from spending the night on the hard wooden floor.

"Ugh!" Why wouldn't his arms and legs respond to his brain's commands? His mouth was dry and he dare not try to describe the horrible taste on his tongue.

A chuckle from across the room caused the youth to open one eye and try to focus it. Piercing daggers shot through his sight and into his already aching brain. Another groan escaped his lips, but he was determined get up. He finally was able to accomplish a sitting position and found the edge of the pallet to lean against. His head was splitting in two and it was with extreme effort that he brought his hands up to cradle the throbbing balloon that housed his befuddled brain.

"Ah, we see you are awake, oh prince of the floor!" the grating voice of Hadjii caused another shudder to ripple through Bahuraja's tortured body.

"Did you sleep well?" The tone of the voice indicated no sympathy whatsoever.

Mustering all his remaining strength, Bahuraja opened blood-shot eyes and surveyed the cluttered scene of the room. The remnants of last night's meal lay scattered across the wooden floor.

The table was turned over with all four legs pointed toward the ceiling and the chairs lay on their sides. A few pinefir boughs were scattered near where he had slept and the fur coverlet was a twisted mass at his feet.

"What happened to me?" he managed to croak.

"You apparently did not heed my brother's warning concerning the brew" was the elven's reply. "But then, it was to be expected. Agnor's wine is quite potent and one needs to get used to it slowly. Here, drink this and it will clear your head a little."

Bahuraja reluctantly took the goblet Hadjii held out to him and suspiciously eyed the liquid it contained. "What is this smelly stuff?" he inquired.

"That *'smelly stuff'*, as you call it, is your salvation if you are to travel with me this day. Now drink it up and prepare yourself quickly."

Deciding nothing could be worse than what he was already going through, Bahuraja brought the goblet to his lips and drank its contents down to the last drop. No sooner had the liquid reached his stomach than his head began to clear and the pounding and ringing disappear. He now found he could stand up and move around without muscle and sinew betraying him.

A scratching at the door announced Agnor's arrival. "I have packed some dried gorska meat and a flagon of tasha root tea for the day's journey", he said, producing a medium-sized hide pouch. "How is our guest feeling this fine morning?"

"A great deal better than when I first awakened", the youth's replied. "Whatever was in that drink Hadjii gave me just now is a magic elixir for a hangover."

Agnor's cackling laugh joined that of his brother's. "Ah yes, a little scale of the dragon works every time."

Bahuraja did not dare ask if Agnor's comment held truth concerning the contents of the drink. "I'm sorry about the room", Bahuraja said.

"No harm. I'll have things righted in a twinkling." Sticking his thumb upwards and flexing the small appendage, the dwarf uttered some unintelligible words. Immediately table and chairs righted themselves and the remnants of food disappeared. A fire burst from the newly laid wood within the fireplace and soon a comfortable warmth began to fill the chilly room.

"There, that should do it!"

This time, Bahuraja did not question the action of the elven. He had come to realize that this phase of his world was filled with a great deal of magic, strange happenings and creatures. He was the apparent stranger here and had much to learn. Yet this was his world now and if he was to survive here, he would have to depend on individuals like Hadjii, Agnor and perhaps others for his education.

It was with a renewed energy and determination that the young prince Bahuraja Muebin Sarach followed Hadjii from the forest and into a new day.

As day followed day and became weeks, Bahuraja learned of the many flora and fauna of this new world he would call home. He learned which plants would quench his thirst, what animals were safe to eat and how to prepare them. He found that his mind powers were increasing as well, but caution was a byword in this area. Hadjii told the youth that he should be quite cautious about utilizing this area of himself until he knew how to use his powers better.

Whenever he practiced the use of his mental powers, there was some loss of energy to his system. It required rest, meditation, and practice before he could master even small feats of the use of this akunem.

Hadjii was patient with his young charge, knowing that this handsome youth would someday rule Acarda and its inhabitants. The Ancient One had foretold of future events and for eons the inhabitants and creatures of Acarda had awaited the appearance of Bahuraja although he as yet was unaware of most of his destiny. The continuance and survival of this sphere depended upon him and the knowledge which lay, still dormant for the most part, within him and him alone.

SAILS AND SHIP

One day Bahuraja noticed a decided change in the smell of the air. There was a tangy saltiness that could only have come from the sea. The screeching calls of seabirds filled the skies and faint sounds of crashing surf could be heard.

After a few more minutes of walking, the traveling pair reached a clearing in the trees. There, spread before them, was a vast sea. Blue-green waters ebbed and flowed in majesty while white-capped waves rolled across its surface only to crash upon a beach of beautiful green-hued sand.

A medium sized gurmon lumbered across the sand trying to avoid one of the many seabirds that swooped down to harry this slow moving hard-shelled beast. It eventually reached the waters ebbing onto the beach, the touch of the cool sea urging it ever faster.

As soon as the deeper waters allowed, the gurmon began to swim outward into the sea. No longer a lumbering, clumsy animal, it took on the grace of a dancer. Its strong thick legs and webbed toes were the paddles that swept it along.

Bahuraja watched the gurmon with fascination until it slipped beneath the surface of the sea and disappeared. He then returned his attention to the beach spreading before him in glistening green splendor. Hadjii had informed the youth that the sand got its greenish tinge from a type of sea coral, that, when it died, was ground by the bashing of the sea and washed up on the beaches.

Other creatures also made the beach their habitat. Tiny sandcrebs scooted sideways across the warm sands, stopping occasionally to pick up some tiny morsel of food with one of many armored appendages that extended from beneath a curved, hardened shell body. Three finger-like eye appendages protruded from the front of the shell to rotate in all directions in order to better locate food and the presence of danger.

If the latter presented its self, the sandcreb would simply use its many armored legs to burrow into the sand and cover itself up. When it wanted to see if the danger had passed, it would extend one of the eyes out of the sand and have a look about. If the coast was clear, up popped the sandcreb to resume its side-gaited search for food.

The seabirds, crantions, were strange looking, half feathered, half scaled creatures. The leather-like feathers helped the bird fly. These feathers were predominately layered on the wings, but four very long and tufted feathers adorned the tail. These allowed the bird to bank and swerve in flight and also keep level.

A long curved beak extended from the head that helped the crantion dig out the many varieties of sand animals that resided on the beach. The rest of the bird's body was covered in red hued scales that changed to a brighter red during mating season.

The females, slightly smaller and duller in color, would select one of the many strutting suitors after several days of their special mating rituals. When this selection had been made, it was for life.

The mating took place in the air with much screeching and flapping and pecking. After about a week, the female would deposit two eggs in a nest built of sand, mud, and sea grasses near the water's edge. The male would take turns sitting on the eggs until, about a month later, the leather-like eggs would begin to hatch.

When the fledglings had come forth, the parents would do a waddling dance around the nest to welcome their offspring and then begin the tedious task of feeding the ever hungry chicks to maturity.

All these things Bahuraja learned from his companion as they stood at the edge of the sands. The day had nearly disappeared and the sun was beginning its descent into the horizon. It cast a reddish glow over the landscape and the sea and sand took on a deep rust-green hue. The sky was streaked with deep reds, yellows, oranges and further up into the atmosphere, pale blues.

A deep sigh escaped the young man.

"Do you find this beautiful, young prince?" Hadjii, too felt the majesty of the scene before them.

"Oh, Hadjii, if you only knew the peace and contentment I feel at this moment." Bahuraja had to sit down, he was so overwhelmed.

"I feel...I feel...so at peace. There is something...I cannot describe it. It's as if an artist painted this wonder upon a giant canvas."

"You did", was Hadjii's soft reply.

"What?" The shock of Hadjii's statement caused Bahuraja to jerk his head around.

"You were an artist in your former life, Bahuraja. When you were creating this world, you did paint many of your ideas on canvas before putting them into actual being. Sometimes you would even use the walls of your home. Later on, as your skills progressed, you used the very air as your canvas. You had developed your powers greatly before leaving that past life, my prince. Much of this world had been created so exactly in your own mind that all you had to do was think it and it appeared here."

The impact of this revelation was great on Bahuraja. He could only view the scene before him in wonderment. With softly spoken awe he whispered, "I created this beauty. From my then known experiences and mind came forth all of this. Hadjii, I am having a difficult time absorbing all this."

"I have some knowledge of your other world", Hadjii replied. "It was a beautiful sphere; the only one of its kind in its vast area of many planets. I've been told your Earth was the only inhabited world in your solar system.

"Much of Acarda must reflect your knowledge and feelings of that world you inhabited; yet the Old One has told me there was much ugliness and pain in that world. You did not find much comfort in it, I am thinking."

"Will I ever remember that other world, Hadjii?"

"I know not the answers to that. Perhaps it is better not to remember." Rising, the elven looked with wizened old eyes towards his young ward. "Now, enough of this star gazing. Night falls and we must make camp in yonder glade. Tomorrow we will set sail."

"Sail?" Bahuraja rose to standing and again questions assailed his mind. "We are going across these waters? But where is there a boat? Do you have one hidden nearby? Are we going to conjure one up?"

"By the scales of Sjogai", groaned the dwarf, "Questions, questions. Can you not be content to take one thing at a time and not drown me with words more deafening than yonder sea breaking upon the shore?"

Bahuraja wanted to ask what the scales of Sjogai meant, but after taking a look at Hadjii's darkening countenance, thought better of it and began helping him set up a night camp.

The new day broke with another beautiful sky and the promise of good weather. Hadjii was already at the fire and the aroma of oaku, an herbal brew having a roasted nutty taste, was strong.

Bahuraja stretched and rose up on one elbow to see whether his companion might be so accommodating as to bring him a cup. After a few minutes had passed, however, and Hadjii had not looked his way, Bahuraja sighed and pushed back the blanket skins.

Looking down, he saw his manhood looking up at him and a distended bladder let him know he had better quickly find a bush to go behind.

Hadjii, hearing his young charge, turned and also viewed the handsome body's dilemma. "Me thinks you'd better pay heed to your staff before imbibing this steaming brew, young prince." Then chuckling, he returned to his work.

Bahuraja hurriedly walked away a few paces and relieved himself behind the trunk of a small tree. While the warm steaming body fluids released themselves upon the ground, the young man's mind wandered randomly. *Funny,* he thought, *how this part of the body ruled the rest of a man with such force.*

He remembered how it reacted to the charms of so many women of his tribe and how, when he had taken a few to bed, his manhood had reacted almost as if it had a mind of its own.

In a sudden rush of rare embarrassment, his thoughts reminded him of how his member had reacted to that girl - Sjhanara? - yes, that was her name, as she had administered to him after the Gholac had nearly overwhelmed him.

Although Bahuraja was quite finished in his emptying his bladder, he just stood there remembering. He wondered where she was at this moment; what she might be doing. Had she continued on her quest, or had she returned home and perhaps married some bumbling young fool of her village? He certainly hoped not. For some reason, he desperately wanted to see this vision again.

He began to feel himself stir again at the thought of making love to her beautiful body, when Hadjii's voice brought him back to reality.

"Are you going to stand there all day holding yourself? I"ll admit it is a gallant looking thing, but a sail billows on the horizon and we'd better make haste with our breakfast!"

Startled back to an embarrassing reality, Bahuraja quickly returned his manhood to its resting place inside his chausses. After quickly splashing some water from the sea on his face and hands, he turned his attention to the hot brew and food awaiting him.

The sun was only a quarter way into the heavens when the full body of the ship began to take shape over the horizon. The sky was fully alight now and a slight breeze made the already heating day more tolerable.

As the wooden hulk took shape, one could see several small, but huskily built crewmen busily at their tasks. Several were climbing the ropes and reefing in the sails prior to coming to anchor. The ship had entered a small bay from the open sea and sails were being tied down.

One lone figure stood against the pointed bow. Even from the distance, Bahuraja could see he had to be the one in authority. Occasionally he would bellow out an order, but he never took his eyes off the shore.

The ship was an impressive object in its own right. The bow was an intricately carved dragon's head, viciously glaring at the shore. Its wings were part of the sides of the ship and the tail curved at the stern. In other words, it was as if the entire ship itself was a ferocious dragon and its occupants rode upon its back. Bahuraja gazed in awe at the ornate carvings and colors of the craft as it approached.

"Drop anchor!" echoed across to the shore and a huge ball dropped from the side to splash into the water. At one side of the ship a much smaller rendition of the sailing vessel was being lowered to the rippling waters below.

Several of the crew members hopped into the craft and as soon as it hit the water, began to row toward the two waiting on shore.

Bahuraja noticed that the one he assumed was the captain stood proudly on a platform at the back of the longboat and continued to holler orders to his crew to guide them. He didn't even wait until the boat had fully come to a halt on the sandy beach before he jumped into the water and waded towards Hadjii and the young man beside him.

"Hadjii, you old son of a seaserpent", he bellowed, "What a sight for these old eyes."

As soon as he reached Hadjii, he grabbed him in a strong armed embrace that looked as if it could crush a stone wall. For a man who was only about four feet tall, the captain of the dragon ship was very well built.

"AArjono, you scaly old sea dragon, you are ugly as ever!" Hadjii's greeting was as full of affection.

There was much backslapping and friendly epithets before Aarjono unwrapped himself from Hadjii and turned toward Bahuraja.

"So, I see the Old One's predictions have materialized. Prince Bahuraja, I presume?" With a sweep of his crushed metal helmet, AArjono gave a deep bow.

Bahuraja was surprised that he was recognized by the sea captain and his surprise must have shown on his face. AArjono roared in laughter and strode over to the boy and kneeling before him, reached for Bahuraja's right hand and kissed the clan signet that rested on his middle finger.

"I greet you, Prince Bahuraja, Lord and Creator of the planet Acarda."

It was then that Bahuraja noticed that the rest of the crew had their faces pressed into the sand.

"I, I, that is, I.....", Bahuraja stammered.

"Prince Bahuraja of the Clan Sarach greets the mighty AArjono and his crew and places his presence in the protective arms of The Ultimate Keeper and the ship Vagasha for this seaward journey!" Hadjii had taken charge of the moment, to which the young prince was grateful. It seemed as though his tongue had taken flight elsewhere.

Finally finding himself, Bahuraja thanked AArjono for his welcome and for his providing the means for travel across these strange seas.

"Now that the formalities are dispensed with", said the captain replacing his horned and battered helmet, "I don't suppose you have anything stronger to drink to this occasion other than bitter oaku?"

"Do you think me a Septurian worm, oh mighty AArjono", laughed Hadjii. "You know I would never journey without some of my clan's famous flummet! Come, come, you and your crew over to our fire!"

Hadjii hopped quickly to his knapsack and produced a flagon and handed it to the captain. Pulling the stopper, the captain tilted his head back and took a long draught of the amber liquid.

"Haaaahhh", belched AArjono, "Now there is a brew for the gods!" He handed the container to Bahuraja, but the young prince, remembering his night at Agnor's, shook his head and declined.

"What's this?" bellowed AArjono, "You mean to tell this old seawort that our young prince is a teetotaler?"

"No, no, no", protested the youth, "I am just not yet accustomed to the strength of your wine is all."

"Not used to it is an understatement", laughed Hadjii. Wherein followed a much embellished tale of Bahuraja's night at Agnor's and the horrible hangover of the following day.

Although the young man felt great embarrassment, he realized the chiding and guffawing of the little men was in good fun and not meant to be disrespectful. The elvens were fun-loving people for the most part and yet took their lives seriously when necessary.

There was still great respect for the young prince through it all and the knowledge that he had that respect was humbling to him. So he took his turn at laughing at himself and despite his protestations, soon was encouraged to take a few sips from Hadjii's flagon. He was just careful to only swallow smaller portions.

As the three had continued celebrating, the crew of the dragon ship had begun gathering up wood and fresh water, had packed up the belongings of Hadjii and Bahuraja and placed them in the longboat. When finished, they sat nearby on the sand in readiness of further commands. Hadjii made sure, however, that the crew also had a bit of wine before they had to return to their duties aboard the ship. After all, it would be a rather long journey and the crew worked hard.

Seeing that everything was in readiness for departure, the captain tipped the flagon to his lips and downed the last few remaining drops of wine. "Ahoy there, me gippers, it be time to head to sea!"

Leading the way to the longboat, he bellowed orders to the crew and they jumped to command. Hadjii and Bahuraja were shown where they were to sit amidships and AArjono once again stood at the stern.

The longboat was shoved back into the water and the crew began the short row back to the Vagasha.

Bahuraja looked back at the receding shore and wondered where this next adventure was going to take him.

CONSULTATION WITH THE OLD ONE

In the meanwhile, Sjogai had covered a great distance; it had been some time since he had come to this part of the world.

In the Old Time, before the arrival of Bahuraja, the dragon had lived in the valley his eyes were seeking. In fact, he had come into being in that valley at the creation of this sphere.

Sjogai had been a very young fledgling dragon in that distant time. He had slithered at the feet of the Old One and been taught the magic due his kind.

As he had grown, his wings had strengthened and Sjogai had learned the mastery of the skies. He had been very clumsy at first, like all young, but he was quite intelligent and an apt pupil. The Old One would not tolerate disobedience or slothfulness in his charges. Besides, as he so often reminded Sjogai, "Thou art as he who comes created thee in his other world. Thou hast a destiny unlike all others of thy kind. Thou wast created from his own substance. Thou art to be the protector of all which is to be precious to him. Heed thy teachings well, Sjogai, for to fail the coming master is to fail thyself. Selah!"

Sjogai instinctively knew that his was a great destiny. As he grew and learned, he realized the importance of his existence. He took it seriously and sought always to please the Old One.

Now, as he neared the valley of the Old One's castle, Sjogai began his descent. He sounded a series of short shrieking barks, almost code like in tone. The Old One had summoned Sjogai, now he would know he had arrived.

The rock-hewn spires of the castle poked through clouds where lightening bolts played. As Sjogai winged into the far southernmost tip of the valley, he could discern the outline of the Old One standing near the doorway of the highest tower. There was a wide flat stone platform where Sjogai could land nearby.

As he neared the platform, Sjogai extended his clawed feet to help him drop effortlessly from the sky onto the wide flagstone. The huge wide wings folded against the scaled body and once again, the mighty dragon was at rest.

"Sjogai, my old friend", the Old One tottered over to view the huge scaled creature that had just landed. "Thou art as glorious as ever. Wouldst thou care to join me in my chambers for a repast? I imagine thy long flight hast hungered and thirsted thee."

In a twinkling of an eye, the form of the dragon Sjogai began to shimmer and change. He seemed to shrink as his huge scaled frame slowly took the shape of a human body. When the metamorphosis was completed, a veritable beauty of a man stood muscular and handsome almost beyond description.

"Well, I see thou hasn't forgotten thy power of molecular transformation", chuckled the ancient old wizard.

"No, Old One", replied the man in a deep, slightly hissing voice, "I have not forgotten even one lesson learned at your feet. I must admit, however, I have not taken this shape for many eons. I much prefer my dragon body. It is far more suitable to my needs. Now, what about that food and drink you promised?"

The two disappeared into the doorway of the tower and soon sat before a warm hearth fire and held cups of hot steaming broth.

They talked long into the night; neither of the two seeming to tire. They discussed many things, catching up on the happenings of their world.

As the pale moons began to descend into a lightening sky, however, the old wizard rose from his fur padded chair and shuffled over to a side table. From an intricately carved box he pulled out a deep maroon-dyed leather pouch.

Carefully opening the thongs that enclosed the top of the pouch, he peered inside as if to satisfy himself the contents were still there. Seemingly satisfied, he shuffled over to Sjogai and offered the pouch to the man-dragon.

From within the opened pouch a glimmer gave light to the darkened room. Pouring the contents onto his hand, Sjogai admired the medallion which glimmered and cast its glow into the room. The circled piece resembled the Namu with wings outstretched upward to encircle its head.

The eye of the Namu was a flawless diamond whose fire pierced the gaze of the two men who examined it. The pure gold medallion was carved so that the feathers of the Namu seemed able to take wing and break away from the thick gold chain which ran through the medallion's bail.

"Thou recognize the piece?" slowly lighting a gnarled and blackened pipe with his finger, the wizard watched the medallion cast its myriad of rainbow lights upon the walls.

"Yes", hissed his companion. "The mighty Namu of my master Bahuraja. It has not lost its magnificence over the eons. Am I to take it then, that the time is nearing for the Gathering?"

Taking another long draught from his pipe, the old one let its smoke encircle his head before answering. "All the signs point towards it. At this very moment, he crosses the Sea of Nopshu. Upon reaching the distant shore, he will accompany Hadjii inland for a few miles still unknowing as to his destination. Thou hast the lovely Sjhanara at thy castle still?"

"Of course", was the hissed reply.

"Thou knowest then where thou must take her?"

A nodding head again acknowledged an answer.

"Then, Sjogai, my old friend and ally, Destiny is in its rebirth." Putting the gleaming medallion back into its pouch and richly carved box, the Old One accompanied the man-dragon up the long stone staircase to the tower above. Reaching the flagstone platform, Sjogai raised his hand in farewell and immediately began his transformation back into his dragon form.

The transformation completed, Sjogai unfolded his magnificent wings, walked to the edge of the parapet and stepped off. As the air beneath pushed against his wings, the dragon ascended into the sky. He took one banking turn of the castle tower before rising higher and taking a position on the distant horizon.

The Old One watched as the golden form retreated from his view. A long sigh escaped his lips as he viewed the valley below. Spring was beginning its slow reclamation of the trees and grasses. Always changing and yet always the same, its beauty never seemed to be lost on the old rheumy eyes that gazed upon it now.

How many eons had passed since he began his long watch.; even he had forgotten. So many seasons of spring, winter, summer and fall, each with its own beauty.

The ancient mage had guarded this valley and taught those who sought his wisdom for all time and now he knew his time was nearing an end. Oh, not that he wasn't going to welcome it, but he was very tired. However, there was still much to do before Bahuraja would be able to take over and rule this sphere he had created in his former life.

The old wizard knew the time was not yet at hand when the young prince would be ready to handle everything. "One thing at a time", sighed the withered old wizard, "One thing at a time."

DANGER FROM THE DEPTHS

Bahuraja leaned over the railing of the dragon ship and watched the rippling waters as the bow cut through the sea. He was a good seaman, having sailed smaller native-made crafts at home. He loved the smell of the salty air and the congenial joking and conversations of the crew.

AArjono would occasionally call out a command to alter a sail or to reprimand one of the crew for some small infringement of duty, but for the most part, all was quiet and serene.

Hadjii and Aarjono had spent a great deal of time in the captain's quarters, going over charts and drinking large tankards of the potent brew kept in kegs in the hold.

Bahuraja ate his meals with the two men, but was not invited to some of the meetings in the captain's quarters.

He never really thought anything of it. He enjoyed getting up at the first watch of the day and after eating a handful of dried gorska jerky washed down with a quick hot cup of oaku, head up to the deck. As often as not, he could be found aloft with one of the crew, trimming the sails, taking a glass and looking out over the sea for any signs that might be important to the journey.

He even coerced the net mender to teach him the knots these seamen used in mending the nets used in catching fish for the daily meals.

The members of the crew accepted him as one of their own, yet as one apart. Bahuraja knew he could never be truly one of them, but enjoyed the fact they liked him and tolerated him in their midst.

One day Bahuraja awoke to a dark sky indicating a change in the weather. There was no wind, however. The sails hung slack and the little ship bobbed in the waters somewhat at the mercy of the unseen tides.

There was a strange feeling in the air and the prince could see the men were nervous and edgy. The captain gave orders to raise more sail in order to catch any breeze that just might happen by, but rather than his usual shouting, he seemed almost to whisper his commands.

About mid-morning, a deep fog appeared. It stretched from horizon to horizon in front of the ship. There was no way to avoid entering this grey soup. As the dragons-head bow of the Vagasha cut into the fog, an immediate bone-chilling cold took over the atmosphere.

Shivering, each member of the ship's occupants took to their lockers to find warm capes of fur lined thick leather to put around their shoulders.

The stillness of the air prevailed and deep creases appeared on the Captain's brow as he lifted his glass and tried to get some kind of bearing. The bowman held up his large lantern to aid in the process, but the light only reflected back at the crew.

Shaking his head, the captain left word with his first mate to inform him if anything changed and went below to take a few long draughts from the contents of his wine cask. He then bent over the rolled charts on his desk to try and figure just where in The Ultimate Keeper's blood his ship was.

An ominous lack of sound kept the crew silent. It was as if no one wanted to disturb the silence. In truth, the elvens were scared. They were used to the call of circling birds, the slap, slap, slap of the waves against the bow as the little ship cut through the water, the friendly chatter of each other as they tended their tasks. In an ominous way, this fog did not invite noise. In fact, when one of the crew accidently dropped a belaying pin, the sound seemed muted.

Slowly, the condition of the black waters began to change. A shimmering of some kind of phosphorescence now covered the surface. It was created by thousands of tiny luminescent sea plankton floating across the top of the waters. The phosphorescence looked like a blanket of silver that shimmered and blinked with light produced from within each tiny plankton.

As Bahuraja watched the shimmering ripples, a large dark object disturbed the luminescent surface about twenty yards off the starboard bow. The watch yelled a warning to the crew below to be on the guard and to inform the captain.

All hands scampered to their stations of battle and the mate went below to tell the captain that something had appeared in the sea.

Both the captain and Hadjii reached the forward deck at the same time and the captain conferred with his mate.

"All hands watch lively now!" came his ordered cry. "Hands aloft - release the tops'l for speed if we can catch any breath of air!"

Hadjii waddled quickly to the rail where Bahuraja stood, hand covering his brow to get a better look at whatever had sunk again below the surface.

"Bahuraja, you had better get below for a time. The captain does not expect trouble, but wants you out of danger just in case."

"I feel no danger, Hadjii. If there is anything that needs fighting, I am just as accomplished with the bhashomhook as any of the crew. I am not some weak wisp of a girl to protect, you know."

"But, my prince, you cannot take a chance on danger getting in the way of your destiny. As my ward...."

"I am not going below!" bellowed the youth. "I am still on my Test of the Zandorn, or have you forgotten? If this is a part of my Test, then so be it! If you want to help protect me, go below and get my weaponry from my cabin, otherwise I close my ears to you!"

Standing at his full height, Bahuraja towered above all and was a force to be reckoned with in his own right. Hadjii knew better than to argue and scampered down the steps to the cabins below to search for the articles of fighting Bahuraja had ordered.

"By the gods", he grumbled, "I hope the Old One can see what I'm up against."

The waters began to roil and heave around the tiny ship, still nothing surfaced. Handaxes, belaying pins, daggers, swords, any type of weapon the crew possessed were brought forth.

Every eye strained to see what the dark shadow was beneath the water. The ship rolled and pitched as each wave hit the sides. Aajorno, at the helm, turned the wheel into the waves so as to keep the ship from turning over.

Suddenly a huge head broke through the surface, followed by a very long, scaled body. Coiled segments covered with drapes of seafoil weeds and barnacles followed the head and glistened with the same phosphorescent light as the plankton. Only one huge eye adorned the center of the head of the apparition, but its gaze turned the insides of the crew to jelly.

As the head swerved from one side to the other, it missed nothing. From a gaping maw, two rows of vicious teeth attested to the creature's ability to tear to shreds anything coming in contact with them; the stench emanating from this--*thing*--was gagging.

For the first time since he had come on board, Bahuraja felt like making for the rail to retch the contents of his belly.

Spying the ship and its crew, the creature turned and slowly began to swim towards it. The gaping maw seemed to be smiling in anticipation of its next meal.

"Crew to the ready!" came Aajorno's command. "Aladono, man the foredeck spear!"

"Aye, Cap'n!" the first mate scrambled to the foredeck where a part of the craft's dragon head was stripped away to reveal two large mounted ramming spears. Coiled beneath them on the planks of the deck were two lengths of heavy rope.

Aladono manned a spring-loaded lever devise attached to each end of these ropes.

"Ready, Cap'n!" came his reply as the water beast approached the ship.

The crew began to holler and beat their shields and whatever else would make noise. At first Bahuraja thought it was a cry to battle, but then he realized they were trying to confuse the beast into turning away without attacking the ship. For a moment, it seemed as though it just might work. The beast slowed and its ugly head swerved from side to side as if trying to shake away the noise.

It was only a few yards from the ship now and its rotting smell was overwhelming. Sweat poured from beneath the helmets of every member of the crew and many tied squares of neck cloth to their faces to help keep the smell from being so over-whelming.

Hadjii had turned several shades of green while trying to keep a stance near his ward in a protective manner.

"By the Gods, Hadjii", choked the prince, that is the vilest creature I've ever imagined. What could possibly have created this monster? Surely not I when making this world."

"Who knows, my prince", gagged Hadjii. If you were only more developed in thy skills, perchance you could at least get rid of it!"

If only he was more developed in his skills! That was it! But what skills did Bahuraja have that could eliminate this, this whatever it was? He could heal small animals and had even healed a horrible wound on his beloved Kaibara. He had, as a child been able to levitate and become invisible, but he had not practiced many of these things for years.

The creature, despite the noise of the crew, renewed its approach to the tiny ship.

"Ready the for'd spears!" The Captain's orders pierced through the heavy air and the crew stood ever more solidly upon the main deck.

Aldorno grabbed hold of the handle to the spring lever and waited for just the right moment to release one of the spears. If the creature veered to the right, then the mate would turn the handle to the right; if to the left, then the handle could be turned that direction. At the moment, the ugly head of the creature was too far away for an effective hit, so Aldorno held his ground.

His grip on the lever was so tight, his knuckles were white. The salt from the sweat pouring from beneath his battle helmet burned his eyes, but he held a steady gaze upon the approaching monster.

Meanwhile, Bahuraja was drastically trying to look back into his mind for some answer to help the crew. He knew he had the knowledge, but what knowledge? He was still so young, so untried. Possibly his life and the lives of these funny little men that he now called his friends and companions would depend on something only he could do.

"Hadjii", Bahuraja's voice was strangled, "You've got to help me!"

"Help you, master? What do you mean, help you?" Hadjii's puzzled gaze swept over the tortured features of his ward. He could see the struggle going on within the mind of the handsome prince and allowed his mind to seek the meaning of the request.

"Power! I've got the power! What can I do? How do I bring it forth?"

The thoughts were jumbled and erratic, but Hadjii knew what Bahuraja was trying to do. Closing his eyes, Hadjii allowed his mind to enter into Bahuraja's.

"Calm yourself, Master", he soothed mentally. *"Allow your mind to concentrate. Block out the din that surrounds you. Search inwardly to find your former self and the knowledge contained there."*

Bahuraja forced himself to calm down and closed his eyes. Outwardly he was aware of the Captain's command to fire one of the spears. He heard the heavy spring and slight rocking of the craft as Aldorno released the first spear at the sea monster. He also heard the cries of despair when that first spear missed its mark and only glanced off the side scales of the creature.

A roar of anger spewed forth from the monster's gaping maw and the stench of its breath was a wind in itself and almost enough to kill the tiny crew. It dove beneath the waters for an instant and suddenly rose up beneath the ship spilling the crew into the churning black sea.

Bahuraja felt the jolt and felt himself falling. He opened his eyes and tried to grab for the rail, but it hit him in the back and he fell overboard. He could see the tiny ship rock for an instant on the curved back of the monster before it spilled over onto the other side into the roiling sea.

The screams of the crew were heard over the roar of the creature as it sought to grasp them from the sea with its horrible gnashing teeth.

"Ultimate Keeper, help me", prayed the prince as he searched for Hadjii in the churning waves.

From within, he felt a surge of something he could not explain. His whole body seemed to be on fire and yet he did not burn. He felt as though every part of his body was coming apart, yet there was no pain. There was no sea, no ship, no monster, only this powerful surge.

Bahuraja was within a swirling whirlwind of fire. He could not think and yet everything seemed clear and precise. He tried to concentrate and discovered he could create pictures. *The monster! Yes, he had to destroy the monster!* Another picture appeared, a dragon. If he was a dragon he could destroy the monster!

Suddenly he was aware of sky and a wind rushing past his face. No, it was not a face. There was a long snout pointing in front of his eyes. He was flying! He was high above the waters and diving towards the scene of destruction below. He tried to open his mouth to yell for Hadjii, yet only a bellow and a piercing screech came forth.

The black sea creature lifted its ugly head at the sound and bellowed its own answer of battle. Temporarily forgetting its easy meal of flesh bobbing around in the sea, it turned to answer a more ancient call, the call of creature against creature.

Folding his wings back slightly, Bahuraja - now dragon - swooped lower and lower towards the rising head of the sea monster. As he neared, he grabbed for a spot just behind the hard skull and clamped down hard with his jaws. The sickening stench and taste of bloody ooze had no effect upon him in this dragon form. He dug his claws into the heaving snake-like body and began to drag it from the sea.

The serpent shook its head and tried to twist itself to an advantage where it could get a jaw-hold of its own, but the dragon had a choke hold that would not allow the serpent's head to turn enough.

The creature felt itself being lifted from its sea environment. It screamed and writhed. The long tail wrapped itself around the dragon's body and squeezed. The muscles of the sea creature rippled and the scales dug into the torso of the dragon. If it was able to wrap itself around the flapping wings, the dragon would not have the advantage of the air.

By now the dragon had reached a height several yards above the sea and had to struggle to keep balance. Shaking the head of the creature within its own strong jaws, the dragon sought land to no avail. It was nearly out of breath due to the squeezing grasp of the sea creature's writhing body.

With its hind claws, the dragon raked at the serpent's sides. The dragon's front claw arms were short and did not have the advantage of reaching backwards, but its hind legs were very powerful.

The serpent's strength was ebbing as its life's blood oozed from the wounds caused by the dragon's hold on its neck and the raking claws to its body. Try as it might, it could not shake this flying demon. Its breath came in short gasps because it was out of its element - the sea; it was not used to being out of water for such a long period. It did not possess a thinking brain to plan a strategy. It only fought with the basic instincts of survival of the fittest.

The horrid black sea creature had never met its match before and yet it knew somehow that it must fight this foe with all of its might or it would surely die.

Within the dragon's brain, however, Bahuraja could see and feel everything. A power he had never known surged within him. His muscles flexed, his teeth bit even deeper into the neck of this vile serpent, and his wings held and beat against the hot air.

Now, with seemingly little effort, he lifted this dragon body even higher, rising above the thick black fog. Banking toward the burning light of the sun, its light pierced the eye of the sea monster and it recoiled in pain, temporarily releasing its coiling hold on the dragon.

This release enabled the dragon to take a firmer hold of the creature's mid body with its back talons. The dragon extended those talons and pierced deeply into the serpent's bare underbelly. It then ripped the creature wide open, spilling entrails and blood through the air.

With one last screeching howl of pain, the sea monster writhed in its death throes. The one eye clouded over, the giant maw with its rows of gnashing teeth hung limp, the tail dropped. Now, only the flapping of the dragon's wings thundered in the sky.

Elation surged through Bahuraja and his mind sang a battle song of triumph as he banked his dragon body back towards the remains of the tiny ship.

Making sure the sea creature was thoroughly dead by chomping off the head, the dragon dropped its burden into the sea from whence it had come. Bahuraja, in his dragon form, watched as the pieces of the serpent splashed into the waters and sank, never to surface again. It now would become a part of the food chain that fed all creatures from the watered depths. That is, if anything would be able to stomach such a vile mess.

As he neared the wrecked ship, Bahuraja, looking through the dragon's eyes, could see members of the crew hanging onto pieces of the mast. Several were sitting atop of the overturned hull. Swooping down lower, he could see fear in the eyes of the little elvens. They must think he was also an enemy bent on taking over where the sea monster left off! How could he help them? It would do no good to change back into Prince Bahuraja. Then he would be just as helpless as they were.

The dragon felt the mind of another reaching towards him. "*Bahuraja, my prince!*" It was Hadjii! His voice was very weak, but he was alive. "*Seek land. Send help from the land. It is not far the way you can fly. Hurry!*"

The dragon ascended once again into the bright sky and veered westward. Traveling the direction the ship had been heading, in no time the pale outline of mountains came into vision. As the land became more pronounced, the dragon sought an area near a small village, yet not where the villagers would be able to see its landing upon the shores.

There were several small fishing boats bobbing in the water, but their concentration was to their nets and not to what might be flying above it.

Spying a secluded beach, the dragon dropped to earth and settled its wide feet upon the sand. Just as soon as it touched down, Bahuraja again felt the surging power within him and the swirling tunnel of light. He felt all pulled apart, yet for whatever reason, again felt no fear. It was as if every molecule of his body was dissipated. Somehow he instinctively knew to calm his mind and concentrate on becoming himself again. Then with a rush, there he stood, on a strange beach with the sun burning down.

As he turned around to survey his position, there also stood a magnificent golden dragon! Immediately, Bahuraja reached for his bhashomhook.

"Prince Bahuraja", it spoke in his mind! *"Let me introduce myself. I am Sjogai, another of your creations."*

After all he had just been through, this was almost too much for the young man to fathom. With his left hand still on the hilt of his bhashomhook, Bahuraja stood his ground and stared at this vision towering above him.

"It is obvious you do not remember me", Sjogai continued, this time out loud. "But it is I with whom you merged, fought that horrible sea creature and flew to the safety of this beach. We can discuss the how later. Right now I highly suggest we return and save your shipmates."

Hadjii! The captain Aarjono! Bahuraja quickly turned his eyes to the sea behind him.

"You need not fear", Sjogai spoke again. "If you will follow my instructions, we can be there in a very short bit of time and can rescue the entire crew."

Bahuraja turned to face the dragon, questions clearly evident on his young face.

Sjogai lowered his head and neck to the ground. "Climb aboard, my young master. There is a curved scale not unlike a saddle just behind my thocks - those two horn-like appendages on the top of my head and behind my eyes. I do believe you will be quite comfortable and protected there. I will be able to travel much faster without our being merged into one. Merging two bodies does require quite a bit of concentration and energy."

Bahuraja, still full of questions, climbed up Sjogai's snout and, using the small scales as footholds, soon was comfortably situated at the top of the dragon's head.

Using his powerful wings, Sjogai ascended quickly into the sky and turned seaward towards the wreckage of the tiny dragonship and its crew.

During the flight, Sjogai mentally enlightened Bahuraja in the methods he had used to dissipate his molecular structure and become one with the dragon. The dragon knew the knowledge was buried deep within the prince's memory but had not been fully developed in this world and this life. Due to the crisis, Bahuraja had instinctively turned his mind inward to bring forth this power that had engulfed him and brought him forth from the wreckage of the ship.

Bahuraja listened and realized he had to remember more. The tiny crew, its captain and his friend Hadjii depended upon him now. With the death of the sea monster, the fog began to lift, making it easier to see the sea below.

As Sjogai sped through the air, Bahuraja struggled to remember. In his conscious mind, he began chanting the ancient tomes taught by the Old One, "*Nam Myho Renge Kyo*", over and over. He felt a sort of weightlessness begin to come over him. The surging of power began to flow through him once again.

"*Not just yet, my prince*", Sjogai's thoughts reached through. "*We are almost at the wreckage sight. You will know what to do when we get there, I doubt you not.*"

Almost at that instant, pieces of floating debris began to appear below. Upon some of the larger pieces, a figure or two could be seen holding on for dear life. Bahuraja, both mentally and with his eyes, searched for Hadjii, but could not see him during the dragon's first pass above.

Sjogai banked and made a twenty-five degree turn to the left and indicated to Bahuraja it was time to use his powers; by this time, the youth knew exactly what to do.

Gathering up the power within him, Bahuraja raised his arms above his head. During the dragon's next close pass, Bahuraja began to chant and direct those powers through his hands. A strange blue-white light shot through his fingers and downwards. As the dragon continued to circle, this light became like a net. It dipped into the sea and gathered first one bobbing figure and then another until nearly the entire crew was suspended in midair.

Their cries for help had turned to fear over the strange phenomena at first, but when they saw Bahuraja perched on top of the dragon's head, they knew they were being rescued.

Seeing he now had the crew gathered safely into the net, Bahuraja then concentrated on the pieces of the wrecked ship. He created a maelstrom of power in which all the sections of the wreckage were plucked out of the sea. One by one, just like pieces of a puzzle, the ship was put back together.

When he was finished, it was as if it had never been wrecked by the horrible sea monster. It bobbed on the sea waters, its dragon-headed bow and dragon-tailed stern ready to take on a crew.

Guiding the suspended power net to the ship, Bahuraja carefully allowed each crew member to scramble aboard. A cheer went up as the last one was deposited on deck. One tiny fellow even did a jig.

During another pass over the ship, Bahuraja counted the elvens he had plucked from the sea, but did not find the captain or Hadjii among them.

"I've got to find them, Sjogai", his worried concern was evident to the dragon without his having voiced it.

"Use your powers to find them, Bahuraja. You have the knowledge now."

Again, turning his mind inward, the youth blanked out his own thoughts and began to search. There! Another voice! It was not the elated scrabble of the crew as they celebrated their miraculous rescue. It was weak, but he heard it.

Reaching outwardly, even further now, Bahuraja searched until his mind again touched that of another mind. Hadjii! It was Hadjii! There was another mind as well, but it was unconscious. The thought patterns indicated that this person was nearly dead.

Sjogai had followed Bahuraja's thoughts and turned into the direction of the distant thought patterns. The currents had carried Hadjii and the captain quite a distance away from the rest of the crew. The only thing keeping them from sinking into the sea was the top of the captain's desk.

"*Hadjii, my friend*", Bahuraja's mind-thought went out to him, "*I am coming. Hold on!*"

Soon the diminutive bodies of the captain and Hadjii could be seen bobbing half in and half out of the dark waters. The captain was lying on his back on the largest part of his cabin desk, his feet and one hand dangling into the water. Hadjii was desperately trying to keep the captain from slipping off and still hang onto the desk himself. It was apparent there was little strength left in either elven.

Bahuraja created the power net once more. This time he directed it to slip deeply beneath the water's surface and wrap around the desk and the two tiny men.

As he lifted the net from the sea, he created a shield of warm air to protect the two nearly spent men from the chilled sea air.

Needing no orders, Sjogai carefully banked and turned back towards the now repaired dragonship. When close enough to lower the power net, Bahuraja directed Sjogai so that he could jump onto the ship and personally guide the net and its contents to the deck.

Those of the crew, who were still able to walk, crowded around to help carry the captain below to his bunk. Bahuraja personally lifted his friend Hadjii and laid him upon the deck. He had to pry Hadjii's tiny fingers from the captain's coat and the desk.

"Are....am I?" Hadjii's voice croaked the question.

"Yes, my dear friend, you and the Captain are both safe aboard the ship and after I check you over, you will be sound as well. The prince slowly guided his hands over Hadjii's body and felt the elven's heartbeat return to normal as the healing powers warmed his blood and chilled arms and legs.

With a command to a couple of the crew to also take Hadjii below to his bunk, the prince followed them to check on the captain.

During the breaking up of the dragonship, the captain had suffered a severe blow to the head. A large gash reached from the top of his head to just above his right eye. On closer inspection, Bahuraja could see that the salt water had cleansed the wound somewhat and stopped the bleeding, but there was a great deal of swelling. It was obvious that the captain was also suffering a concussion.

Bahuraja closed his eyes and slowly waved his hands over the wound. He imagined each damaged molecule and directed his healing powers to return those molecules to normal. Slowly, the swelling was reduced and the gash began to disappear.

"Let him rest now", the youth directed the first mate. "He soon will be up and about. He's just very tired from his ordeal in the sea."

"I'll just remove his wet clothes, Prince Bahuraja", the first mate was already removing the Captain's soaked fur jerkin, "and then pop the Cap'n right into his bunk here." The first mate's awe of seeing the healing powers of this tall youth wasn't going to deter his first duty to his captain.

Feeling a little drained himself, Bahuraja trudged up the steps to the deck once more to see if there were any more wounded who required his help. There were the occasional cuts and bruises, but, fortunately, no one had been badly hurt.

He found a bench next to the foredeck and sank to it wearily, closing his own eyes.

"*Bahuraja*", the voice of Sjogai reached his mind. "*You must come with me now.*"

"I need some rest, Sjogai. I didn't realize how much energy all this would take out of a person. Besides, there is Hadjii and the captain who may need my help again."

"*No, my prince. They are well enough to guide the ship to yon shore. Your destiny is now to go with me. Hadjii knows this. You may rest as I fly you to your next destination.*"

Too tired to question Sjogai further, Bahuraja arose from the bench and looked into the skies for the circling dragon. However, Sjogai was floating like a huge golden ship himself upon the shining waters of the sea. His gigantic wings were folded against the scaled body and the taloned feet were being used as the rudders beneath the waterline.

How magnificent a creature, thought the youth as he walked to the rail. He found it difficult to imagine that he had created such a beautiful thing - and in another lifetime as well!

"Thank you for your admiration, Master", Sjogai's smile appeared more like a grimace. Now, if you would again climb upon my snout and find your seating, we will be on our way."

As soon as Bahuraja was secured upon the scaled saddle behind Sjogai's horned ears, the giant creature unfolded his wings and began to ascend into the sky. Taking one more glance below to the dragonship, Bahuraja waved goodbye to the crew who stood by the rails cheering. He was only slightly surprised to see that Hadjii stood among them, waving a smiling goodbye and his blessings to the young prince's forthcoming adventure.

THE CAVES OF SJOGAI

For the first few days after Sjogai's departure from his crystal cave, Sjhanara was content to just enjoy the luxury of her near surroundings. Every morning, the tinkling of the crystal walls would softly awaken her.

Shortly after her awakening, Elvandora would bring a tray of various sliced fruits and juices as well as some sort of freshly baked bread. This tasty repast was enjoyed in the huge poster bed where the girl slept at night.

It was the most beautiful bed Sjhanara had ever seen. At home, she had enjoyed luxury of sorts, being the daughter of a Clan leader, but nothing like the surroundings provided by the dragon Sjogai.

Where her bed at home had been carved from wood of the surrounding forests and had bedclothes of finely hand-woven linens, Sjogai's guest had been allowed to sleep on a bed of sheer silks and soft cushions. A veil of gossamer silk fell from the ceiling to enclose the bed at night. A colorful hand-embroidered quilt covered the girl as she slept and she was never too chilled or too warm.

Each morning, after breaking fast, Elvandora would accompany Sjhanara to an adjoining room where a large steaming pool of scented water awaited for her bath.

Stepping into its freshness, was sheer pleasure to the girl. She could almost swim in it, it was so large and the feeling of the warmed scented waters against her naked skin made her tingle with delight.

Elvandora had explained to Sjhanara that the waters were warmed from underground volcanic steam vents and kept a proper temperature by the addition of fresh, cooling spring waters.

After her bath, Sjhanara was given a soothing massage of scented oils that gave a lovely sheen to her already beautiful body.

Sjhanara got used to the tiny woman's administrations of dressing and undressing her although it had been strange at first. Each day, a new gown or seshu was ready for her after her bath and massage. Cloth of the most unusual weaving or texture and colors would cause the girl's eyes to widen and she marveled at herself in the crystal mirrored walls of her room.

She had to admit that she was fair to gaze upon. Beauty was not something one dwelled upon in her clan - at least not outwardly.

Sjhanara had never really thought about her looks while growing up. Her main purpose then was developing her skills as a warrior. Of course, she was aware of the subtle metamorphosis of her body as she changed from a girl into a young woman, but even the admiring glances of the young men had been wasted on her.

Now, however, seeing herself as another might, Sjhanara began to sense rather strange sensations within herself. Gazing at her reflections in these crystal walls, she would often feel a blush rising to her cheeks.

One morning, just after her bath, she viewed her naked body in her mirror. The face staring back at her was oval, with slightly wide-set eyes. A cascade of golden blonde hair framed the face in waves and soft, damp ringlets. The eyes were green with golden-brown flecks that she knew sometimes danced with mischief and daring. The nose was slightly small and pert.

It was the mouth, however, that really drew attention. The lips were full and sensuous. *'Made for kissing.'* This thought brought a real blush to the girl's cheeks. She found she blushed easily these days.

Gazing downward at the rest of her body, Sjhanara saw the full breasts. A baby would have no problem suckling these. The thought caused her to catch her breath.

As she surveyed the remainder of her body, no part of her beauty escaped her. She had never given thought to herself like this before.

It was not uncommon in Sjhanara's tribe for men and women to mate before marriage. It was even allowed for one child to be born without a marriage union. There was no shame in that, but Sjhanara had never wanted that kind of union. She had not even willingly allowed any of the village youths to kiss her, though many had tried. Somehow, deep inside, she knew that the man she made union with would be special. She would save herself for this man or have none at all!

Her mother had explained much about the union of a man and woman, and of course, Sjhanara had witnessed the mating of animals, but none of this had affected her regarding herself. *Until now.*

Her examination caused her whole body to become inflamed. Grabbing a robe of silk, she quickly wrapped it around her. *Well,* she decided, *this was not for her!* She could not allow herself to be involved in such practices.

She still had the Test of the Zandorn to complete. Then there would be more training to become the leader of her Clan. Having a mate could be decided on then, if absolutely necessary, but not until then!

As the days continued, however, Sjhanara became more and more nervous and discontented with inactivity. She begged Elvandora for something to do to take up the time waiting for Sjogai's return.

The older elven woman knew what was bothering Sjhanara and chuckled to herself. *Ahh, the cravings of youth,* she would think to herself. She remembered her first encounters with the ways of elven men. Then she remembered her marriage to her own beloved Dorsoro. What a rutter he was! This slip of a girl didn't know what she was missing. But then, she was human.

Elvandora decided it wouldn't hurt to take Sjhanara to the cave of the fledgling dragons. Perhaps it would help her to forget her unease. She also needed to check on the conditions there and to see if Othux and Othorn were behaving themselves in the Master's absence.

Sjhanara was delighted at the opportunity to go outside the crystal halls of Sjogai's cave and accompany Elvandora. She was up and ready long before the sun had risen above the horizon and only nibbled at the fruits and the bread Elvandora brought for her breakfast.

She dogged the elven woman's heels so full of questions about the journey that Elvandora was almost sorry she had suggested her coming.

Soon, however, they were on their way. It would take a half day's journey by foot. Elvandora could have secured the use of one of the young, lesser land dragons to carry them, but she felt Sjhanara needed the exercise to take away some of her restlessness.

The day started out with a beautiful sky and a slight, fresh breeze. By the time the sun had risen fully, the pair had already traveled several miles. It was difficult for Sjhanara to keep her pace at the slower rate of her companion, but she had to allow for the other woman's shorter legs.

She used the pace to thoroughly examine the flora and fauna of the area. There were many different species here than she had knowledge of. She plied Elvandora with questions about the existence of healing herbs and botanicals, of which the elven woman replied the area was virtually a healer's paradise.

They would stop often to examine some plant or other that contained healing powers. Tangawort root - when ground to a powder and brewed into a tea healed stomach aches. The milk-like juices from the Lumlum weed aided cuts and bruises. The young needles of the banyon tree could be brewed into a tea and mixed with certain mosses to provide a poultice for respiratory problems. A rare type of Orris grew, whose petals, when mixed with tangawort root, helped ease pains in the joints and head. The flowers of the multi-blossomed stalks of the Dragonhead plant could be dried and when ground into a powder, used to relax the nerves and even induce sleep.

At one stop, Elvandora stooped to gather several whole plants of a low growing variety near a clump of furry-leaved bushes. She put them, dirt and all into her leather pack she carried. She also examined and gathered several of the furry leaves from the larger bushes. At Sjhanara's query, the elven only murmured something about them being useful for woman's complaint, but refused to explain any further.

She had not had to use their qualities for years, but felt they might come in handy soon. It was not for the girl to know that an elixir from these plants could prohibit pregnancy. Elven women with too many children sometimes used the elixir to keep from conceiving. Just how much a human would have to consume to accomplish the same result was beyond Elvandora's scope of knowledge. She would seek the counsel of her village shaman before enlightening the girl as to its powers.

Sjhanara was very curious why Elvandora refused to tell her the use of these particular plants when she had been so careful about explaining all of the others, but she had found out that to badger the older woman would get her nothing. The pair traveled silently after that for some time before her curiosity caused the girl to speak again.

"Elvandora", even though you are Elven, your womenfolk have children, do they not?"

"Of course, girl. We must survive as do humans. We marry and eventually children begin to come. Why do you ask?"

"I...I am just curious. Please do not think me prying, but is the way of Elven men the same as human?"

The Elven woman kept on walking silently for several moments and Sjhanara began to think she had asked a forbidden question.

Elvandora eventually halted near a large flat ledge of rock protected from the hot sun by a large-leaved tree.

"Sit down on yonder rock, Sjhanara", commanded the tiny woman. "Me thinks you've a great deal on your mind concerning the ways of men and women and have need of counseling. Am I right?"

Sjhanara hesitated, but was firmly directed to sit when the pair reached the small outcropping. She kept silent as Elvandora also found a comfortable spot to ease onto.

Her short legs stuck out in front, her tiny cobbled shoes showing well-worn bottoms. Sjhanara realized she had no idea how old this diminutive woman was. Her face showed signs of weathering, yet seemed softly youthful and there was usually a hint of merriment in her eyes. Now, those eyes had a questioning look as they gazed deeply into the eyes of her young charge.

"Now, while we have a brief rest, girl, what is it that troubles your mind about the ways of sex?"

With the word 'sex', Sjhanara's cheeks tinged a faint pink and she quickly looked down at her nervous hands. "I..I.. didn't really mean...I..mean...I know about that, but, what I mean...."

Elvandora looked hard into the girl's eyes. "Have you ever been with a man, Sjhanara?"

The girl's head jerked up and she stared into the tiny woman's eyes. "No, never!" she exclaimed. "I mean, not as you imply. It's just that lately strange things have come upon me...feelings...that I can't explain. I am not totally unwise to the ways of coupling, but, well, my mother talked to me about it some, but I am confused about the importance of it all. I know there is great love between my mother and my father and I know that they must have joy in their coupling or there would not have been children, but...." At that, the girl stopped. Her face was a mixture of question and torture.

The elven woman pondered for a moment and then knew what she must say.

"Sjhanara, you are a very young woman. Your body is going through changes that are a mystery to you, not unlike the magic of the sages. You have set a goal for yourself that is different from the normal ways of womankind."

At the defensive look which came to Sjhanara's eyes, Elvandora put up her hand to stop a response. "All I am saying, girl, is that by now, most women your age are married and bearing children and tending to the hearth fires of their husbands."

"I don't want that kind of life, Elvandora. Not for a long time at least. I want to be a warrior like my father and brothers. I want to rule my family's clan when my father passes on. I have spent all my life training for this and I don't want the life of most women to hinder what I want!"

Sjhanara had risen from her rock seat and been stomping around the area. Each stomp emphasizing her resolve.

"Sit down, girl!" Elvandora's command was sharp and declared no nonsense. "Did the fact that your father was ruler of his clan keep him from taking a wife? Did it keep him from casting his seed to produce children? Was he not able to rule his people and raise a family at the same time? What is the matter with you, you silly gootling?"

Sjhanara pondered the woman's words and realized there was no argument with what she said. It was just that how would she know?

"You are wondering how you will know the right man when he comes along, Sjhanara", echoed Elvandora to the girl's thoughts. "Girl, how can I tell you one of life's great mysteries? In the Elven world, coupling is as natural as eating. I enjoyed several elven men when I was a young girl. The way of a man and woman is a beautiful thing when done correctly. But..." here, Elvandora got a dreamy look in her eyes. "When my Dorsoro...that's my beloved husband... came into my life, well, that was different."

Elvandora shifted a little on her rock and clasped her hands to her bosom. "One day I was out gathering herbs for my mother's house. I was happy with my life. Life was carefree and good. Elvens are by the most part, a happy lot. We don't allow the same concerns about life to bother us as you humans do.

"However, back to my story. I was bent over selecting the leaves from a certain plant when a shadow shut out the sun. When I looked up, there was the handsomest elven I had ever laid eyes on. My heart did a flipflop and I felt it clear down into my toes. I must have looked very silly indeed with my mouth wide open, dirt on my face and clothing, but I didn't care. All I could see or feel was that handsome face and the beating of my heart in my pointed ears.

"Well, Dorsoro - as he soon told me his name - had darker hair than most of my people, and laughing eyes. He asked me if there was a place nearby where he could get something to eat and drink before traveling on. All I could do was point in the direction of our village nestled within the roots and branches of a grove of tall tonka trees to the north of here.

"Dorsoro laughed and took my hand, dirty as it was, and kissed it and then asked me if I would accompany him to the village. My feet never touched the ground from that point on. Do you know that he never let my hand go the whole way back to the village?

"I took him to my father's house and Dorsoro was immediately welcomed and invited to dinner. It is the way of all elvens. No stranger is ever turned away.

"All through the meal, Dorsoro's eyes would follow me as I helped serve. I had made sure I had on my prettiest dresher and had brushed my hair to a fine sheen. When it's not braided in elven fashion for women, it is quite long. In fact, mine hangs down to the floor.

"When the dinner was over, my father brought out pipes and lit one for himself and our guest while mother and I cleaned up. I was so nervous I kept dropping plates and our eating spoons. My mother finally booted me out of the kitchen for being such a ninny, but she knew.

"As the nightbirds began their drowsy twittering, my father invited Dorsoro to stay the night and continue his journey the following day. Dorsoro was happy to accept the invitation.

"Now, the elven custom, when a guest stays, is to put him up with one of the children. If that child happens to be a nearly grown daughter, such as I was, there is no problem. The family accepts that there might be an attraction or not. It is up to the couple.

"I was so shy. Like you, I felt stirrings within my body that I'd never felt before. I told you, I had coupled with elven boys before, but they had not made me feel like what was going on within me with Dorsoro.

"When we got into my bed, I was shivering like a quakeleaf. I laid there like a stone, afraid to even look at the handsome elven beside me. Then he reached over and took my hand and kissed it again, as in the meadow. His eyes had the question. I knew, deep within, that I would submit to this man because on the morrow he would leave and I might never see him again.

"I was going to blow out the candle, but he said to let it glow. He wanted to watch my face as he made love to me and then he kissed me."

There was ecstasy written on Elvandora's face even now, as she recalled that first kiss. "Oh, Sjhanara, how gentle Dorsoro was to me. All through that night he made such wonderful love to me; a love such as I had never known with the others. I dreaded the coming of morning, but I knew I would always have that night.

"With the morning, I awoke to find Dorsoro already gone. For days I wore a lump of rock where my heart is. I only half performed my duties. No more did I want a romp in the bushes with any of the village boys. I sent them all away with a sharp tongue. I cried into my pillow every night and didn't want to even change my bedding because I wanted to hold on to whatever I had had with Dorsoro.

"My mother and father kept silent and let me suffer through my pain, but there were lots of hugs and squeezes to let me know they were there for me. The pain finally became a dull ache, but I knew what love was by then, or at least I thought I did. I thought it was either ecstasy or pain. I wasn't sure I wanted any of it, if this was what it did to an elven.

"About half a year later, who should show up in our village again, but Dorsoro! He came directly to our home and approached my father. He told him that, if accepted, he would like to take me to wife. He showed my father a pouch of coin worth a king's ransom as dowry for my hand.

My father then called me to him and told me of Dorsoro's offer. I was so surprised, but seeing him brought back the night of wonder and I knew with no doubts whatsoever that I wanted to be his wife.

"I've never been sorry, Sjhanara," an unbidden tear traveled down Elvandora's cheek. "Dorsoro has treated me like a queen every day of my life and every night when we lay in each other's arms, it is as the first night."

"How long have you been married?" came the girl's soft question.

"A long time", Elvandora answered. "We elvens do not measure time in the same manner as you humans. In fact, we live much longer. What I want you to understand, Sjhanara, is that when Destiny brings two people together who belong together, they will know it.

"Dorsoro knew it that first time we came together, but he also knew that he wanted to be able to provide well for me. That is why he went away. He went to sea and earned what he hoped would be enough dowry to ask my father for my hand. I would have gone with him for nothing, but he loved me too much for that. He wanted all in our village to know that the man Elvandora married would provide well for her. He has been a loving husband and we have had six wonderful children together. All of them are grown now, but our sex life has never diminished."

Her story finished, Elvandora got up, picked up her pack and with a glance at the thoughtful girl, started walking again. As she followed, Sjhanara mulled over and over in her mind what this tiny woman had told her. *'When Destiny brings two people together who belong together, they will know it'*, she had said.

The sun was high when the caves of Sjogai's young came into view. Several fledglings were outside, sunning themselves upon the rocks and ledges. When the elven woman and her taller companion were detected, a loud ruckus ensued. All of the young dragons began hissing and blowing puffs of smoke from their nostrils. They lashed the ground with their tails and tried to look ferocious. The smaller ones could only squeak and look ridiculous, but they tried to emulate their older peers as best they could.

Sjhanara could not suppress the giggle the scene produced. The young dragons were so cute and yet she knew they would grow into very large and dangerous beings.

Elvandora waved the staff she had used for walking and spoke a command in the elven tongue. Immediately the young dragons quieted down, yet kept their full attention on the two women. Who knew, these visitors just might have a snack or two to share with them. As young dragons, they were always hungry.

As the pair came closer to the entrance to the main cave, a very strong odor met their sense of smell. Sjhanara had to hold a corner of her seshu to her nose to keep from gagging. From deep within, the sound of scuffling and arguing could be heard.

"It is your turn to clean this section!"

"Oh, no, I cleaned it last time, it's your turn to clean it!"

"You're not going to bamboozle me this time, Othorn, you lazy dragon fart. I'm not doing your work and mine too! Now take this spade and get to it!"

"Ouch! How dare you hit me with that spade, Othux!" I'm going to tell the Master when he returns, and just who are you calling a dragon fart, you paddle-faced turd-eared .... Ayyee, Elvandora!"

By this time, Elvandora and Sjhanara had made a turn inside the cave and there before them were the two elvens who had been banished to the caves by Sjogai as punishment for their constant arguing.

Their jerkins were filthy. Dragon dung stained their leggings and their feet were disgustingly covered with the smelly stuff. Their round faces were smudged and even their hair contained bits of straw and no telling what else.

"Enough, you two!" Elvandora's angry command stopped the pair in mid sentence. "From the looks and smell of things, neither one of you has cleaned anything since you got here. Perhaps I should tell Sjogai myself how you have bungled even this lowly job. He may decide you deserve something even more distasteful than cleaning dragon caves!"

"Oh, oh, oh! Please, Elvandora, mercy on us!" wailed the pair, as they groveled at her tiny feet. The elven woman had to back up to keep from some of their filthiness transferring to her!

"We are not arguing. We are but making important decisions of the day!"

Even as they plead their cause, the two pitiful elvens, scrambled for their spades and sweeps and began to raise such a dust the two women had to make a dash back to the entrance in order to breathe.

Elvandora shook the dirt and dust from her skirts and grumbled epithets in her elven language that even Sjhanara could imagine the meanings of.

"Those two will never amount to anything!" Elvandora grumbled.

After filling her lungs again with the fresher air outside and dusting herself off, Sjhanara couldn't help smiling. "But they are so cute! They couldn't possibly be as bad as you say."

"Cute, you say! Cute! Only their poor aged mothers, bless them, could care about those two. The gods protect them when Sjogai returns and sees the conditions of these caves! One thing you don't do is anger Sjogai."

Elvandora then began to inspect the contents of four other caves of the young of Sjogai. In the first cave, several eggs lay in clusters in nests of twigs, sand and the occasional discarded dragon scale. When the baby dragons hatched, they were moved to a second cave where they were nursed by a few smaller drab gray female dragons who were the occasional mates of Sjogai, but who were usually mated by other lesser male dragons.

It was obvious to Sjhanara that the male dragons must be the ones who developed the beautiful colors. Even the youngest males sported scales of various shades of green, purple, red, rust and even tinges of gold.

Elvandora explained to the young girl that the true golden dragons were singled out for special training as they matured. Each prominent color held certain rank of higher or lesser importance. Golden dragons were very rare and were given dominion over various special areas of the planet. It was also explained that golden dragons were the sole result of Sjogai's seed. That was the reason they were of such exalted status.

Sjhanara was fascinated to learn how many different types of dragons there were; fire dragons, water wurms, air and land dragons. The mating habits were rather complex and she wasn't sure she understood just how one male dragon could have so many different types of offspring, but she guessed it had to do with the female he selected.

Elvandora explained that Sjogai was very different from all the other dragons; that he had been formed in another lifetime from the very flesh of the creator of this sphere. Sjogai had been the first living creature here after the creation. It was Sjogai who guarded the possessions of the creator.

All this was too much for Sjhanara to comprehend. *Other lifetime? creator's possessions?* Wasn't the Creator The Ultimate Keeper? Was that not the teachings of the priests? No, now that she thought back on it, that was not quite the wording of the ancient writings.

Sjhanara had not been an apt pupil of the scriptures during her upbringing. All that mystery and ritual was confusing to her and yet she believed in a superior being who created all things. Her mind began to fill with more and more questions. She knew that when Sjogai returned, she would ask much of him concerning all of this. For what end, she knew not. All that she did know, was it all now was important. Her destiny seemed to be linked to knowing.

While Sjhanara reflected on these mysteries, Elvandora continued to inspect the caves and the fledglings. She could be heard barking out this order or that to the workers. Othux and Othorn were not the only elvens in the service of Sjogai concerning the raising of his offspring. In fact, with the exception of the two battling bantyweights, most of the elvens considered it an honor to work for the ancient dragon and attended to their duties cheerfully and with diligence.

There were the hunters who searched the forests for just the right game for feeding the young dragons. Most female dragons usually laid their eggs in a nest of their own making in the caves and cared for them until they hatched. Some of the wilder females, however, laid their eggs wherever they were disposed to and then often left them to the elements and fate. It was up to the gatherer elvens to find these eggs and bring them back to the caves.

Not all these eggs were from the seed of Sjogai directly, but in a sense belonged to him in one way or another since he was responsible for the entire dragon population of Acarda.

The females Sjogai personally impregnated were kept in a separate cave a distance away from here and were treated with royal care. They became very fat and lazy, therefore being unable to feed their young themselves.

Dragons did not mate often - usually about once every forty years. It was another three years before the eggs were laid. After that, it depended on the surrounding conditions as to when the eggs hatched. If left in the open and untended, some never matured - the fetus dying within the leather- like shell. Sometimes roving animals would come upon a nest and steal an egg while the female was out hunting food.

This is why Sjogai had instructed the elvens to gather as many as could be found and bring them to these caves. He knew that without special attention, the existence of dragons could become extinct, just as it had in his former world.

As Sjhanara followed Elvandora through the *'nurseries'*, one small fire dragon fledgling slithered near and jumped upon the toes of her right foot. It startled her and she kicked her foot causing the tiny reptile to be flung across the dusty cave floor and against a small rock. The action didn't hurt it much, but the squeaking and hissing was so pitiful that Sjhanara rushed over immediately, gathered the tiny creature into her arms and cuddled it.

As she cooed and caressed the fledgling, it snuggled against her, raised its pointed little nose to her cheek and gave her a lick with its tiny forked tongue. The girl laughed and drew it even closer. With an almost inaudible hiss, the dragonlet sighed, closed its eyes and fell fast asleep, its head resting upon Sjhanara's bosom.

"Oh, Elvandora, isn't he just the cutest thing?" she whispered. "Do you suppose Sjogai would allow me to keep it? At least until I leave on my quest again?"

Elvandora looked at the sight of this young woman rocking that baby dragon in the curve of her arms and crooning some tuneless lullaby probably remembered from her own childhood. "*So*", she thought to herself, "*this human female wants no part of motherhood, eh? Wants no babies to suckle at her breast or man to help her produce one?*" Yagenta, Sjhanara's middle name, meant 'gentle'. It was obvious this young woman had a lot to learn about herself.

Elvandora saw no problem with letting Sjhanara keep the dragonlet since it was one of the smaller varieties and would grow slowly. Her consent brought such a smile to the young girl that her face beamed.

Sjhanara named it 'Sneezer' because every time it tried to spit fire, it only sneezed out a small puff of smoke.

The girl carried Sneezer to the door of the cave, sat down on a nearby rock and continued to sing to it. Her voice was clear and the song she sang floated through the air like the tinkling of bellflowers.

Othux and Othorn, emerging from their cave to take a break from their duties, stood in awe at Sjhanara's beauty and the singing.

"How could you have ever thought this human female ugly?" queried Othux, who looked a little in love with the girl himself.

"Me?" argued Othorn, a pained look upon his dirty face. "Me, think her ugly? Why, you wart-nosed son of a gorka's hoof, it was you who thought her ugly. I have always known she was a beauty of great prize!"

"Who's a wart-nosed son of a gorka's hoof, you, you, blat-eared dung fossil!"

Othorn lunged at Othux and the pair wrestled in the dirt, their little fists punching and bare-toed feet kicking at each other for all they were worth.

At the sound of the ruckus, Elvandora came running from the cave she'd been inspecting. "What's going on here?" she hollered. Raising her staff, she began to beat at the pair, not caring where she hit or how hard.

Their cries of 'mercy! mercy!', brought other cave workers out to see what all the noise was about. Even a few of the young dragons showed interest. Their tongues flicked in and out of their long maws and their tails flailed the earth in agitation. Some of the slightly older fire dragons were even able to puff out a small flame or two.

"You two worthless imps!" Elvandora screamed. "When Sjogai returns, I'll make sure he knows about your constant bickering. You'll be lucky to be left on this planet when he gets through with you!" She emphasized each word with a whack of her staff upon whatever part of their bodies came under its torture.

Finally, even Sjhanara couldn't stand it any longer. "Elvandora, please!" her cry stopped Elvandora's hand in mid whack. "Please don't hit them any more!"

The young girl went to the two elvens and they could see tears running down her cheeks. Tears, for them! No one had ever cared enough to shed tears over them before.

"Fine thing!" Elvandora grumbled. "It won't do, you know, Sjhanara, to feel sorry for this pair of lazy good-for-nothings. They'll only take advantage. They'll end up in the Dogar swamps when Sjogai returns, mark my words!"

Othux and Othorn scrambled to their feet and stood in humble shame before the two women. Their bruises were already beginning to swell and dark circles forming where the heavy staff had found its mark. In fact, there was a lump on the top of Othorn's head that nearly matched his bulbous nose.

In spite of her genuine concern over their injuries, Sjhanara couldn't help but giggle. They looked so pitiful - covered with dirt and dragon dung. The girl knelt down before them. "You truly are a pair of rag-a-muffins", she crooned.

Immediately, the two were smitten. At that moment, they both would gladly have walked into the mouth of Sjogai and become his meal. Their little hearts began to thump within their tiny chests and they were Sjhanara's slaves forever.

"We're truly sorry, Elvandora", they shuffled their feet and bowed their heads low. "Please don't let us be sent to the Dogar swamps!" At the mere thought of that dreadful place, the two shuddered.

"Hummph!" was Elvandora's only reply.

"By the eyes of The Ultimate Keeper, we won't fight each other any more." Othux peeked up at Sjhanara and a tiny smile came to his bruised lips, causing him to wince a little.

"Oh, you are truly in pain", Sjhanara reached out and touched the swollen lower lip of Othux and caressed his cheek. "Elvandora, have we no salve to soothe these wounds?"

By now the two Elvens were so enthralled with the young princess that they were near faint.

"Sjhanara, you are completely playing into their hands", the diminutive elven woman tried to sound harsh, but even as she spoke, she began to dig around in her herb bag until she found some of the fresh moanna leaves she had just gathered. Rubbing them together between her tiny palms, the leaves began to juice up until a pulp was formed.

"Now, you two, go to the stream and wash all that filth from your bodies - clothes and all. Only when you are clean will I take care of those bruises. The Ultimate Keeper knows why I even offer. If it weren't for Sjhanara's sympathy, you two would have been allowed to suffer."

When Orthux and Othorn returned, much cleaner from their bathing, the pulp was thinly applied to the cuts and bruises of the two errant elvens.

"There, you two. It's more than you deserve, but you have found a savior in the princess here. It's to her you owe your salvation. Beware, however, I will not allow any elven antics in the future out of either of you. I will still make a report to Sjogai upon his return. You may not be out of the swamp yet!"

For once, Othux and Othorn were two very subdued elvens and again mumbled their apologies after thanking Elvandora for putting salve on their wounds.

"Can I trust the two of you to return to your duties in the dragon caves until Sjogai releases you?" Again the two voiced a unified humble response to the affirmative.

Noticing the sun had begun dipping below the horizon, Elvandora made the decision to spend the night at the caves. She led Sjhanara a short distance away to a little hut built for just such a stay.

The small building had only one main room; one wall of which was all fireplace. Sjhanara had to stoop over quite a bit to get inside the doorway, but once in, it seemed roomy enough.

Elvandora busied herself around the fireplace, taking this and that from her huge pouch and dropping it into a cauldron hanging from a hook implanted in the fireplace wall. Soon a delicious spicy smell of something cooking began to fill the room. Sjhanara, offering to help, was told just to sit at the rough hand-hewn table and relax until the meal was completed.

With the warmth of the fire and Sneezer curled around her leg dozing, Sjhanara yawned. She was having a hard time keeping her eyes open when a bowl of steamy soup was placed before her.

"Here, eat this before you fall asleep at the table. We still have some of our unleavened toku bread in our packs to dip into the soup. I'll make up a batch of dough to set for tomorrow's journey home."

Elvandora hastily ate her own bowl of the delicious soup and then set about mixing up a batch of the traditional elven bread - toku. Patting it into little round loaves, she placed them on a shelf about midway up the side of the interior of the fireplace. They would rise and bake during the night and be ready for their breakfast. Any leftovers would pack nicely into their knapsacks for the journey home.

Sjhanara was so sleepy, she hardly had any energy to eat, but the soup was good and warmed her stomach. Barely had she finished when she sought one of the straw pallets that lined the walls; she was asleep before her head rested on her arm. Sneezer snuggled into the curve of the her body, sneezed a little sigh and followed her into a deep sleep.

Elvandora, by now quite weary herself, made sure that one of the warm furs, folded neatly in one corner of the hut, was placed over the girl to take off the chill of the night after the fire died down.

As she tucked the fur beneath the girl's chin, the elven woman gazed for a moment into the sleeping face. "Ah, Sjhanara", she crooned. "Sleep the sleep of youth and innocence for your tomorrows are filled with Destiny. Soon, my sweet girl, soon you will know the answers to so many of your questions. Soon you will meet your heart's fire. Be prepared, Princess Sjhanara, your prince awaits you."

For a long while, Sjhanara slept the deep sleep of no dreams, but after awhile, strange scenes began to emerge. From the cloudy fog of sleep marched strange creatures and places. Sjhanara stirred in her sleep, but not enough to waken. She clutched the bedfurs close as she seemed to feel an icy chill of a deep cold surround her. Before her was a wall of ice. She knew that she must go beyond this wall to meet her destiny. However, there was no doorway, no cracks, nothing she could find that would allow her through.

All she had was the wooden sword her father had carved for her as a little girl. She was hacking away at the wall of ice with all her strength, yet the wall held. Her nails and fingers were bleeding from her trying to find even the tiniest of cracks in which to place a wedge. Shadows followed her and she was frightened. *"Oh mighty warrior, Sjhanara"*, the shadows mocked. *"Where is thy sword?"*

"I hold it in my grasp", she cried, "But its edge is dulled."

"That is not thy sword", spoke the shadows. *"It is but a toy. Doest thou believe thou hast a true weapon to dispel yon wall?"*

"It is all I have", came her panting reply. "It is the sword of my father's hand. It will help me overcome this icy fortress. The honor of my clan depends upon my strength."

"Seek not the sword of thy father's clan, Sjhanara. Seek ye the hidden sword of a mightier warrior than Janor Hajatnii. Therein lies thy true destiny!"

More misty scenes invaded the young girl's dreams. A face tried to come into view; a strong, chiseled face, a strong muscular body, yet the touch of that hand to her face was gentle. The face lowered to hers and placed a tender kiss to her lips. Then the kiss became more passionate. She felt her body responding to this strong being whose face she couldn't quite make out in her dream.

"I want you, Sjhanara", a deep voice whispered into the hollow of her neck. "It is I who you have waited for, my heart's desire. Let me carry you to paradise."

Sjhanara shifted in her sleep. Her body was aflame She ached with desire for the promised act of love. At that moment, she awoke.

At first, she was disoriented. Still half asleep, she still felt the urgings of her body. Then, seeing the sleeping elven woman across the room from her and the walls of the hut reality brought her totally awake.

Her cheeks burned with the remembrance of the dream still so fresh in her mind. As the dream slowly faded, Sjhanara shivered.

What manner of dreams were these that made the body respond so? What was the portent of the voices? Was there anything to it, or was it just a dream of no import; yet it had seemed so real.

REVELATIONS

Bahuraja dozed as he flew the skies on the back of Sjogai, the Golden Dragon. His dreams were disoriented and broken. He drifted back and forth between his homeland and the hearth fires of his parents to this strange new land of elvens, dragons, sea monsters and magical powers.

He jerked awake as Sjogai banked and changed direction slightly.

"Where are we headed, Sjogai?"

"We've not far to go now, Prince Bahuraja", the dragon spoke into his mind.

Bahuraja noticed the darkening sky as the sun had already set. There was only a red-orange streak at the horizon and stars were appearing.

He also noticed a keen feeling of hunger beginning in his stomach. He had eaten only sparingly since the saving of his shipboard companions.

Sjogai, mentally sensing the youth's discomfort, let him know that a nice warm meal would be waiting for him when they landed.

The landscape began to change to one of deep forests and rocky outcroppings. It was near one such pinnacle that Sjogai finally came to rest. He folded his huge ribbed wings and lowered his head so that Bahuraja could slide down to the ground.

Bahuraja's legs were stiff after the long flight, but a bit of flexing and walking around soon took away that off-balance feeling. He walked down the small path Sjogai had told him to take that would lead down a slight embankment to a clearing below. In that clearing, he found himself before a nice warm fire with a large eclot roasting on a spit. Large leaf-wrapped tubors roasted in the coals and oaku bubbled in a thick leathern container on a warming rock.

Bahuraja rubbed his hands over the fire and smiled in anticipation of the meal. The smells were enough to cause his stomach to really speak out their distress.

"You'll find a thick leather bowl beside the fire, Prince Bahuraja", a voice spoke from beyond the light of the fire. "Eat your fill and then we will visit for a time."

Bahuraja strained to see where the voice came from and was soon rewarded as a frail wizened figure emerged from the thicket of trees on the other side of the fire. The Old One! How long had it been since Bahuraja had sat in the cave this withered ancient called home? He took a step towards the old wizard, but the latter held out his hand.

"Eat, eat, Bahuraja, I might even have a morsel myself, what say you, Sjogai? Care to join us in a bit of eclot and tubor?"

In the moments that had passed, the dragon had transformed himself into his man-shape and was already slicing off thick pieces of eclot into one of the leathern bowls. "I'm way ahead of everyone - flying is tiring and hungry business. Better hurry, Bahuraja, last one to the feast eats the leavings!"

Bahuraja spun around to face the imposing handsome features of a stranger, yet the voice was that of Sjogai. Warily keeping his eyes on this smiling being, he picked up the proffered bowl and absentmindedly began to fill it. A hot tubor brought him to his senses.

"Sjogai?" he exclaimed as he dropped the steaming hot vegetable onto the ground. "What manner of magic is this that you have the body of a man as well as a dragon?"

Sjogai exploded into laughter at the perplexed look on Bahuraja's face. It was left up to the ancient one to explain more of the mysteries of this strange world as they ate. Bahuraja listened with rapt attention as more of his planet's mysteries were unfolded before him.

After the initial shock of seeing Sjogai's transformed self, he ate ravishingly, stopping only to ask the occasional question.

In his former life and world, Bahuraja had taken great pains to insure his new world's creations would be as he desired them to be. Sjogai, in the other world, had actually been a recreation of Bahuraja's own molecular self - to create an '*image*'. Bahuraja had transformed himself into this image whenever he wanted to impress the locals or whenever he wanted to observe that world from the air. When Sjogai was transferred to this world, he was still a part of Bahuraja's own molecular structure, and as such, had the power to create 'images' of his own, ie, the ability to change into human form. All other creations of Bahuraja's making were made of other molecular structuring and with only a few exceptions, kept one image only.

All of the humans who inhabited parts of this world had been given certain '*subliminal mental instructions*' before their deaths in their former lives. Upon their demise, their spirits came directly to this new world; all with the Keeper's blessings of course.

These humans kept their original molecular makeup for the most part, yet were endowed with stronger mental capabilities. Part of this was due to the atmosphere of the planet, part was due to the implanted 'suggestions' of the planet's creator, Bahuraja, to utilize their brains to the fullest.

It was long believed on the old Earth that man had originally been created with all the powers of telepathy, teleportation, the ability to heal themselves and others and much more, but lost those powers through degradation and sinful natures over the centuries. In the end, therefore, most of Mankind only used a fraction of their mind capabilities.

The ancient teachers, or sanseis, of the old world had taught Bahuraja how to utilize his own brain's capabilities to the fullest. With practice, he had developed the power to heal, to dematerialize objects (as well as himself) and use the molecules to restructure an object or to create something entirely different.

It was this ability that had eventually caused Bahuraja to become despised in his former life. The ruling powers of his world imagined this quiet, yet imposing figure a threat to their positions. They did not see that Bahuraja only wanted to undo the pain and suffering of the peoples in his world.

Although most of the people he healed and helped loved him, Bahuraja soon became sought after by the authorities. They wanted to eliminate a possible threat to their ways of life.

When Bahuraja finally saw that he could do no more to help the people he had come to love and help, he retreated to his castle island. In constant meditation, he 'created' a new world and put in motion the architecture that would inhabit it.

After he was satisfied that his creation was to his liking, he said one more prayer for this world and those he loved, laid down in front of his huge Gohonzon and put himself into death sleep. As his spirit broke free of the body, it looked down for one last time at this world. There was no longing to return to the peaceful looking body below. The spirit of Bahuraja knew there was no more use for it here.

It had ascended rapidly into the atmosphere and beyond, searching for the rapturous symphony of the spiritual universe. Once again within the peaceful undulation of this river of Time, the spirit tuned into the wave of direction that would take it to its new existence. Hence, Destiny was to begin anew.

The young prince sat in dazed silence before the now dying campfire. He looked into the face of the ancient wizard's face and reeled under the knowledge of his importance. Some of the old mage's words had been told him before when Bahuraja had been taken to his cave and he remembered them now. Yet, somehow he still felt incomplete. It was difficult to absorb all this knowledge. He was a humble prince. He may have been the original creator of this new world, but he felt very insecure at this moment.

Shifting his tired old bones, the wizard took another puff from his long, ornately carved pipe. "Well, young prince, thou now art ready for thy next adventure. My time here is nearly finished, but thee still hast one or two more duties to perform before I canst leave this existence. I know thy thoughts. It is true, thou art not yet complete. Thee canst not take full rule over this world until thee finishes thy Test of the Zandorn.

"As it is now, there art two planes, still slightly out of phase. Thou must bring them together. Thou wast born into one plane, and thee remembers thy fall into the second. They exist side-by-side ignorant of each other. For some reason, when thou created this new world, it came into being out of phase. Who knowest the reason. The humans for the most part, came into existence in the first phase and thy other creatures, the elvens and such, ended up in the second. Only a few of us hast the ability to travel from one phase to another. We kept an eye on thee from birth to now so that thy destiny could mature in this world, but the time for thy taking over is at hand. Thee must bring the two phases into one or Acarda may not continue."

"But how is that to be done?" despite his new knowledge of the existence of his growing powers, Bahuraja could not quite grasp this new challenge.

The ancient one sighed. Why wast the young prince so difficult? Ah, well, in time he wouldst get it together. "Thou wilt soon have the answers, Bahuraja", was the reply.

"Enough for now. I am tired and needst to rest these old bones for awhile. On the morrow we wilt continue." With that, the old man wrapped his cloak around him and in moments, a soft snoring emanated from the folds.

Sjogai had been silent during the meal and following conversation between Bahuraja and the wizard. His thoughts were far away. He had been monitoring the events of his elven housekeeper, Elvandora and the young princess Sjhanara.

The man-dragon was well aware of his part in this world. Sjogai had actually been the first creature to inhabit Acarda after its creation. He had been the one to welcome the Old One and direct him to the cave-castle where he had overseen the rest of the building and inhabiting. The original Bahuraja had sent Sjogai for just such purpose.

The dragon loved Bahuraja because he was a part of him from the beginning. He owed his existence to the young prince, although this Bahuraja was not yet quite aware of the significance. When he changed into man form, Sjogai became as the original Bahuraja of the old world; tall, lean of body, with golden hair instead of dark yet still with a deep widow's peak at the forehead. The eyes were of a golden hue instead of Bahuaraja's blue and seemed to pierce whatever they gazed upon. The mouth was somewhat sensual and rested above a slightly weak chin. This did not mean that the person was weak, however.

Sjogai's shoulders were broad and muscular and narrowed down to a lean waist and hips supported by long legs. If the young prince were to have really studied Sjogai, he would see much of the man he would grow into. One would have thought them brothers in fact, one dark, one light.

Bahuraja was already quite muscular of build and his handsome features would mold into an even more handsome countenance as he grew older. His eyes would take on more and more wisdom as his reign over this planet taught him. He would become a very wise and benevolent ruler and his subjects would love him as he never had known in his former world. All this was known by Sjogai, but as yet this knowledge was held back from the young prince.

Bahuraja stared into the firelight silently for some time and then turned to Sjogai. He examined the man-dragon's features for a moment before speaking.

"Sjogai, I am still confused over the knowledge I have received, yet I feel at peace for the first time in my life. Do you know that ever since a small child, I felt something was missing. There are still several gaps in my memory, but it is all beginning to come together.

"I know now, also, that you are a very special part of my life, Sjogai. Will you always be, I mean,...."

"Will I always be around, Bahuraja? Yes, I will be there whenever you have need of me, young prince. I have my own dominions to maintain, of course, but being a part of you, you take precedence. I actually prefer my dragon form, believe it or not, although this body takes up less space. As Sjogai, the dragon, however, I am more an imposing figure when the need arises, as you well know. Yes, you need never fear, I will be only a thought away. That is another lesson you may want to heed. If ever a time comes you do not wish me to be privy to your thoughts, you will have to learn how to block those thoughts from me."

Sjogai picked up a stick and poked at the fire for a moment.

"By the way, Bahuraja, have you given any thought to who you would rule your world with? I mean, a king must have a queen, is this not true?"

The sudden question caused a frown to spread quickly over the young prince's face. "I haven't had much time to think of such things", was his muttered response.

"You should give it thought." Sjogai continued to stir the coals with his stick. "This is a large world to rule and a ruler should have a helpmate. Have you any idea what type of woman you would like as a wife?"

As he stirred the coals, Sjogai stared into the flames. Bahuraja also turned his eyes to the small flames and sparks rising toward the night skies.

Forms seemed to dance on the tips of the flames. As Bahuraja stared, the voluptuous body of a young girl came into focus. Her long red-blonde hair flowed around her face as she danced a slow undulating rhythm. Her seshu barely covered her smooth hips and thighs. Her breasts were bare of covering and were full and inviting. She turned and gazed into his eyes and her lips seemed to invite a kiss. They were full and red and opened into a soundless laugh as if she knew of the desire she could create.

Bahuraja could feel an ache begin as he recognized the beautiful body of the girl who had helped him overcome the dreaded Gholac. Without thinking, he reached for her only to feel the hot flame on his fingers. With an epithet, Bahuraja jerked back his hand, licking his singed fingers.

Sjogai laughed until his sides ached. He had thrown the stick into the fire when Bahuraja swore, causing the image of the beautiful Sjhanara to disappear. Bahuraja's frowns in his direction only caused more laughter. Tears flowed down the man-dragon's face as he continued to snicker at the young prince's discomfort.

"Not very amusing from my point of view, Sjogai." Bahuraja continued to nurse his throbbing fingers.

"Methinks you do have someone in mind, young prince Bahuraja", Sjogai blurted out between his chuckles. "Could it be that the damsel might also find you as comely as you find her?"

Bahuraja looked at Sjogai with a mixture of anger and confusion. "I don't have time to consider a wife. I am young yet and have many adventures before I can settle down. Besides, there is so much to do to this world. You heard the Old One." A frown creased his brow as he paused for a moment. "Yet, yet..."

"Yet you have met someone who keeps coming to your thoughts. Bahuraja, let me advise you. You will meet this girl again. She is a part of your Destiny. You do have your free agency, however. You may or may not find her worthy of your future, but beware, young prince, you are not the only one with strong powers."

With that last statement, Sjogai stretched, yawned and rose from the log he had been sitting on. Muttering something about having to get rid of the wine he had partaken of during the evening, he disappeared into the darkness. Soon, the sound of water hitting the side of a tree came to Bahuraja's ears.

Feeling a rather full bladder himself, he arose and went to the other side of the camp to relieve himself. When he returned, Sjogai was already asleep in his furs.

Bahuraja unfolded his sleeping furs and wrapped them around him. The night had turned rather chilly and the fire had now died down to only a few glowing embers. Before lying down, he added a few sticks of wood to the coals. As he laid there staring into the fire, trying to go to sleep, disturbing thoughts kept bombarding his mind. It was a long time before the young prince's breathing slipped into the same rhythmic pattern of his sleeping companions.

Even in his sleep, however, the dreams continued to disturb him.

TO JOURNEY RETURNED

In the morning, back at the dragon caves, Elvandora was already up and preparing a light breakfast before Sjhanara finally awoke. The smell of food had stirred Sneezer first and his wriggling beneath the young girl's arm awakened her.

Stretching and yawning, Sjhanara smiled to the elven woman. "Good morning, Elvandora", she yawned. "Did you have a good sleep?"

"I always sleep well", was the older woman's reply. "I see you had no problem dropping off last night either. Now, gather yourself to the table and eat this porridge, girl. We must be on the trail soon."

Ravenous, Sjhanara needed no prodding to eat her morning meal. Sneezer got tiny bits of seeds and toku bread from Sjhanara's fingers and even managed to beg a few morsels from Elvandora. The elven woman warned her young charge that feeding this tiny dragon at the table could become a dangerous habit. As if in response, Sneezer sneezed and a tiny puff of smoke tendriled from the nostrils at the end of his long snout.

Sjhanara's laughter at her little pet was as the sound of tinkling bells. She hugged Sneezer and crooned soothing words to him as she left the table and went outside to wash her face from a nearby spring. The small dragon scampered after her and the girl tried splashing water at him, causing him to sneeze and puff. Sneezer decided water wasn't much fun.

Elvandora mumbled something derogatory about the wisdom of having a fire dragon as a pet as she cleaned up the tiny hut and readied for departure.

In no time, the two women were on the trail back to Sjogai's cave. There was little talking, as Sjhanara was very thoughtful during the trip. She wondered how long she would be delayed on her journeys. She had already spent nearly a month at Sjogai's cave and was anxious to get on with her Test of the Zandorn. Sjogai had been very insistent that she await his return, however, and she knew she did not want to anger him by leaving beforehand.

Instinctively, the young girl seemed to know that this huge gentle dragon was a part of her destiny and she was curious to know what that was. Sjhanara had no way of knowing that Sjogai had been in blocked mental contact with Elvandora and was already winging his way back to his lair.

Elvandora, having received her master's message, hurried the young girl along the trail stopping only long enough for short rests. She wanted to get back before moonrise as she knew Sjogai would be arriving within that time frame.

The pair arrived at Sjogai's home cave shortly after the sun had set, having made better time than expected. Elvandora made sure the other elven servants of the dragon had a nice bath readied for Sjhanara before she, herself, looked to her own refreshments. Giving orders left and right, she had the servants scurrying to her will even before she looked to her own bathing. All would be ready for Sjogai upon his return or she would know the reason why. Even returning to her beloved husband, Dorsoro, was not as important as seeing to Sjogai's comforts.

Dukor, the night watchman, announced sighting the master on the horizon only within minutes before the sound of his thundering wings beating the air caused the crystal walls to vibrate. All the servants gathered on the floor in the huge cavern where Sjogai would enter from the sky.

As he lowered himself from the opening at the top of the cavern, his huge shadow darkened the view below. Folding his wings as he settled upon his huge cushioned bed, Sjogai eyed with approval the heavily laden table of food prepared for his benefit. He sought Elvandora from the crowd of servants and mentally asked if all was well.

Elvandora bowed and looked back with the thought that the master need have no worries and that the girl Sjhanara was resting in her room and awaited audience with him at his request. Sjogai nodded and proceeded to devour the food before him.

Only after every morsel had disappeared into the large maw and the area cleaned and tidied, did Sjogai motion for Sjhanara to be presented to him. It would have been very easy for Sjogai to again change into his man form and go to the girl's rooms, but he did not want to reveal this part of himself to her; at least not at this time.

Moments later, Sjhanara entered the crystal room. Her beauty caused even this dragon to an intake of breath. She was as a fresh breath of spring air.

Her seshu was of pale sage greens and apricot colorings. It set off her tanned skin and reddish golden hair. And those green eyes!

Sjogai almost wished... no, it was nonsense to think such thoughts. This girl was not destined for him. It did not stop him from looking and appreciating her fine qualities, however.

Lowering his head so as to be able to be more or less at eye level with the girl, he mentally inquired as to her well-being. Sjhanara curtsied and verbally informed her host that she was well and had enjoyed her stay. She directly met Sjogai's gaze and he could see the questions in her eyes. Here was a strong, intelligent woman as well as a beautiful one. She would be an asset to any man, but to a world ruler...well, now.

Most women would have lowered their eyes after a moment, but Sjhanara continued to look boldly into Sjogai's large reptilian eyes without flinching. She knew he could read her mind. She reached out with her own and he felt her probing for answers. He let her enter partially into his thoughts before closing them to her. She stepped back a step and had a startled look on her face almost as if she had been struck.

"You are very talented, Sjhanara, as well as beautiful, but all my thoughts are not for you to know until I impart them to you. I do not wish you to be alarmed. You will know the answers to your questions soon enough. Now, please sit and we will talk for awhile."

Only then did Sjhanara look away from the dragon's face. She sought one of the huge comfortable cushions surrounding Sjogai's bed and sat upon it. The pictures within Sjogai's mind that she had been allowed to see disturbed her a great deal, but she was too polite and also in awe to push Sjogai too far with her questions.

"Now, I see you are anxious to return to your journey and your Test of the Zandorn, Sjhanara. Do you have any idea what your future might have in store for you? Has your upbringing led you to any conclusions as to what you want in life?"

Sjhanara felt a little disturbed by Sjogai's questioning. She had known he could read her thoughts, of course, but to be able to reach her innermost thoughts and questions was unnerving. Sitting up as straight as possible, she met Sjogai's gaze once more.

"I do wish to return to my Test of the Zandorn as soon as possible, Sjogai. It is not that I have not enjoyed my stay or your generosity, but I must find my destiny and return to my clan. My father is growing old and will need me. My mother will be missing me."

"Have you not needs of your own, Sjhanara; husband, hearth, children?"

Sjhanara felt a warmth surge up her neck to her face. She shook her golden mane of hair in defiance. "I have no need of these things. I am not just a mere woman. I will challenge my brothers for the throne of my father when he becomes too old to rule. I am not going to be made servant to some man's whims. My breasts will not sag from the nursing of too many children.

"Since a child, I have learned the ways of the warrior and I will defy any man to beat me in battle. I have gifts of powers my brothers do not possess. I have no fear of wild beasts. I have killed many for the table of my father." She would have gone on but for the hissing of Sjogai.

"Enough, child!" the dragon's voice thundered within the walls of the cavern. The crystal walls clanged and nearly deafened the young girl. "You lie even to yourself, Sjhanara. Yes, you are Learned in the ways of the warrior. It is to be commended that you can defend yourself when needed. A man is not the only creature in need of physical strengths. And yes, you do have certain mental powers that others in your clan have not, but your body was created to bear children as well. Do you not think that takes a certain special type of strength? Do you not realize that all women possess this power that men are not born to possess? "How do you think even the ugliest of women can snare a husband if she wants one?

"But, you, Sjhanara, are right about one thing. Yours is a different destiny. Yet not quite the way you are thinking. On the morrow I will take you to the next leg of your journey. From there you will continue your Test of the Zandorn. But beware, Sjhanara. I know what your future is supposed to be.

"You do, of course, have your free agency and the right to choose your own path of life. If you are not careful, however, you will not make the right choice and you could be the destruction of a very peaceful world. Use your powers wisely."

Sjogai's words struck Sjhanara with great impact. Each word tore into her as the blade of a bhalock. She paled and fought to keep welling tears from coursing down her cheeks. This angered her. A womanly trait - tears! She would not let this enormous snake see tears from her! A body made for bearing children! Hah! Well, her body would not suffer the rough fumbling of some ignorant oaf of a man!

"Snake, eh?" Sjogai's laughter caused Sjhanara to jump. He had read her thoughts and they had amused him. "Sjhanara, if I were a man and had the inclination, you would learn to enjoy my 'rough fumbling', but I am not the one to teach you the ways of love. Keeper grant that I were. That lesson is reserved for one much better than I. You will welcome it when the time comes, believe you me or you are not the woman I perceive you to be!"

"Now, go. You will need your rest for the morrow. Elvandora will prepare food for your travels. The chimes will awaken you before sunrise."

Sjhanara arose and stalked from the room. Her back straight, hips swaying haughtily, fists clenched, she refused to even thank the dragon for his hospitality. Sjogai smiled at her retreating back. Yes, he decided, she was definitely the right one for the young prince. He would have a fight on his hands taming that one, but she could be a true queen for his kingdom.

In the early hours of the next morning, before sunrise, Elvandora stepped into Sjhanara's room just before the chimes began their calming melody to awaken her. The young princess was curled up on top of the bed, still fully clothed. It was obvious to the elven woman that the girl had cried herself to sleep. Although her eyes were closed in heavy slumber, there were dark circles beneath them and the lids were quite puffy. Even the soft chiming of the crystal walls had failed to awaken her.

For a few moments, Elvandora stood gazing at the sleeping girl. She was a beauty, there was no doubt. She was also very headstrong and quite intelligent. Either one of those qualities would have served her well in life, but to have all three was not something that came along every day.

Elvandora wondered just what had ever possessed Sjhanara to desire the life of a warrior, a man's position, instead of the life of a wife and mother. Both positions required strength and character. But men and women were created differently. Their bodies functioned differently. Creation, in its wisdom, had intended this difference for the purpose of continued existence.

As if in some unconscious response, Sjhanara sighed softly and turned over onto her back. Even in sleep and to the female elven, it was obvious that this young woman was a beauty born to be a wife. What man could resist that temptation?

Yet Sjhanara claimed she wanted no part of that way of life. Would The Ultimate Keeper intervene and change her mind before she was too old to attract a man?

Elvandora shook her head as she reached out to softly shake the girl awake. Life dealt some strange hands when it came to personalities. It would take a very strong and wise, yet gentle man to overcome the strange ideas of this young female, the elven woman decided. Pray that it happened soon.

Sjhanara awakened and was hurried to a quick bathing and breakfast. Sjogai was already impatient to be off. Barely had Sjhanara finished her bowl of porridge when the chiming of the walls summoned her to the giant cavern of Sjogai.

"Did you rest well, Sjhanara?" the dragon barely glanced at the girl as he was busy issuing final orders to the elven servants before his departure.

"As well as could be expected." Sjhanara was not going to let Sjogai forget that she was still a little miffed at him for last night's reprimand.

The dragon paid no attention to her response. With a final word to Elvandora, Sjogai turned his head to the girl and lowered it to the floor. "Fine, fine. Now if you will climb up my snout to the saddle crest just behind my horned ears, we can be off. You can hang on to the two small thocks jutting from behind my eyes. There is no danger of your falling, I assure you."

His manner suggested no more argument, only obedience, so the girl did as she was directed. She found, to her amazement, that the hard leather crest at the top of Sjogai's head did indeed make a perfect saddle. She fit her toes into one of the horny scales on each side of the saddle and grasped the slightly curved spurs with her hands.

As soon as she was in place, Sjogai arose from his bed and stretched his wings upward towards the huge opening above. With only two sweeps of his wings, the dragon began his ascent to the skies. Sjhanara felt the pressure bearing down upon her and she had to nearly ly upon the saddle.

Once clear of the roof of the cavern, Sjogai clung to the ledge for a few moments with his large clawed feet. "Comfortable, Sjhanara?"

"Yes, thank you", came her breathless reply.

"Hang on, then, we fly!"

Slowly, the dragon began to rise from the ledge. The stretched-out wings rose and fell slowly, but with each undulation, the dragon rose higher and higher into the morning sky. Sjhanara felt the air becoming lighter and began to wonder if she would be able to continue breathing, but no sooner had the thought come to her, Sjogai mentally telepathed his reassurance.

"I will not fly higher than you can breathe, little one. I must reach a height to where my body will fly easier on the air streams, but you will have no problems. Trust me."

Trust him! Did she have a choice? He demanded and she had to obey. But the young girl had to admit this ride was thrilling. As the wind pulled her flowing hair back from her face and made her thin clothing flow and flap behind her, Sjhanara felt an exhilaration never before experienced. Her heart pounded in her ears, her face flushed. She looked down at the speeding scenery below her. It didn't seem they were going very fast, but the ground beneath her was mostly a blur.

Everything looked so different from this height. Trees, trails, lakes and streams were so tiny. They were not more than dots and ribbons. The girl laughed out loud as they passed over a herd of gorskas. As the shadow of the huge dragon covered them, they began to stampede, their bawling snorts and curling tails evidence of their fear.

Sjogai banked slightly to the east and the change of direction brought the sun's rays directly in front of them.

The golden scales gleamed in the bright light, almost blinding Sjhanara.

Being unable to continue her examination of the ground below, she concentrated on thoughts of her future. So far, Sjogai had not revealed their destination. As far as she knew, the dragon was taking her back to where Othux and Othorn had found her.

"Oh, no!" the wind whisked her words from her lips and carried them away. She had not had time to say goodbye to the two chubby little elvens. She had loved their impish ways and said a quick prayer to The Ultimate Keeper that Sjogai would not punish them too harshly. She had nearly forgotten Sneezer, too, in the haste to leave, but he had curled tightly around one of her ankles to make sure he was not left behind.

"Othux and Othorn have already had punishment enough in the caves of the young dragons." Sjogai's answering thoughts entered her mind. *"They are not a bad pair, just a thorn in my side occasionally. I have to punish them once in awhile to keep them from killing each other with their foolish arguing."* A chuckling rumble came from Sjogai's throat.

Sjhanara had been so engrossed in her thoughts, she had temporarily forgotten Sjogai could read them. At first she was irritated, but to stay angry was not her nature. As the flight continued, she allowed the dragon to read her thoughts and questions and thus they conversed until the sun was near its zenith.

Sjogai began a wide circle, dropping several feet with each bank of the huge wings. The ground below rushed up to meet them and when only a few feet were left, the large clawed feet jutted out to grasp the thickly carpeted ground. Slowly the wings folded against Sjogai's sides and the long neck and head lowered to the ground so that Sjhanara could climb down.

The girl was a little shaky on her feet after the long thrilling flight. She found a stump and sat for a moment to catch her breath and get her bearings. This gave Sneezer a chance to unwind also, and he scrambled quickly, sneezing and puffing all the way to a soft mound of dirt where he quickly relieved himself.

Sjhanara saw nothing familiar in the landscape. There were a few trees here and there upon a wide expanse of rolling plain. No buildings or paths or roads that she could see. She turned a questioning gaze to Sjogai.

"You will continue your quest from this point, Sjhanara. I cannot tell you all that you will encounter, but I will tell you this. Your true Destiny begins now.

"You have had dreams. Dreams with portents of things to come. Heed them well. You are brave, my little one, but do not allow foolish pride to be mistaken for bravery. You were born for a purpose in this world. In the days to come, this purpose will begin to take shape. There will be signs along the way to guide you. Be careful and watchful and no harm will come to you."

"Will I ever see you again, Sjogai?" For some reason, Sjhanara now had no desire to part the dragon's company or protection.

Sjogai's head tilted back and his hissing laughter nearly deafened the girl. "Do you miss me already then?" The dragon's smiling grimace only showed the girl that he, too, was sorry they must part.

"Farewell, Sjhanara Yagenta. Who knows what the future has in store for us? One day we may meet again, to be sure. Until then, take care and remember that not all is as it seems. A dragon, too has his dreams."

Sjogai shook his giant body until a few small golden scales fell to the ground. "Take these scales and put them in your pack. If ever you have need of exchange, they are each worth a king's ransom." With those last parting words, Sjogai reached out with his long forked tongue and lightly touched Sjhanara's cheek. It felt just like a kiss to the young girl.

With a turn of his head, Sjogai lifted his wings once again and began his ascent into the afternoon skies. He circled the clearing once and in her mind, Sjhanara heard a soft *"Farewell, little princess, farewell."* and then he was gone.

Sjhanara continued to look into the fading sunlit skies until Sjogai's form had disappeared into the horizon. The rustling of the leaves of the few nearby trees and an occasional twitter of some creature were the only sounds. For some reason, she didn't feel very brave right now.

Finally, Sjhanara arose from the stump, gathered the scales Sjogai had given her, her pack and travel gear and put the sun to her back. West they had traveled so far, west she would continue. She said a prayer to The Ultimate Keeper to protect her on this leg of her journey and started walking.

Sneezer, emerging from under a rock where he had found some tasty grubs, scampered after the girl. His squeaks and sneezes caused her to slow down and scoop him up. Crooning that she would not leave him behind, she put him on top of her pack where the rhythm of her walking caused the tiny dragon to soon nod off to sleep.

TIME TO EXPERIMENT

When Bahuraja awoke the next morning, a breakfast of young tender eclot was already roasting on the fire. A hard leathern bowl of oaku bubbled gently at the side of the coals.

After relieving himself, Bahuraja ate his meal and sat back to drink the steaming oaku. No sign of the old wizard or Sjogai existed. Their sleeping furs were gone as were their eating utensils.

With a start, Bahuraja realized that he was now alone. In fact, he began to wonder if the others had been with him at all. But no, he had gained too much knowledge from them.

Then he remembered that the Old One had told him the end of his Test of the Zandorn was near. There was one more adventure, the most important one of all. He must keep his wits about him, he had been told. Be alert and use wisdom at all times and practice the use of his powers until he was strong in them. There would be danger, but also great reward.

The young prince felt a sadness flow over him. In a way, he loved the Old One like a father. Sometimes he had brief glimpses of his past life and he remembered an old sansei who taught him. The Old One was much like that sansei.

Then there was Sjogai. Well, *that* was one of this world's greatest mysteries. Sjogai was a part of him and yet an entity in his own right. Much like a twin brother, the young man thought.

Still pondering all of this, Bahuraja began to put his belongings together. Covering the fire and stirring it, making sure every hot coal was dowsed, he drank the last of the oaku and put the cup into his pack.

The sun was just jutting the topmost part of its rim into the morning sky when Bahuraja left the camp and began trekking toward its spreading rays. *Eastward ho*, thought the youth. He began to whistle in time to his stride and in no time had set up a good pace.

Nightfall found him several miles to the east and quite hungry and tired. A small grove of trees near a gurgling stream seemed an inviting place for spending the night. Soon a small campfire blazed cheerily and a brace of fat thoads roasted on a spit.

While waiting for the evening meal to finish roasting, Bahuraja practiced some of his powers by making his backpack rise into the air and down again. With his mind, he caused his bhalok to cut branches from one of the trees and chop them up for the fire.

A large beetle made the mistake of wandering into camp and became an experiment in molecular transformation. Unfortunately, the experiment failed because Bahuraja could not quite put all the molecules back into their right places. The beetle dragged itself into the bushes with all of its legs on one side and its head and tail reversed.

"Better luck next time", snickered the youth.

The intrigue of his multi-faceted powers enticed Bahuraja to stay a few days more at this campsite to practice. Little by little, he improved on each skill tried. When it came to changing himself, however, the young man held back. He was not sure enough of his abilities to take a chance on turning himself into a human rendition of the beetle.

When he had utilized his powers saving his comrades from that horrible sea serpent and plucked them from the water, he had Sjogai to guide him. In some way he felt the power had not been entirely his to command. Confidence was not yet his in this manipulation of matter business.

Each day followed with another. Bahuraja, traveling in a southeasterly direction, noticed the land was changing. There was less lush undergrowth now. The land sloped and rose gently and instead of mountains, low hills edged the horizon. What rock formations did exist were lined with bright color as if a lake had, at one time covered the area and left its mark.

One morning as Bahuraja trudged along a faint track, he heard the grunting sounds of a herd of wild gorkas. Putting his hand to his brow to keep the sun's rays from his eyes, he searched to see where the sound was coming from.

He remembered his beloved Kaibara who had been lost in the earthquake so long ago. How long had it been? There had been so much that had happened since that dreadful day. The youth who had started out on his journey of the Test of Zandorn, was now a tanned, muscled young man whose travels had brought him far and taught him a great deal.

It was not long before a small herd of the lizard-like animals appeared to Bahuraja's left. There appeared to be one large adult male, a couple very young males, and several females along with three or four young folts.

The gorkas were grazing, seemingly unaware of the young man's presence. Eventually, the adult male raised his head and ceased its grazing. The huge snout sniffed the air. Turning towards Bahuraja, the gorka snorted and stamped his broad flat feet. The females ceased their grazing and began to bleat to their young who immediately scampered to their respective mothers' hind legs for protection.

The male took a few menacing steps forward, grunting its warning to the human intruder. Bahuraja just stood there quietly, not wanting to cause the herd to stampede. There was something vaguely familiar about the male gorka, a certain turn of its head, the way.....,all of a sudden, Bahuraja gasped! It was.... yes, it was Kaibara!

"Kaibara! My friend", softly Bahuraja called to the bristling animal. "Do you not know me, Kaibara?" Holding his hand out, Bahuraja began to move slowly towards the gorka.

Kaibara's long fringed ears tilted forward, but he still held his menacing stance of protection for his little herd.

"It's alright, Kaibara", crooned the youth. "It's me, Bahuraja, who raised you from a folt."

Kaibara seemed to calm down a little, but kept a wary eye on this strange creature approaching. In the back of its tiny brain, however, images began to come forward. This two-legged creature did look familiar. The animal could picture a warm shed full of hay and grain. A young boy groomed him and rode him over the lush green countryside. His grey-green skin rippled and found the scar that had been caused by dreadful thorns when the Mists had nearly destroyed his master.

Kaibara took a few steps towards Bahuraja. He sniffed the odor of the stranger and remembered. Trotting forward, he screeched his recognition and nearly knocked Bahuraja over in his exuberance.

"Kaibara, Kaibara!" Bahuraja could not hold back the tears of joy over discovering that his beloved pet had not perished in the earthquake after all. He hugged the lowered neck of the animal and let the tears flow freely.

Kaibara, in turn, nuzzled the cheek and hair of his newly found master.

The snorts and tiny screeches of the rest of the herd finally brought both man and animal back to the present. "Well, Kaibara, it looks like you have taken on a family while we've been apart."

The male gorka snorted, stamped his feet and took on a stance, looking very much like a proud husband and father. This caused Bahuraja to laugh out loud. Kaibara snorted to the herd in several short barks. Nuzzling his former master one more time, the gorka then returned to the herd. There was much snorting and stamping. It was as if Kaibara was creating a welcome home song for Bahuraja.

Bahuraja decided to camp for the night near Kaibara's herd and family and then see if the animal would possibly stay with him on the journey tomorrow. To have a mount to ride again would make the traveling much more enjoyable. It would be nice as well to have the company, even if it was an animal.

The young gorkas were very curious about this strange two legged creature their herd master had accepted into their midst. They wandered close to his camp several times, but never close enough for him to touch them. They were very wary of the heat of his cooking fire. Fire to them meant danger and they did not know the difference from this small blaze and the raging inferno of a flash plains fire.

In the morning, Bahuraja awoke to the nudging of Kaibara. Stretching, he gazed at this beast with love. The animal was chewing its cud and its eyes were half closed, yet it still kept a keen eye on the herd of females and their young.

Bahuraja arose, folded his bedding furs and began packing up. Kaibara followed closely and seemed to know that departure was close at hand.

"I want you to go with me, Kaibara." Bahuraja had his pack in order and had eaten a couple of the hard camp biscuits from his food supply for breakfast. He reached out and touched the snout of the beast.

"What say you, Kaibara? Will you be my companion again, or does the lure of your family have more to offer?"

Kaibara made deep throated sounds that had always been his way of letting his master know how much he appreciated and loved him. He turned his scaly head toward the herd of grazing gorkas and then back to the youth. He thumped his tail on the ground a few times and the heads of the other gorkas popped up as if to a command.

Ambling over to the females, Kaibara nudged them and their squeaks, snortles and coughs were a language of their own. The male nuzzled each young folt as any proud father and snorted at the young male gorkas loudly and defiantly. He then turned once again towards Bahuraja. His place was with his herd and family, but his heart was with his master of old. The decision was made. They would all go.

Of course, Bahuraja did not understand all of this until he had fashioned a makeshift saddle for Kaibara, climbed upon his back and urged him forward. As soon as Kaibara began his rambling gate eastward, his master riding comfortably upon his broad back, he snorted and squealed to his family to follow. Looking back, Bahuraja saw that the small herd of gorkas were following at a discreet distance, grabbing what fodder they could find along the way. What a fine parade we present, grinned the youth to himself.

Day followed day as the two young travelers, man and woman, wended their respective ways closer and closer towards each other. Bahuraja traveled slowly due to Kaibara's little herd family being with him; their need to graze at whatever grasses they came upon slowed their pace. Sjhanara, not as lucky to have a mount, walked about the same distance each day by foot.

Sjhanara stopped often as well to gather herbs for her supply. Many new varieties grew in the areas she walked and she tested most of them for their medicinal qualities. Moanna leaves, orris flowers and roots, plus some species she had never seen, therefore named them herself.

She instinctively seemed to know how they were to be used and kept each one separate from the others by wrapping them in the broad leaves of the low growing portrae trees that grew in abundance. The lush countryside was a virtual garden of scented flowers, trailing vines, clumps of broad-leaved plants and needled trees.

Bahuraja kept a keen eye on the land and watched for the possibility of any dangers that might befall him and the herd. Each night he would make camp, preferably near a lake or stream if available, where the water bags could be refilled and the bodies of both man and beast refreshed. The gorkas were helpful in finding water as they could smell it from several miles away.

The nights were filled with strange dreams for both man and woman. Vague forms and faces floated in and out; strange prophesies and omens warned them of things to come. With the coming of dawn, both found themselves tired and puzzled. What did the dreams mean? Were they truly a portent of the future, or just the fruits of overactive young minds?

Bahuraja would rise from his sleeping furs early each morning and perform his ritual of thanking The Ultimate Keeper for the gift of life and for protection. He would also unroll the Gohonzon and beads the Old One had given him and chant the words he had been taught. This strengthened his spirit and he noticed his powers improved as well. He would then spend about an hour practicing the use of his growing powers.

One such morning, he spied another small beetle scurrying across the bare ground. Chuckling to himself, Bahuraja decided to play a little trick on Kaibara and the herd.

Hoping he would be more successful this time, Bahuraja directed his mind toward the beetle. It came to a shuddering stop in its race across the bare ground and turned towards him. The youth raised one hand and pointed a finger toward the insect. Slowly the beetle's form began to dissipate. The molecular structure of the small creature flowed outward into the air until nothing could be seen with the naked eye.

With a slight movement of his finger, Bahuraja began to reassemble the beetle within a few feet of the grazing gorkas. Only the beetle did not reappear as a tiny insect as before. This time, it was many times larger, and, much more fierce looking. Its many faceted eyes rotated and flashed, two huge mandibles clasped and unclasped in front of the beetle's opened mouth. The legs bristled with hairy spines.

Climbing upon its hard armor-like back, Bahuraja nudged his knees into the beetle's sides, trying to get it to move. "Hai!, Kaibara, Hai!" he yelled, waving his arms.

With a snort, Kaibara took a stance between this sudden apparition and the herd. His tail flailed the air and he stomped the earth in defiance of the intruder. The fact that his master was astride this monstrosity only made it more imposing. In Kaibara's mind, it appeared as though his master was being attacked by this strange black creature. Being alerted to their leader's alarm, the herd began to shuffle and trumpet their fear.

The beetle, on the other hand, just stood there trembling. It had suddenly been pulled apart from its small world of grass blades and gravel and now faced large creatures it had never before Seen, at least from this angle. It was confused. That is, if it had a brain large enough to even feel emotion. It felt the weight of something strange upon its back that kept it from unfolding its wings and flying away.

The long hairy legs trembled violently, nearly knocking Bahuraja from its back. The antennae suspended from its multi-eyed head quivered and sought familiar surroundings. It was unaware of the ground beneath him, only the menacing sounds and thumping of several strange large creatures in front of him. It quickly began to back up, causing Bahuraja to slide off onto the ground.

He could not contain his laughter at the sight before him. Snorting gorkas, a shaking beetle and a hysterically laughing human. The picture in his mind of how they must look only brought fresh guffaws.

Finally feeling merciful, the youth returned the beetle to its original size and watched as it scampered quickly to a nearby torpa bush and hide beneath its wide thick leaves.

Kaibara, startled by the sudden appearance and disappearance of the black foe, was not amused by his master's trick. The gorka turned his back on the youth and stomped towards his herd. He nudged each female and folt into a tight circle and then brayed his defiance and outrage. The other gorkas took up the cries and soon the surrounding countryside echoed with their brays, snorts, and screams.

Bahuraja had never in his life heard such a clamor. "All right, Kaibara!, I get the message!" he cried, covering his ears. It was some time before he could get his friend to come to him and allow the saddle to be put on for the day's journey.

THE MEETING

The sun was nearing the horizon, its rays shooting a myriad of orange and red colors over the evening sky. The landscape seemed ablaze as the sun cast its rays sideways across the trees and grasses.

Bahuraja was both hot and tired. There had not been a hint of a lake or stream for several days. Even the gorkas were beginning to show signs of fatigue and need of water. If none was found soon, the young gorkas would start to weaken and die. Then the youth's new dream of raising a herd for profit would not come to pass. Without water, he might have to change the direction they had been heading.

Suddenly, Kaibara's head jerked upwards, his nostrils flaring. Bahuraja, who had been dozing, was immediately on guard, fearing an attack of some sort. The gorka began stamping his feet, alerting the rest of the herd. They began snuffling and bellowing in response.

Without any urging from his master, Kaibara turned slightly to the southwest and began leading the herd to an unseen destination.

"What is it, my friend?" Bahuraja did not sense any danger, yet knew his gorkas were able to hear much farther distances than he.

The animals were now beginning to pick up speed in their shuffling sort of gate. Even the little ones were hard pressed to keep up with their mothers. Occasionally one of the mothers would slow down and call to her young as if urging it to hurry up. Just as soon as the baby caught up, however, the parent would nudge it with her long snout and begin catching up with the rest of the herd.

Bahuraja reached out with his mind and soon found the source of the herd's destination. A lake of some size, still some distance away, came into his mind's eye. Water! No wonder all of the gorkas were in such a hurry.

"I guess I don't need to urge you to hurry, Kaibara", the youth laughed at his mount. "Last one into the water is dirty gorka dung!"

It was true that Kaibara needed no urging. He was already ahead of the herd by several tail lengths.

Eventually the lake came into view. It was wide and long. In fact, Bahuraja could barely see the far shore. Kaibara and the herd could have cared less if all it had been was a mud puddle. The closer the water came, the wider their nostrils flared. Their trumpeting filled the air. Kaibara did not even wait for his master to dismount before hurtling into the cool refreshing waters of the lake. The rest of the herd followed suit and soon all were splashing, wallowing and drinking.

For a time Bahuraja frolicked with the gorkas, washing the dust of travel from his sweating body and clothes. He then swam to the shore, feeling greatly refreshed. The edge of the lake sloped gently upward from the water towards a grove of trees, leaving a generous sandy shore basking in the sun.

Bahuraja emerged from the lake, stripped off his now soaked and dripping clothing, letting it lay where it fell. He then dove back into the lake, letting the wavelets of water ripple over every inch of his sun parched skin.

It felt good to swim naked. The weeks of traveling over semi-desert land and not being able to really bathe, had begun to make his skin dry and uncomfortable. Not to mention the tiny insects that had taken refuge in his sweat-soaked jerkin and had been using him for a dining table.

After his nice long cleansing swim, Bahuraja spread his blankets upon the shore and stretched out for a nap. By now the sun had fallen well below the horizon and night stars were twinkling above.

As the young man laid on his back, hands folded behind his head, he couldn't remember when he felt so relaxed. It didn't take long for him to doze off, his quiet snoring adding to the other night sounds beginning to fill the air.

There was no need to fear beasts that might inhabit the area, for the gorkas would sound the alarm of anything even remotely smelling of danger. The herd was, for the most part now, settled down in a nice grassy pasture they had discovered near the lake. Only Kaibara and the young bucks were guarding the perimeters. Once or twice Kaibara shuffled over to his sleeping master to make sure all was well before returning to take his fill of the sweet and tender grasses.

During the night, a slight breeze came in from the lake. Hardly wakening, Bahuraja rolled up in his blanket. Dawn found him thus, all curled up with only one foot sticking out.

As the sun's first rays dispelled the night fog from the lake, warm tendrils reached the sleeping youth's face. Bahuraja was reluctant to open his eyes, for he knew it meant leaving the lake to continue on with his journey.

"Why doest thou have to leave this day?" The thought entering his mind jerked him upright.

"Who are you? Who enters my thoughts?" Alert and on his feet, the youth stood slightly crouched, bhalok in hand.

He could see only Kaibara and the gorka herd nearby, not at all alarmed. The words had been uttered into his mind only and the deliverer's presence was not yet to be seen.

"It is such a lovely lake, is it not? Thou enjoyed thy swim yesterday in its cool waters. Wouldn't another be just as refreshing?"

By now Bahuraja was getting really angry. He did not like being played with. If the voice did not identify itself soon, Bahuraja would begin tearing out every bush and blade of grass until he discovered where it came from.

"Bahuraja", the voice continued. *"It is I, the Old One. Doest thou not recognize my voice by now, even in thy thoughts? Rest beside this lake awhile. Thy destiny is close at hand, my son. Enjoy a brief respite from thy long journey. I promise thee, it will reward thee."*

Bewildered by the Old One's words, Bahuraja stood there, still naked, still holding his bhalok at readiness. His *'destiny was close at hand'*, the voice had said. Glancing around him, the young man did not see anything which could remotely be construed as adventurous. If his destiny was here, then where or what, by the sharp toes of a thoad, was it?

Kaibara, seeing that his master had risen from his sleeping blankets, shuffled over and gave a soft nudge to Bahuraja's buttocks and then tried to lay his huge head on his master's shoulder.

Laughing at the picture he must make, Bahuraja wrapped his arm around the gorka's thick neck and hugged him. "Ah, Kaibara, what do you think? Should we dally here awhile and rest? "

As if he totally understood, Kaibara nodded his scaled head and snorted. He turned to his grazing herd and bellowed. The heads of the bucks jerked up and they began to circle the females as if to keep them in line.

"What a taskmaster you are, Kaibara", chuckled the youth. Be careful lest one of those young bucks decides to claim one of your prize females as his own. Again a snorting reply emitted from Kaibara's throat.

"I know, my friend. There are many females in your herd, are there not? One is as good as another; would that I had a choice female at hand right now. I am feeling rather randy at the moment. All this rest will make me a soft man. What say you, Kaibara? How about a swim in this inviting lake to temper our male egos?"

With a turn, Bahuraja ran into the lake and dove into its depths. Surfacing, he looked back at the shore to see if Kaibara was following, but the gorka's attentions had turned elsewhere. A young female had separated herself from the herd and was slowly advancing toward the head buck. The arch of her tail indicated she was in heat. Kaibara was primed for a romp in the grasses with her.

Sighing, Bahuraja turned and began slowly swimming outward, letting the cooling waters brush away the heat within.

He had swum some distance when he decided to go ashore and explore the area. There were dense trees here and a nice stretch of beach. Emerging from the water, Bahuraja found a soft grassy spot and stretched out to let the sun dry him. It was then that the sound of singing came to him.

Sitting up, he tried to get the direction the sound was coming from. The singing did not seem too far away, but the wind might have carried it some distance.

Taking to the nearby trees, Bahuraja began following the sound, keeping the shoreline to his right. He had only walked a short distance when the object of his quest came into view.

There, bathing in the lake, was a woman! Her back was towards him, but he could see she was as naked as he was. With a start, he realized he hadn't bothered to even put on his chassuses when he had gone swimming; he hadn't planned on meeting anyone, but then, what did it matter anyway. This female wasn't even aware of his presence. He would just observe her for awhile from the cover of the bushes and then return to the herd on his side of the lake.

The woman's voice was crystal clear and the song she sang was vibrant with a tale of long ago battles and historical heroes. As she sang, she bathed her arms and body, giving the view a sensuous meaning. Her long hair caught the sunlight and it glowed as gold. Bahuraja found he was captivated with this vision. He could not take his eyes from her.

The woman turned and emerged from the lake. Her full ripe breasts gleamed with droplets of water. Her curved hips swayed as she walked onto the sandy beach. Bahuraja caught his breath. It was she! The lovely Sjhanara; the young woman who had come to his aid when the Gholac had nearly taken him! By the gods, she was beautiful!

Sjhanara had taken a soft cloth and was rubbing the water from her naked body. Each motion affected Bahuraja as if he had been subjected to an electric shock. He could feel himself respond to the ancient desires of body and flesh. If he didn't leave this place quickly, he would explode. Yet he stood bound to the spot as if rooted there.

The young woman suddenly stopped her motions and looked directly in Bahuraja's direction. He was discovered! Looking for anything with which to hide himself, the youth realized she couldn't possibly see him in the dense foliage, yet she knew something or someone was there!

"Who are you? I sense you, yet your mind is not open to me. Come out or be prepared to fight!" Paying no heed to her own nakedness, Sjhanara reached for her small bhashomhook and shield. She took a battle stance and began to advance toward the edge of the trees. A small fire dragon that had been dozing near her bedding started squeaking and tiny spurts of smoke came from its nose.

"Do not enter, my lady", Bahuraja was able to croak. "I was swimming the lake and came ashore to discover the person who sang such a lovely song. I am ashamed to admit it, but I did not know I would discover a woman. I...I am not clothed."

As if realizing her own condition, Sjhanara looked down at herself and began to blush, then smiled. "It seems as you have me at a disadvantage. You can see my nakedness, yet do not allow me to see yours. A very one-sided situation, do you not agree?"

"Throw me one of your sleeping furs and I will show myself."

Sjhanara tossed one of the neatly folded furs into the thicket near where Bahuraja crouched. He had to expose his head and chest in order to reach it, but the woman had discreetly turned and was wrapping herself in a seshu in order to cover her own nakedness.

Coming out of the trees, Bahuraja finished wrapping the fur around his waist and walked as bravely as possible into Sjhanara's camp. As she turned to face him, her green eyes looked him up and down. Her gaze was bold and did not betray the pounding heart within her breast.

Bahuraja blushed in spite of himself. How ridiculous he must appear - naked except for a rather small sleeping fur wrapped around his hips!

"Well, mighty warrior, we meet again!" A smile still played around the girl's full mouth. She was playing with him!

At first, anger began to rise, but realizing how ridiculous he must look, he laughed, albeit a bit nervously.

"It seems we must always meet under difficult circumstances, Sjhanara. Yet, I must admit, this time the circumstances are far more pleasing to me than the last time." This time it was his eyes that traveled over her body and it was Sjhanara's turn to blush. She tried to hide her embarrassment by picking up her little dragon pet and calming it.

She turned quickly to a small fire burning within a ring of rocks. "Are you hungry after your swim? I have a small eclot on a spit that I'm sure is quite tender by now. You would be welcome to share it with me."

She put Sneezer down and gave him a slight nudge in the direction of her sleeping furs where he promptly curled up and returned to his dozing.

Bahuraja's growling stomach let him know it would be an insult to refuse a meal.

Sjhanara lifted the sizzling eclot from the fire by its roasting stick. Another stick on which strips of coarse flattened bread dough had been wrapped was also propped near the fire to bake.

Reaching for a small ankle dagger strapped to her slender calf, Sjhanara sliced a thick slab of the hot juice-dripping meat and placed it on a wide leaf from a nearby tatha tree. Tearing a chunk of the hot bread from the pole and placing it over the meat, she handed it to Bahuraja. After doing the same for herself, she sat down on one of her spread out sleeping furs and proceeded to eat without further ceremony. Sneezer, having roused himself at the smell of the food, teased Sjhanara for tidbits.

Bahuraja reveled over how wonderful the meat tasted. No eclot he had ever roasted had tasted like this. "This is excellent. It has an unusual flavor for eclot."

"It's the herbs I seasoned it with - whitesage and catmuff seed", Sjhanara licked her fingers and reached for a leather drinking pouch. "Here", she said, handing the pouch to Bahuraja "Wash your meal down with a drought of this."

Taking a healthy swig, the youth realized he was drinking a very delightful wine. "Where did you get such a wine in this wilderness?"

"A dragon gave it to me."

"A dragon?" Bahuraja nearly dropped the pouch.

"Don't spill it, for Zorn's sake!" The girl reached across her blankets and grabbed the pouch from his hands. "I told you a dragon gave it to me. On the trail I usually quench my thirst with spring water if I can find it, but since I have a dinner guest, I thought 'twould be nice to share the wine."

She rambled on something about its being made from some kind of yellow flower that grew atop some mountain or other and that was set to age with honey and berries. All Bahuraja could do was stare wide-eyed at this slip of a girl prattling on and on as if her statement was an everyday occurrence.

"Wait - WAIT a minute!" Bahuraja's bellow stopped Sjhanara in mid sentence. "You say some dragon gave you this wine; that he made this and you act as though it happens all of the time?"

All of a sudden, laughter burst from the bushes behind the pair.

Startled, both man and woman sat up and grabbed for a weapon, but of course, Bahuaja did not have one. It only caused a more healthy raucous bellow of glee to come forth. The bushes quivered and shook.

The pair stood and began to carefully advance to the sound. Before they reached the bushes, however, the leaves parted and a very teary-eyed and laughing Hadjii emerged.

"Hadjii!" Bahuraja grabbed up the elven from the ground. He hugged him in a grip that would have crushed the tiny man's bones had he not squealed his protests.

The youth put Hadjii back onto the ground. Sjhanara stood a pace or two aside, with her dagger still in hand. It was now her turn to be puzzled.

"Well, this is a cozy setting, if I do say so", Hadjii was still having a hard time containing his mirth.

"Do not be alarmed, Sjhanara, the young lord here and I are old acquaintances."

Realizing their near state of nakedness, both man and woman looked blushingly at each other while tightening their wraps about them.

"Ah, ah, ah!" the elven shook a finger, "No need for explanations. I know all and would not have even let you know my presence, but for the comedy you two presented."

"Hadjii", Bahuraja found his voice again, "Have you been following me? Why are you here, spying on us? What do you mean, *'you know all'?*"

Sjhanara also found her voice. "How dare you spy upon me as I bathed. Have I no privacy in this wild land? First this young buck blunders into my camp, naked as a featherless Cawja bird, and then I find you were hiding in yonder bush.....Why, for two skellers, I'd split both your gullets!"

"Now, now, me lady", Hadjii raised his stubby little palms towards her. "Calm yourself. Both of you; sit and hear my words. I have news from the Old One."

These words brought Bahuraja to attention, but Sjhanara had never heard of the Old One and wasn't prepared to be told by anyone to sit down.

Hadjii looked into her eyes and she had an image form in her mind. A very thin and wrinkled personage, wrapped in flowing, shimmering robes took over her thoughts. She immediately sat down, dropping her daggerhook beside her.

The same image had taken over Bahuraja's mind as well. He, however, recognized the ancient wizard and was more prepared for the message that followed.

"*Bahuraja, Sjhanara*", the thin reedy voice echoed in their thoughts."*Thee both hast done well in thy quests, but now it is time for thee to join forces. Thy destinies art at hand. It is the will of The Ultimate Keeper that you follow the rest of the path together.*"

Sjhanara's fists clenched in her lap at these words.

"*Yes, my daughter*", the mental voice continued, "*thou must heed my words. Doest not let thy womanly pride cloud thy destiny.*

"*In the days to come, both thou and Bahuraja will need thy combined gifts to fulfill thy quests. Hadjii will guide thee both to the Lake of Illusions. I warn thee, this lake is full of deceits. Thou must follow Hadjii's instructions or thou wilt fail in crossing to the Island Aka.*"

The Ancient One's voice droned on with each bit of instruction seemingly more difficult than the one before.

When at last his voice began to fade, he left them with a blessing. It seemed a strange and haunting one.

"*When at last the Sword is revealed, thy lives will be twined and the world and all its treasures thine.*"

For many moments after the vision of the Old One had left their minds, both man and woman sat staring at the now dying embers of the fire. The sun was high in the sky, halfway between the horizons.

A crashing from within the trees brought the couple back to their senses. The vision still vivid in their minds only heightened their sense of warning. Each again grabbed for a weapon.

A large greenish head thrust through the thick-leaved branches of the trees. Kaibara!

Snorting in pleasure at having finally found his master, he pushed through to the beach, stomping on blankets, cooking pots and all to nudge the now laughing prince.

"Kaibara, you old gorka, was I away so long?"

Nudging and pushing at Bahuraja, the gorka let the youth know that his place in the herd had been missed.

Sjhanara, on the other hand was bristling with anger over the mess this overgrown lizard had created in her camp. She tried to sidestep the huge thick legs and tail of the gorka to grab blankets and gear. Her language became more colorful with each moment. Sneezer, also protesting with much sneezing and puffs of smoke, scampered to her and wrapped himself around her ankle in trying to avoid the huge feet of the large beast.

"By the horned araks of Morn, it's little enough I possess. But to have it ruined by some green, scaly-skinned beasty while it moons over some.....OH!"

Kaibara, noticing the slip of a girl darting around his legs, carefully swung his tail around and swept her off her feet. Sjhanara, blankets and pots flying, fell unceremoniously on the sand in a very unseemly position. Then the gorka leaned his massive head down and licked her right across the face with his long forked tongue. He liked her.

Bahuraja, seeing that his gorka's affections were not being well received, tugged at Kaibara's ear knot. "Not so fast, Kaibara", he laughed. "I don't think the lady is ready for your greetings."

"This, this beast is known to you?" sputtered the girl, wiping the slobber from her angry face. Her stormy countenance was ready to burst forth with more colorful epithets when a cackling Hadjii intervened.

"Alright, both of you! It's time to cease this confusion. We must prepare for tomorrow's journey; the day wanes. Bahuraja, take your over-zealous pet and return to your camp. Pack your gear and return here before moonrise. We will leave at first light.

"Sjhanara, I will help you restore your camp", Then, with another gleeful cackle, "and your temper!"

Bahuraja jumped upon Kaibara's back. The squat little elven had made it perfectly clear, despite his amusement, that he now was in command of the situation. The Old One's words returned to the young prince again to remind him that more adventure was at hand. Turning back one more time as he left the camp, Bahuraja saw that Sjhanara, too, was remembering. Standing barefoot in the sand, a cooking pot in one hand, a daggerhook in the other, her hair in complete disarray, the youth felt at that moment that he had never seen a more beautiful woman in his entire life.

"I'm sorry my gorka made such a mess of your camp, Sjhanara. I think he remembers you from the time you helped me fight the dreaded Gholac and when we healed his wounds. Please, don't blame him too much." Then holding up a corner of the blanket wrapped around his torso, he added,"I will bring your fur when I return."

Sjhanara's green eyes met his own. All of a sudden she seemed so vulnerable. Tears sparkled, but her pride held them fast. Her shoulders betrayed her in that they drooped slightly. There was no prideful female warrior standing at that moment, only a tired and slightly frightened little girl.

Something warm broke in Bahuraja's breast. She needed his protection! If they were to travel together, he would do all in his power to keep her from harm. With one more glance, he gave Kaibara's side a slight kick. Gorka and man trotted back into the trees and headed toward Bahuraja's camp and the rest of the herd.

Hadjii sighed as he began to restore order to the small camp sight. He prayed in his mind that he would have the strength to guide these two young and willful humans to their destiny.

Sjhanara, wiped one tiny tear away that was bound and determined to escape her will. She still did not know what this day's portent was to her. There was so much mystery. Pulling herself together, Sjhanara began helping Hadjii restore order to the camp, but she was lost in her own thoughts. It seemed she was destined to have men govern her life in some way or another despite her own will. She didn't claim to like it, but there was no denying the tugging of her heart in Bahuraja's presence. The strange words of this 'Old One' also intrigued her. Bahuraja seemed comfortable about all of this. For the life of her, however, why was she to be a part of this quest? There were so many questions and so little answers.

Hadjii looked upon her with some compassion. He knew the days ahead would try her, but the rewards, if she obeyed her destiny, would bring her happiness beyond measure.

FINDING THE HEART

Two days passed and again the countryside began to change. The trees became stumpy, as if something had held them down so they could only grow so high. Their branches were twisted and needles or leaves were scattered haphazardly across their limbs.

Scrub brush and tough-leaved tufts of grass dotted the landscape. What animals did occasionally appear were small scaled things that scurried for cover beneath a bush or dart into an almost undistinguishable hole in the ground. Some of those Sneezer tried to chase, but never caught anything. Either they were too quick or he was too slow. It seemed more of a game to Sneezer anyway.

Kaibara and his herd had a hard time finding forage to feed upon. By this time Sjhanara had chosen one of Kaibara's females for her mount and Hadjii, complaining all the way, rode one of the younger, smaller gorkas.

Bahuraja would have left the herd behind but for their persistence to stay with Kaibara. There was no questioning the need for Kaibara and the two others for mounts. Whatever came to be, it appeared they would all be in it together.

On the evening of the second day, as the trio was making camp for the night, Bahuraja sat cross-legged before the fire near Hadjii. The pudgy elven was stirring some type of stew over a small fire and Sjhanara was trying to scrub some of the day's sweat and dirt from her body with some soap leaves from her pack. There was precious little water about the area and this was saved for drinking.

"Hadjii, this island the Old One spoke of. How much farther must we go? The gorkas will not be able to continue much longer without sufficient grazing or water. Neither will we, for that matter."

"Have you so little faith in the wisdom of the Old One?" Hadjii's heavily browed eyes held Bahuraja's. He tossed his little top-knot as he warned, "You are about to make the turning point of your existence and all you are concerned for is your stomach?"

"You know that is not true. If it were just myself, I would manage with what I could find, but we are three people with a herd of gorkas. Even if the three of us could survive on this land, the gorkas are hard pressed. I am not doubting the wisdom of the Old One, just trying to understand how we are going to make it to this -- destiny of ours."

Hadjii continued to stir his pot for several moments before turning to the youth sitting beside him. "If you are in so great a hurry to meet your destiny reach into your mind and seek it. Many of the answers are there."

Before the puzzled Bahuraja could reply, Sjhanara came into the firelight. She had managed to comb some of the tangles from her thick hair and had tied it back from her face with a thong. An escaped tendril fell softly near her right temple and ringlets cascaded over her shoulders and down her back. One thigh was exposed from the slit in her seshu and it gleamed in the firelight, softly rounded, yet strong.

Glancing up, Bahuraja saw Sjhanara's eyes softly looking at him also. For a moment both minds met and passion stirred. Bahuraja felt his loins tighten. A blush fused Sjhanara's cheeks before her mind closed tightly. She quickly reached for her small herb pouch and pretended to be looking for something.

Hadjii, having ladled some of his stew into small wooden bowls, chuckled as he handed one of them to Bahuraja. The youth was so flustered he almost dropped the bowl. "Too hot for you to handle, prince?" Gleefully, Hadjii waddled back to the fire to fill a bowl for the girl.

Dinner was eaten in a strained silence with only Hadjii making comments about the surrounding landscape, the coming travels for tomorrow and how tired his backside was from riding gorkas. The man and woman carefully avoided looking at each other until time to spread their sleeping furs.

The bedding was strapped to one of the gorkas at the edge of the camp sight, and while Hadjii cleaned up from the dinner, Bahuraja and Sjhanara went to get the furs. The gorka stood quietly, chewing its cud while the pair undid the straps and let the bedding fall to the ground. Both reached for the same bundle at the same time.

Bahuraja's hand covered the girl's as the bundle was lifted. She tried to pull it back, but he held firmly

Looking up at his face, Sjhanara could see desire etched across his features. Her own heart began to race. That strange heat surged through her

For several moments the two stood as if in stone. They let their mind guards down and the thoughts poured forth as if from an opened dam gate. The forgotten bundle of furs slipped from their fingers and plopped quietly to the ground.

Running his hands up her arms, Bahuraja marveled at how soft her skin was and yet he could feel the firmness of her muscles beneath. At his touch, Sjhanara trembled, her eyes, ah those eyes, holding his gaze - drawing him inside - drowning him.

Pulling her closer, he could smell the herbal sweetness of her hair. Despite the traveling, she was so clean, so beautiful. His gaze dropped to her lips. They were slightly open - soft, full. Finding them with his own, his kiss was light at first, savoring her taste, then gathering her tightly to his firm muscular body, his desire increased. His kiss became more urgent.

For several moments, she responded in kind. She felt every muscle in Bahuraja's body pressed tightly to her. She let her thoughts blend with his and felt his desire and let hers mix with his. A groan escaped from Bahuraja's throat and suddenly she pulled her lips from his and tried to push him away.

"Please, stop!" her voice was husky and still filled with desire, but she was insistent. "Please, Bahuraja, I can't."

Still holding her shoulders, the youth had trouble containing himself. He looked at her slightly bruised lips and felt desire even more. "Sjhanara, walk with me."

"No, please." Her protest was not convincing, however.

"If you do not consent to walk with me, I will carry you."

His eyes would not leave hers. She knew he was serious. This moment was too strong. Something was drawing her and she really did not want to resist. All the warnings she had been so careful to develop over the years meant nothing. She was not able to stop her heart or the blood coursing through her veins. It was as if she was already becoming a part of this strong man holding her. She had no strength of her own.

She nodded, as if in a dream. His eyes never leaving her face, he carefully lifted her. He did not want to let loose of her. She was so light and yet the arms she raised and wrapped around his neck burned into his flesh as if iron from the metal maker's fires. As he carried her away from the firelight, her features became shadowed, but he could still feel those eyes, he could still feel her burning thoughts.

Reaching a small patch of trees, Bahuraja again let Sjhanara's feet touch the ground, but he would not release her. With one hand, he undid the thong that tied her hair. It cascaded around her shoulders and framed her pale face.

"You are so beautiful, my Sjhanara, you are as a flower blooming in a desert." Again he kissed her passionately.

Only with his kiss did Sjhanara close her eyes. By the gods, his touch inflamed her, she thought. I should not allow him to ....but her thoughts were again too merged with his to be singular.

She felt him lower her gently to the ground. His kisses were more insistent now. Sjhanara began to moan softly. She was innocent in the play of love. She had resisted all the advances of other men. *But not this man.* She did not have the strength or the desire to resist. It was as if her body did not belong to her. It responded even when parts of her mind tried to warn her to stop. "*More, more!*", her body seemed to cry. She wanted this man, and no other. The realization hit her like a blast of air from the smith's forge. She knew this was the one and no logic would convince her otherwise. All the years of saving herself, of denial had not been wasted. As their thoughts blended, all that mattered was this night.

Bahuraja's mind was also a jumble of thought and desire. Oh Zorn! What was happening to him? He was on fire. No other woman had ever brought such fire, such desire to him before.

"Please, please", she begged. "Love me now!" Sjhanara's voice was soft but insistent. She was beyond being afraid of what was to come. She only knew it must be. Her eyes opened and searched his face. There was no turning back now, but yet his held the question. "Yes", she whispered and arched toward him.

Time and space dissolved. Only the passion of the two mattered. Two minds melded into one. Two bodies no longer separate. Worlds collided. There was no other place, no other time, only now.

Bahuraja knew that this woman was his match. Inexperienced in the art of love though she may be, she instinctively knew. She was the other part of him and he now knew it. There was no turning back to anything else now.

With passion quenched, Bahuraja lay upon the grass, still holding her close to him. "My Lamish, my beautiful love, my god, what have you done to me?"

Softly, she traced his chest with her lips. "What have I done to you, my lord? What have you done to me?"

Looking down at her face, Bahuraja saw the smile curving upward. The act of love had made this beautiful woman even more wonderful to look upon. All the feelings of manhood surged through him. He wanted to make her totally his. He wanted to protect her forever. He wanted to build her a home. Have her children.

"Wait, Bahuraja," softly her finger touched his lips. "Perhaps the woman does not desire your protection."

However, looking at her, the man could only see that this woman and he had melded into one being. This was a part of their respective destinies. Whatever was to come, they would be together in thought and presence. Their physical union was only the beginning.

Sjhanara knew this too. It was frightening and yet, she, like Bahuraja felt this was right. Whatever forces governed this world, the two were meant to be as one. There was no questioning these powers at this point, only acceptance.

As these thoughts raced between them, they gazed into each other's eyes. Only moments passed, yet lifetimes were shared. The night was only a passing thing, but the days to come would take on new meaning.

Much later they lay beside each other, exhausted, but relaxed. Little by little the outside world began to invade their senses. The chirping of some night bird, the soft sounds the breezes made as they swept through the trees above them.

Content with their newly found discovery, the two lay wrapped together in each other's arms and let their thoughts and feelings flow together. With each revelation, they felt closer to each other. A strength of bonding was being formed that would outlast the ages to come. It was humbling and exhilarating at the same time.

Finally, Sjhanara shivered. The night had nearly passed away and lying out in the open, the heat of passion set aside, the flesh once again noticed outside influence.

"My love, methinks it is time to return to camp."

"Must we?" Bahuraja was seriously considering another delving into Sjhanara's mysteries. Sjhanara pushed his hand away reluctantly.

"No more, Bahuraja." Rising, a shivering Sjhanara retrieved her seshu "The day is fast coming upon us and Hadjii will be searching for us. Even now, I detect him stirring in his sleeping furs."

"You are right, of course." Bahuraja quickly rose and slipped into his own clothing, and once again gathered the now fully dressed Sjhanara to him. "You know that there is no turning back, Sjhanara. What we have experienced is now as much a part of us as is this world. I do not claim to have all the mysteries solved. I only know that you and I are a part of each other's destinies. I also know that I don't want to lose you again. Can you accept this?"

Looking deeply into Bahuraja's piercing blue eyes and feeling the strength of his arms around her, Sjhanara knew without thinking that there was truth in his words. There was no turning back. Their lives were one now as much as if they had participated in the marriage ceremony with priest and all present. Her thoughts were his answer. This she sealed by standing on tiptoe and brushing his lips with her own.

Turning toward camp, the pair walked quietly and slowly so as not to break the spell. Stirring in his bed, Hadjii smiled and pulled the furs up over his long pointed ears and drifted off into a few more moments of sleep. The Quest had begun anew and was going right on schedule.

THE CAVE

Day dawned with the sun brightly slipping into the sky and warming the night's chilled air with its warm rays. After a quick breakfast, the trio and trailing herd of gorkas were well on their way toward their next Test of the Zandorn.

About mid-day, two days out, by some miracle, they came upon a lush area of sweet grasses and a small stream. The gorkas smelled the water first, of course, and their shuffling gate became faster. The young gorkas screeched to their mothers and waddled as fast as their tiny legs would waddle trying to keep up.

As the green of the grasses began to fill the landscape before them and the stream came into view, gorkas and human alike hurried forward.

Slipping from their mounts, the trio ran to the stream and splashed in up to their hips. The water was still cold from the night, but it refreshed their sweat soaked and dust covered bodies.

The gorkas pressed their heads in clear up to their horns and filled their thirsty bodies with the cool liquid. Once their thirst was quenched, they wandered a short distance from the still bathing people to graze on the sweet grasses.

Hadjii set up a small camp and built a fire, even though it was only mid day. From his seemingly bottomless pack he extracted his cooking pots and bowls and began to prepare a meal.

Bahuraja and Sjhanara were always amazed at how Hadjii was able to fix a stew or soup from practically nothing. Neither knew or wanted to ask what all was in that pouch. As long as it tasted good and was nourishing, that was enough.

It was apparent that a change had come over the man and woman sitting next to each other at the campfire. They could barely take their eyes from each other. Sjhanara speared a tender morsel from her bowl and teased it into Bahuraja's willing mouth. Bahuraja sat so close that Hadjii feared he would crush the girl by sitting on her.

"Ah, youth and love!" he smiled to himself. It brought back thoughts of his own youth so long ago. There was no need for words. He knew the bonding had taken place. It was as the Ancient One had foretold. The Prince had his bride. Only the formalities were yet to be performed. The days and adventures ahead would be softened by their love. Their combined talents and skills would create the knowledge needed to pierce the Hidden.

Hadjii did not need to enlighten Bahuraja that it was the youth's own desire to provide for the little troupe that had caused this small paradise to form. The prince's knowledge was awakening more as time passed. Soon now, full enlightenment would emerge and Destiny would be realized. The Ancient Sage was never wrong. Besides, who was Hadjii to question wisdom? It was to his advantage that his creator persevere for it was his destiny as well.

As he cleaned up after the meal, Hadjii hummed an ancient tune under his breath and from time to time he would take a sidelong glance at the couple who seemed oblivious to anything other than each other.

The little group decided to spend a few days in that lush environment to give the gorkas time to rest and fill their bellies with fodder and water. Gorkas could travel great distances without eating or drinking, but even they had their limits. Especially the young needed time to recuperate from the long dry trek.

In the evenings, after the sun slipped into the horizon and lengthening shadows spread darkening fingers across the land, Bahuraja and Sjhanara would take their sleeping furs and move away from camp.

Hadjii knew that their passions would keep them more warm than any fire he could build with sticks and mosses. He also knew that they did not want to disturb him with their lovemaking - as if anything could bother him when once asleep. But it was a private thing and he respected that.

He did remember to add a few pinches of the fuzzy leafed herb mixture into Sjhanara's tea each night. Elvandora had pressed them into his hands before his leaving to follow the paths of the two humans. She had insisted, stating it would not be wise for Sjhanara to become impregnated before the proper rites had been performed.

Each night together meant new experiences and newly found passions for the couple. Bahuraja marveled more and more at the way Sjhanara fit into his body and mind. She matched him in every way, every movement. If he had had the stamina, he felt he could have made love to her all night every night. As it was, the pair got precious little sleep.

Even in sleep, they lay wrapped in each other's arms, Sjhanara curved in front of Bahuraja's longer body.

Sjhanara, too, could not believe the change that had come over her feelings. Where was the woman who would not allow any man to touch her - to take away that power that was hers and hers alone? Had she turned away suitor after suitor in her homeland who offered honorable marriage and home and security only to be taken body and soul in the desert by a stranger? Where was that strong resolve to stay single and rule as queen on her father's throne when the time came for him to step down? All those years of strenuous training and discipline. Had they also been in vain?

All Sjhanara had to do was look upon her lover to know the answer. He filled her eyes with his strength and masculinity. When his eyes turned towards her, she could feel every sinew melt within her. The beating of her heart was as the drums of the Ebonnu warriors going into battle. One did not question the heart. The soul dwelt there and it was not ruled by the mind. Bahuraja was right, there was no turning back now.

The weather changed about a week later. Clouds began to form on the horizon and a brisk wind whisked across the plain. At first it was a refreshing change from the hot sweaty days with little or no breeze. But as the day progressed, the temperature began to drop and a few drops of rain started to fall.

"Better stop and unwrap our water capes", Hadjii's advise was almost too late to obey. No sooner had they tied the layered capes around their shoulders than a torrent ripped open from the heavens and dumped to the world below. Lightening flashed and the wind howled, sounding for all the world like a pack of wounded Cheenas.

"Is there any shelter anywhere?" shouted Bahuraja through the howling wind. The gorkas may like all this rain, but we are getting soaked in spite of the rain capes."

No trees grew within sight, the land was flat and there did not seem to be anything to offer shelter.

"Let us go forward a little more", Hadjii pointed ahead. "I seem to remember an outcropping of rock just a little farther."

Gouging the gorkas with their heels, the trio pushed forward. A few yards ahead, a rocky rise appeared. Steering their mounts towards the huge boulders, Hadjii guided them to a cave-like opening. At first glance, the opening appeared shallow, but at least would offer some shelter form the storm.

After alighting from Kaibara and helping Sjhanara from her mount, Bahuraja removed the saddles and let the gorkas return to the herd. The rain did not bother them and it gave them time to find grazing. The trio unloaded the carpas and gear from the pack gorka and made haste to the cover of the outcropping.

Hadjii had already gathered wind-blown brush and sticks just inside the entrance to build a fire. Sjhanara stood with hair streaming and looking much like a drowned ratche, but still beautiful to the young prince. Sneezer was wrapped around her ankle still, but had one eye on Hadjii and the small blaze he was creating. Fire dragons didn't favor cold weather much.

The fire quickly dispelled the gloom of the wind and rain. Wet clothing was quickly shed and laid out to dry near the fire. Sleeping furs were wrapped around shoulders and while Hadjii brewed some hot water for oaku, Bahuraja and Sjhanara went exploring.

Near the rear of the cave was a small indentation. When approached, one could see that it became a break in the wall that would allow one person to slip through.

"Wait, my love, I will get a torch to light our way." In moments, Bahuraja returned with a small rag-wrapped stick with flames burning brightly enough to chase away the dark of the tunnel entrance.

At first Bahuraja just stuck his head through the opening and let the torch show what was beyond. What it revealed was a huge cavern with long stalagmites and stalactites forming cathedrals in stone. The light played along the walls causing a reflection of flashing lights from thousands of crystals to create the appearance of jewels.

Bahuraja slipped through the opening and motioned for Sjhanara to follow. Lifting the torch high, they stood in awe of the natural beauty of the cavern. The walls glistened with multicolored iridescence which testified the presence of many minerals suffused within them. Neither had seen the like before.

Standing on a platform of rock and looking down, they could see gigantic crystal columns rising from the floor. Many faceted jewels winked in a myriad of colors from every notch along the huge cave's walls.

"It's like a palace in stone." Sjhanara's whisper echoed throughout the cavern as if she had shouted. Her gasp was as audible as her statement.

Bahuraja wrapped her close to him as moved as she was by the magnificence of such a place. Something stirred within his mind and yet stayed just beyond his reach. It was as if he knew of this place. He had never been here before, that was certain, yet it seemed familiar.

It was his world, he had created it in his former life. The realization sent a shock through him.

Sjhanara felt him tremble and looked up to see the surprise appear in his eyes. "What is it, Bahuraja?"

"I made this for you, Lamish. I dedicate its beauty to the most beautiful creature upon this world." He bent down and kissed her lightly on the forehead.

Searching his mind, she did not need to question. She could feel it all. Her awe then turned towards the man beside her. She had not yet learned all about him, but their mind melding had told her enough to know he was more than just a warrior of the realm. He *was* this world they stood in. He had not revealed yet to this woman the full extent of his existence. She did not know that he had created this world in a former life and world. Something inside her silenced her questions, however. It was enough for now to know that whatever was to come, whatever greatness was in store for him was also to include her.

They stood in silence for several more moments before turning back to the opening of the outer cave and Hadjii.

A very quiet couple sipped the hot oaku. They stared into the flames of the tiny fire and let their thoughts wander as they may. Hadjii observed the pair in solemn reflection. Their thoughts were also open to him. "*Yes*", he told himself, "*the knowledge emerges stronger each day.*"

The storm lasted through the rest of that day. Bahuraja checked on the gorka herd and was assured they were not bothered by the torrent. They grazed on whatever grasses they could find or stood, tails to the wind, chewing their cuds, letting the wind and rain wash their dusty backs.

Noting the youth's irritation at yet another halt in their progress, Hadjii felt it was time to offer advice. "The cavern beyond, have you examined it well?"

Bahuraja turned a questioning eye to the pudgy old elven. His mind was closed but for a picture of the huge cavern beyond. What did Hadjii know of this place? Was it more than mere chance that the storm drove them to it?

"The gorkas can be left for a time in my care, Bahuraja", Hadjii's voice again interrupted the youth's thoughts. "The cavern is the doorway to the Lake of Illusion. Your quest is at the threshold and the way is for you and Sjhanara to explore alone. I will abide here until the first moon comes into its full phase - three months hence. If you have not emerged by then, I will come for you. Me thinks it will not be necessary, however." The elven returned to his pipe.

Sjhanara looked from one to the other. She was learning that to question the aged elven was to question the stars as to their orbits. He would divulge only that which was necessary and no more. His was the role of a guide, not a discoverer.

Bahuraja, and she, too, in a small way, was the secret. The mystery and magic surrounding them was so strong one could almost reach out and touch it. Each day she could see new wisdom emerging from her lover's countenance.

He was turning from a young inexperienced youth into a man of knowledge and greatness. The aura surrounding him was bright and full of color. What little Sjhanara had gleaned from their mind melding, was somewhat unsettling. There was a depth to Bahuraja that went beyond anything she had ever experienced. He was more than just a man. A great power that slept within was awakening. It scared her a little, yet she knew that power was also to be a part of her. As she watched the thoughts play across her lover's face, she began to prepare herself mentally and spiritually for what was to come.

Sensing her thoughts, Bahuraja turned and gazed into her lovely face. *'She does not question as I do. Already she is preparing and she knows not what is ahead. This woman has placed her trust in me and yet I am the one who trembles. What manner of woman has the gods placed in my care? She has strengths of her own. Where I falter, she will stand strong. Where she needs, I will be - two as one. The brink of the precipice is before us. We stand at the door of our Destiny and knock. What will we find on the other side? Only The Ultimate Keeper knows. What did the Old One tell me? I am the key.*

Sjhanara is the one who will interpret the key. Where is the meaning?

The air surrounding the trio became electric with the thoughts that formed. Could anyone have observed, they would have seen three auras blended into a myriad of bright color, swirling and filling the cave. A buzzing and snapping sound accompanied the swirling colors, yet no one was listening. Nothing else moved. The world was waiting.

A shudder within the bowels of the earth brought the trio back to the present. Time had hung suspended for a moment and had created a small void. As their thoughts filled the void, it had begun to change the space around them.

Bahuraja rose from the cave floor. Reaching for Sjhanara's upraised hand, he pulled her towards him. "You feel it too." It was a statement, not a question.

"Yes."

Both turned towards Hadjii who remained in his squatting position near the small fire. His wise old eyes searched the faces above him. "Remember the words of the Old One, Bahuraja. They will guide you the rest of the way. When you feel you do not have the answers, search within yourself. They are there. It is all there, my prince."

Facing Sjhanara, his face softened and a smile played across his withered old lips. "The Keeper go with you, my child. You have chosen wisely your husband and consort. You will have many strong babes from his loins and your love and powers will grow with his. Do not fear that your training has been in vain. You will need all your strengths to sustain yourself with this man and the world and life beyond. All your training of the past will serve you well."

Sjhanara bent to place a kiss on the elven's bald head just in front of his topknot. His blush was apparent and he snapped his fingers and cackled. "Get along with the two of you now, before I forget meself and take this wench to *my* sleeping furs."

The somber mood broken, Bahuraja and Sjhanara smiled, gathered their packs, making sure there was food and water enough for several days. Hadjii knew there was no need for such provisions, but he kept that secret well hidden. The path ahead would be full of magic and mystery, but the pair before him was now well able to handle it all.

A small sigh escaped the small dwarf as he watched the pair head once again towards the crack at the rear of the cave. This world would soon never be the same. Times were changing rapidly. He felt the thoughts of the Old One confirming his own. "*Yes*", in unison, "*Yes, it has begun!*"

LAKE OF ILLUSIONS

Entering the huge cavern once more, the couple looked upon its beauty anew.

Bahuraja had brought a larger torch to guide their way, but it really was not necessary. The cavern had a luminescence of its own and, as soon as their eyes adjusted, the pair could see very well. Soon the torch was extinguished and Sjhanara strapped it to Bahuraja's back in case of future need. Without the torchlight, the full brilliance of the minerals and jewels of the cavern seemed as if they, too, were in anticipation of the coming events and were helping by lighting the way.

Searching carefully for a pathway down from the edge near the crack to the cave where Hadjii waited, the pair finally found a narrow ledge to the left that sloped downward. Bahuraja led the way down, cautioning to watch for stones that might turn an ankle or cause one to slip and fall. The path was smooth, however, a soft padding of powdery sand covered everything.

When they finally reached the bottom, the immense size of the cavern took their breath away anew. They seemed as pebbles themselves in the vastness. The pair was dwarfed by the giant stalagmites towering above them from the cavern floor.

Sjhanara stood close to Bahuraja and he drew her to him as they drank in the multicolored beauty for a few moments.

Then they began picking their way around the stalagmites and boulders strewn across the cavern.

It was several hours later when the walls of the far side of the cavern were finally reached.

Finding a wide section of rock on which to sit and rest, the couple shared a few sips of water from a water bladder and took in the cavern from this other angle.

For the first time, they noticed that a breeze stirred within the walls, creating a musical effect as it wound through the cavern. A soft tinkling and singing sound; a soothing sound, calming and spellbinding as if the very rock of the cavern was urging them on.

"How wonderful it would be to make love to you right now", Bahuraja squeezed Sjhanara's shoulder and kissed her forehead.

"Methinks you would be able to make love anywhere", she giggled, snuggling closer. "But is this truly the time or place?"

"Unfortunately, you are probably right." Another squeeze and he rose. "But I can kiss you." Pulling her towards him, he kissed her long and hard until her breath caught.

Pushing him away, she looked as if she was going to faint. "That was not at all fair! Do you think I can resist the strength of your kisses when such magic surrounds? Bahuraja, you go too far!" Try as she might, however, Sjhanara could not look too convincing. Laughing she tugged at his sleeve and turned. "Come on, my horny lord, we have a quest to pursue!"

Before he could grab her again, she had sprinted ahead towards a break in the wall that appeared to be a natural exit from the cavern.

Breathless, the pair stopped as the exit of the cavern widened before them. The sound of rushing water crashing against a shore could be heard above the sound of wind rushing through the doorway.

There was a short tunnel, whose walls were covered with more sparkling gems and crystals, that traveled from the exit of the cavern to a point of light some distance away.

Something skittered across Sjhanara's foot causing her to jump. Without thinking, she grabbed her bhashomhook. Bahuraja also reached for his daggerhook, but whatever the tiny animal was, it was long gone; only their quick glimpse of two beady red eyes noted the direction it had taken. A more cautious couple picked their way forward towards the pinpoint of light at the end of the tunnel.

The rushing sound of the wind and water became louder the closer to the light they came. Soon another opening loomed before them.

Blinking in the brighter light outside of the tunnel, the couple viewed another strange sight.

Stretched before them was a large lake, its waves slapping the shore in tiny ripples. In the center rose an enormous many-faceted crystal. It rose upward and disappeared into clouds. The surrounding light entered and was bent within the facets changing into ribbons of rainbows that appeared to shoot forth as a beacon. The whole area was bathed in reds, blues, purples, greens, yellows, golds - all ever changing.

The water of the lake swirled and eddied and seemed to whisper. It, too, changed colors, first grey, then marbled in various hues, then black.

There was no sky, for this phenomena was all underground. Yet upon gazing upwards, it seemed like sky. There were clouds and pinpoints of light, but it was not blue as normal sky was. It was black or different shades of grey. There was no sun or moon to show a change from night into day or day into night. The light came from the crystal and returned to be changed and emanate once again.

Moving forward cautiously, the couple searched the land for any danger. There did not appear to be any living creatures, for other than the ever changing colors and whispers of the lake, nothing seemed to move. The ground was hard with only a thin covering of powdery sand that puffed upwards like dust with their steps.

As soon as the couple exited the tunnel and walked a short distance into this strange plain, the colors began to change more rapidly and sounds like the clanging of hundreds of bells nearly deafened them.

Bahuraja grabbed Sjhanara by the arm and pulled her behind him, but she pushed forward to stand by his side, bhashomhook still in hand. Whatever dangers might emerge, she, too, was ready to fight.

From an outcropping of rock near the lake four figures moved. As they came nearer, the couple could not tell what they were. The figures walked on two leg-like appendages and seemed to have two arms, but looked as if made from stone. Their gait was stilted and awkward - stiff-legged. The structures seemed as jagged rocks stacked one on another and made to come alive.

The heads were the strangest of all. A solid square block of stone sat upon rock-like shoulders but did not seem attached. They rolled around the shoulders so that a band of what appeared to be eyes could view from all angles.

"What manner of creature could these be?" Sjhanara's quavering voice denied the stance of courage she had taken.

Onward toward Bahuraja and Sjhanara the creatures came. They did not appear to carry weaponry, nor did they seem to threaten, but the man and woman were not about to be fooled. This was too strange a land and their every nerve was tensed for what might come.

The clanging sounds began to fade away and soon all that could be heard was the stomping of the creatures' stony feet. When they were only a few feet away from the couple, they stopped. The heads rolled this way and that across the broad rocklike shoulders. The thick pebbled fists clenched and unclenched.

"What or who are you?" Bahuraja voiced the question, but no answer came forth. "I am Bahuraja Muebin Sarach of the Clan Sarach, speak or prepare to die!" A bold approach might be better than submission, he told himself.

Still the creatures stood, heads rolling. They came no closer, spoke not a word, but acted as a barrier.

"Stand your ground, my love. I want to test their mettle."

Shifting his daggerhook to his right hand, Bahuraja raised his left in greeting. In his clan, the left hand raised was a show of greeting, yet caution. There was still nothing more coming from the creatures.

Cautiously, the youth advanced until he stood right in front of them. A very slight humming seemed to be passing from one creature to another. The eyes, if you could call the moving bands eyes, pulsed with a reddish glow and seemed to register whatever they viewed.

Again Bahuraja spoke. "What manner of creature are you? We seek entrance to yonder structure. Let us pass!"

More humming, only this time it was much louder.

"Bahuraja! Something more comes from beyond." Sjhanara's warning made the young man turn away from the rock creatures to look where she was pointing.

From behind the rock-like creatures, a small figure could be seen floating across the ground on some kind of thin apparatus. As he came nearer, the rock creatures parted and stood silently in rank.

A twisted and gnarled gnome of indescribable age and ugliness alighted from his craft that looked for all sakes and purposes to be nothing more than a beautifully woven carpet. It, too, changed colors, one fusing into another and creating yet another hue or design.

The gnome, deformed as he appeared, was very nimble. He hopped to the ground and, with a rolling gate, much like the rock creatures, approached Bahuraja. "Ayee! What visions these old eyes strike? Emerge from where did thee to my world?"

Walking right up to the tall youth before him, the gnome poked a gnarled finger at Bahuraja's knee, which was about as high as he could reach. "Speak, human, else yonder gholums on ye I sic!"

Rent speechless by the mere appearance of this twisted creature before him, its words brought Bahuraja back to his senses. "I am Bahuraja Muebin Sarach, of......"

"Oh, heard thee before, I did! The gholums thy speech didst transmit. What art thou doing here at the Lake of Illusions? Thy purpose speak and be quick about it. My nap interrupted thou hast!"

Sjhanara had quietly moved forward to stand just slightly behind Bahuraja. Hearing the gnome speak in a brogue much like those from a village near her home, she gazed upon him with wonder.

Turning his knobby head slightly, the gnome's gaze fell on the girl. His eyes pierced hers and seemed to burn into her mind. She cringed and instinctively pressed against Bahuraja's side.

"Aye, lass, an ugly creature before thee thou seest, doth thou not?

For some reason, the girl could not stay afraid. She felt those eyes bore into her mind again, but this time there was no fear within her. Standing before her was the ugliest creature Sjhanara had ever seen. The gnome stood only four hands high. His short malformed body seemed to have been rammed onto the two stubby legs with feet too large. And the head! Well, that almost denied description. The head was a huge knob of pulpy-looking flesh with bits of wispy hair sticking out at random. The nose protruded from the center of a pockmarked face like a blob of reddish clay and a large hairy mole rested on the right side.

There was no doubt as to the ugliness of the creature, but the eyes, those piercing eyes belied all the rest. Within those eyes radiated intelligence beyond the scope of most. There were worlds hidden within them; universes without beginning or end. Gazing into those eyes was to nearly drown in an abyss of thought and color.

Sjhanara somehow knew the gnome would cause no harm to them. This knowledge had not yet occurred to Bahuraja, who, hand on hilt of daggerhook, was ready to defend. The touch of Sjhanara's hand on his arm caused him to look at her. Seeing a tiny smile cross her lips, he frowned and looked again at the gnome.

"Who, or what are you and why do you bar our way to the Lake of Illusions?" There. A direct approach. If this was Destiny, then attack it head-on.

"Ask who I art, puny mortal? And who gavest thou the authority to question I? Even my golems here question me not!"

It had been an esogi eon since the creature had seen anyone other than his golems and it was a treat to play with these humans. It did seem that his humor was lost on the man before him, however. Always ready to fight battles, these humans were. What a waste. Was there no fun left in this sphere anymore?

Bahuraja advanced on the gnome with the intent of pushing through. The golems, however, immediately closed ranks in front of the ugly little creature and became a barrier. It appeared no one would go anywhere until a small gesture from the gnome caused the golems to step aside once more.

"Enough of this play. For what purpose hast thou sought the Lake of Illusions? Guardian of the crystal tower am I. All who pass this way must pass my test."

Looking into those fathomless eyes, Bahuraja finally realized that this creature was not to be reckoned with by force. He could feel his mind being searched and tried unsuccessfully to close his thoughts. Obviously the gnome had strong powers.

"I come to seek what is within yonder tower. It holds the key to our destinies, Sjhanara's and mine. I pray let us pass."

"Well, now, better this is, thy manners. Respect begets respect, it does. Await thee I hast. Knowest thou comest, I did. Welcome, Bahuraja, creator of Acarda. Follow me and my companions here and showing thee the way I wilt."

Without further ado, the gnome turned and stepped onto his rug-like craft. Motioning the couple to do likewise, they barely had time to settle upon its broad surface before the craft rose and slowly floated towards the lake and the crystal tower looming in the center. The golems lumbered after them at a much slower pace, looking for all the world like moving boulders.

The craft slowed as it neared the lake and finally came to a halt in front of a small stone hut. As it settled to earth, the trio alighted and Bahuraja gazed with awe at the scene before him. The Lake of Illusions and the island at its center were huge. The colors and hues that played across the lake were beyond description.

There was a music swirling around them that was mysteriously calming and alarming at the same time.

"Beautiful, it is, doest thou agree?" The gnome's statement brought the couple back to the present. "Now, the test will begin."

Bahuraja looked down upon the creature before him. "I still would ask your name."

"My name, human, thou couldst not pronounce, but if happy it makes, Blmetrmountitemous called am I."

"Blematm....Blmountit...Belemoutitmos..., well, I guess I did ask for that, now, didn't I?" It was Bahuraja's time to smile. "I'll accept your description as it is and not question it further. Agreed?"

Mumbling almost inaudibly, Blmetrmountitemous sighed, "Thou gavest the name to me beyond Time, and carried it, have I, a name bigger than self. Agree or disagree what need hast I?"

Motioning the couple to sit, the gnome disappeared into the tiny hut only to appear again in an instant. In his hand he carried a thin shard of crystal from which emanated a brilliant blue light.

"Eyes thee wilt close. Palms up place on folded knee. Whatever thee feels or sees in thy minds, open eyes not."

Satisfied that their eyes were closed tightly, the gnome began chanting some ancient words. The blue light began to pulse around the couple. Forms and symbols danced within the light. Sjhanara shivered, but she kept her eyes tightly closed. Bahuraja, sat rigidly, unmoving.

Within his mind pictures formed and disappeared. He could see a world where tall structures stood bunched together. Many bodies of water covered the land. Strange crafts moved across hard ribbons of earth. Hundreds of thousands of peoples inhabited structures of many forms. It was a strange world to Bahuraja, yet he felt that somehow he had known it well once. All was vaguely familiar. There was a sadness that surrounded all he pictured.

As the scenes changed, he viewed a destruction of this world. Huge plumes of fire rained down upon the structures and he saw them disappear into a rubble of twisted metal and rock. He saw the fire consume thousands of the peoples that inhabited the villages and towns. Children cried for dead parents, some laid dead beside them. Animals and human alike roamed the desolate landscape seeking shelter and food.

A groan escaped him and tears ran unchecked from his eyes and fell to the ground. His heart felt as if it would break. He felt a great loss. What manner of place was this and what had happened to cause such destruction?

Sjhanara, too, was envisioning all that was in Bahuraja's mind. Her heart rent with the pictures of dead and dying children. How could the peoples of this world allow such to come to pass? Was it real or imagined? She heard the sobs coming from Bahuraja and she, too cried. For some reason she could not explain, she, as well, seemed to feel loss. She felt a kinship to these people and yet, she could not, for the life of her, imagine why.

The scenes of destruction disappeared and within their minds they saw a beautiful castle of black obsidian built upon an island. It had several towers, each adorned with a dragon head or gargoyle with snarling fangs. It was surrounded by a wide moat. The main entrance was huge, the door was painted a bright red and several strange symbols were carved upon it. Above the door was a gold plaque which proclaimed "THROUGH THIS PORTAL ONLY ONE CAN PASS. HE, WHO CREATED BEYOND TIME."

Strange words and yet Bahuraja felt a stirring within his breast. The words were familiar.

The scene changed again and the couple viewed a large room with ornate carvings within the castle. In the center of the room, an intricately carved dais stood. More strange symbols embraced its sides and seemed to move across it; however, it was the object lying upon the dais that was truly magnificent.

A large sword, with a hilt span of nearly twenty inches, reclined upon a bed of velvet. The hilt was encrusted with jewels, one being quite large and round. The stone appeared to hang suspended between threads of gold. From this jeweled ball emanated rays of light. The blade was long and double edged; it was polished to a fine sheen and was very sharp. Upon the blade were more inscriptions.

At one side of the room a large tapestry hung, richly embroidered with silken threads. Scenes of trees, dragons, human warriors and finely dressed ladies had been intricately embroidered upon its surface. Below this tapestry was a large bed. It, too, was covered with rich fabrics, shimmering and changing colors as the light played across it.

Upon the bed lay the body of a man. Bahuraja felt a jolt go through him as he gazed upon the peaceful face. It was of a man of age, yet there was still a youthfulness about it. The hair was white and long and a carefully trimmed mustache and beard graced at the chin. The alarm was caused, however, because it was his face. Whoever this personage was, or had been, he was the exact likeness of Bahuraja, yet older.

"Open eyes, thee now may." The scene began to fade and once again Bahuraja and Sjhanara were at the edge of the Lake of Illusions with their host, the gnome

Blmetrmountitemous standing before them. The shard of crystal was now white.

Bahuraja sat very still for several moments trying to absorb that which he had seen in his mind. Sjhanara, too, was very quiet and thoughtful.

"Well, thee two", the gnome seemed impatient, "before thee can go forward, interpret thee must the vision."

Bahuraja stood and looked upon the lake and the crystal tower beyond. Thoughts swirled in confusion through his mind. The vision was causing something to occur within him that he was not sure he was ready to accept and yet there was also excitement. He looked down at his lovely Sjhanara, still sitting on the ground, her eyes met his and held. She was waiting, putting full confidence in him. Had she seen all that he had seen? "*Yes*", the answer came to his mind.

Looking down at the ancient figure before him, Bahuraja took a deep breath and spoke. "I am still totally unsure of all that I witnessed, but my instinct tells me those visions seen were of a former world, perhaps my old world. I recognized the figure lying upon that bed and feel it must have been me in my former life. I've been told something about this by another ancient one. He has told me that that other Bahuraja Muebin Sarach had tried to save his world only to be mocked and therefore, he created this one. My destiny now is to correct mistakes made in this creation of Acarda and help change it to the world it is supposed to be and then become its ruler. Is that close enough?"

The tiny dwarf smiled. "Close enough, it is. The crystal verifies all, it does. Now, go forward thou will to solve the rest of thy destiny."

After they had regained their senses, Bahuraja and Sjhanara turned once again to the Lake before them.

Gazing into the lake, the couple saw a myriad of figures. Some headless, some with gaping mouths. Eyes stared back at them in seeming horror.

The water, if that was what it was, swirled and eddied in a variety of colors. The figures almost seemed to move, but did not.

The misshapen gnome spoke once more. "If thou wouldst that lake cross, find the proper path, thou must. Miss thy step and lost in the depths thou will be like those poor souls within."

Bahuraja had Sjhanara stand behind him. Closing his eyes, he reached deeply into his mind and brought forth the power from within. When he again opened his eyes, the path through the shimmering lake was very plain. It rose above the swirling colors several inches, allowing the two to cross without fear.

As the couple neared the crystal, a great door materialized before them. Emblazoned in gold across the mantel were the words Bahuraja had seen in the vision. "THROUGH THIS PORTAL ONLY ONE CAN PASS. HE WHO CREATED BEYOND TIME."

What manner of magic was this? The words were from another time, another world. The tower was not the same, but the door he seemed to recognize. The door was bright red and strange symbols moved across its planks.

Looking more closely, Bahuraja realized he knew the language of the symbols. They, too, had come from that other world. It was, even in that world, an ancient tongue. Searching his awakening mind even farther, the youth knew the language had been known as Mandarin, one of several dialects of a people known as Chinese. It was a royal dialect spoken by the learned.

Tracing his fingers across the symbols, this message emerged: "*The secret of the door is of the mind. He who created all will know the secret. He and he alone can decipher the meaning. He and he alone can change it.*"

"The secret of the door is of the mind", Bahuraja murmured the translation as he pondered the meaning. "I will know the secret, I can decipher the meaning, I and I alone can change it.

"YES!" Sjhanara, my lamish, we are truly at the portals of our destiny! This is the castle of the vision! Don't you see? I and I alone have held the secret. Not even the Old One would have been able to enter."

Sjhanara, looking at her chosen mate, could see the wisdom etched across his face, the coming around full circle to his destiny. The girl was in awe and yet so proud to be accepted as his woman, yet fear also wound its fingers round her heart. The message on the door said only one could pass beyond. Would she have to stay here as Bahuraja entered and searched the depths beyond? If she tried to go with him, what danger would possibly befall her?

Realizing her fears, Bahuraja, wrapped Sjhanara in his arms and kissed her soundly until her trembling stopped. "My Lamish, the warning was for those others who would try to enter. Do not the words also say that I can change it? Are you not as much a part of me now as I? Meld your mind with mine and let us pass these doors together."

Still holding her close to his side, Bahuraja began to chant in the ancient Dao-Mandarin tongue. "Bahuraja Muebin Sarach, woe yah, tioquay - ta so nah ging shiou!" (Open to me, oh mighty door, it is I, Bahuraja Muebin Sarach!) The words flowed easily as if never forgotten. As the chanting rhythm ebbed and flowed around the couple,

Sjhanara, too, felt the words and in her mind also began to chant in unison with Bahuraja.

The doors began to shimmer and sway. The words disappeared and other symbols took their place. Then the doors creaked and slowly began to open. A loud hissing sound escaped as they turned inward on golden hinges. Trapped air from an ancient age rushed forward and escaped into the atmosphere. Then all fell silent.

The couple stepped forward beyond the threshold. The entrance was a huge hall with every manner of ornate tapestry adorning the high walls. The floor was of intricately placed tiles depicting a large picture of a dragon - wings outstretched, fangs bared, breathing fire. Large vases of gold stood in the corners.

Although this area was sparsely furnished, what was there was of the finest and richest of materials.

As the couple proceeded into the hall, they could see several doorways branching off to the sides. Their curiosity to explore them, however, was not for this time. From above and behind them, a beam of light stabbed through the hall from one of the facets of the crystal and centered on a small door of plain wood at the rear of the hall beckoning their attention.

This was most curious. All of the other doors were richly painted and adorned with golden symbols and design. This one door, however, was very plain. It was a solid piece of wood, roughly hewn, and no symbols appeared upon it. A small round knob was in the center right of this door near the edge. It was to this door that Bahuraja steered Sjhanara.

The knob turned in his hand and the door creaked open with great protest. The couple entered a small room that was very sparse. There was a long narrow bed, a plain table and one rickety chair of simple, yet strange design.

Ancient books lined the shelved walls. On the table was a very battered bowl and cup. It was obvious they had been well used. One very small book rested beside the bowl. Its tattered edges attested to having been often read.

Sjhanara, having not seen many books, opened the cover and carefully traced the strange lettering with her fingers. They seemed to burn into her, and she was fascinated. Words formed in her mind and strangely, she could understand. She had never read this language before, or had she?

Bahuraja had been drawn to the bed and the simple woven blankets neatly folded upon it. Who had lived in this room? Was it the being he had seen in his vision? The one, who though aged in appearance, had the same face as his own?

A gasp from Sjhanara brought him around. Her fingers were upon a small book on the table. It was opened to about the center and her eyes were fastened to the words before her. "Bahuraja! Look! I know these words. There is a message here. There are instructions."

Finding her revelation hard to believe, Bahuraja took the book and looked at the writing before him. "*From simple beginnings come wisdom and discovery. Seek that which is hidden by humbling self and the light will guide you.*"

"I, too can read these words, Sjhanara, just as you, even though they be from another time, but the meaning needs searching."

"I understand them, Bahuraja. I don't know how, but I do understand them. Do you not see, this room is plain and simple. Simple beginnings! The former inhabitant obviously was a simple person with little but his books for companions. Was this person your former self? Only you can know this, but if the tales of the Old One are true, then this was your beginnings.

"What is more humbling than prayer? Was not chanting a prayer the means of opening yonder portal doors? It seems this person spent a great deal of time in prayer and meditation. The usual position of prayer is to kneel, is it not? It is meant for us to find something - Discovery. Help me, Bahuraja, I know I am right!"

Down on their knees they went. Bahuraja thought Sjhanara was becoming slightly demented over all of this, but she did have a point. The floor was surprisingly clear of dirt or even dust, having been carefully preserved; even so, the floor was hard on the knees.

Again, it was Sjhanara who made the discovery. There was one small slit of window shining its beam of light into the room. The window was rather high and reading could only have been during the high point of the day when the sun was at its zenith. A candle would have been necessary any other time. Here in this false day, however, the light was constant. From their vantage point on the floor, the light was directed to another small book on a low niche near the floor by the bed.

Carefully, Sjhanara removed the book from the shelf. Leather bound, it, too, had been well used. Gently opening the cover, she saw neatly handwritten text. Questioning, she held out the book to Bahuraja.

Each page was filled with formulas and observations. Neatly outlined were the discoveries by the author into the manipulation of molecular structure by the use of the mind. There were the histories of healing by the use of this method. Detailed descriptions of how the author had discovered and used his power to heal the sick and maimed flowed through the pages. Although the book seemed small, volumes of information came forth with each turning of the pages.

It was the last page that held the couple spellbound, however.

An etching of a beautiful sword, just as they had seen in their vision, stood out from the page as if alive. The words describing its creation came forth.

"As the last days of my existence pass, I see there is nothing more I can do in this world. My healing and powers are misinterpreted by a world of peoples who are bent on destruction. All I have wanted to do was bring peace and happiness to those unfortunate enough to be different and unaccepted. The beautiful children. How I am going to miss them. They were the light of my life.

"The sword I created as a symbol of power for my successor. I molded it from the molecules of the finest and hardest metals known to this world. I have tempered it with some of my own structure so that it will have a life of its own. I pray there will never be a need for its use as a destructive power, but that it will serve its owner in the cause of justice and peace.

"Have I succeeded in creating a world where greed and pain will not reign? Will I succeed in transferring myself to this other world, therefore becoming my own successor?"

The next words caused Sjhanara to gasp in a near faint.

"My lovely Sjhanara, the only one who even tried to understand me and who I tried to save from the jaws of death, are you waiting for me? You were so ill with the flesh-eating cancer in the last days, but would not allow me to cure you. With your last breath you looked into my eyes and bore testimony of your love and faith in me.

"I hope you have forgiven me for my taking liberty to send your spirit forth into my new world. Your spirit was your own, not mine to command. A God higher than anything I could ever attain gave me my abilities, and I dared to use them to send your spirit ahead. I pray He will forgive me for taking license

with His domain. It gives me peace in my last days to think you are waiting there for me.

"From the elements I have created this castle and its contents. This room was the beginning. Through diligence and prayer and study, I was given the power to manipulate the molecular structure of animate and inanimate objects. Through it all, I tried to forget the Self and consider only the good of Mankind. In the end, however, Mankind has tried to destroy me because of lack of understanding.

"I am not a god, I am only a vessel for a work in which my desire was to heal pain. In my own pain, however, I created within my mind my own world and everything in it. A world where being different is not a thing to be despised. A world where fantasy and magic is the accepted. Hopefully a world where I will finally find peace."

Almost as an afterthought, the last inscription was the key to the search.

"Within the least of many find the highest point. The lifeline will guide the hand to discovery."

The signature was bold with a definite left slant. *"Bahuraja Muebin Sarach"* A small icon of a glyph representing the symbol of wisdom encased in a triangle was carefully drawn after the name.

Bahuraja let out a long sigh and looked at Sjhanara. "So, it *was* me in that other life. I am in his presence and yet it is my presence at the same time. It is almost too much to fathom. I have been schooled for this all my present life. The Old One instructed me as well, yet to come face to face with this reality is...is...."

"Humbling. I know. When I read my name and heard how I was.. was..." the words choked in Sjhanara's throat. She had also been loved by this other Bahuraja in the other time and world. No wonder there had been such a bond between them in this one.

Gazing into one another's eyes for several moments, the couple let the realization of their discovery flow between their minds. It was as if Time had stood still.

Finally, Bahuraja rose from the floor. "There is yet another mystery to solve - the search for the highest point within the least of many. When we entered into the great hall, there were many doors, all beautifully ornate. This door we chose because of its difference. It is plain - therefore, the least of many.

"Of course this book was inside the room, but we do not yet know when it was written or for what full purpose intended. I think we should now search upwards for the last mystery."

Searching the walls, the couple discovered that on the far wall, certain niches formed a rough stairway to the ceiling. Removing the books from around these niches, Bahuraja placed his right foot in the first indentation. By shifting slightly, his left foot fit perfectly into another niche only about a foot higher. By this method, he soon was near the ceiling several feet above and near a corner. There were no books near any of the indentations here.

The light was dim and Bahuraja could not see anything that might give them the clue they were looking for. Beside the head of the cot, Sjhanara found a stub of a candle and some small sticks that appeared to have some kind of substance on one end. She was not sure exactly what these sticks were used for, but it seemed logical they had been used to light the candle. She tried hitting one of the sticks on the table's edge, but the substance just broke off. She then tried rubbing the edge of the stick on the board and the stick flared. Sjhanara wrinkled her nose at the acrid smell it emitted, but found that she could now use this to light the candle. What miracle of invention this was - a stick that would light without flint or powder.

Following Bahuraja's steps, she held the candle before her until he could reach down and take it from her. The steps were pretty high for her shorter legs and she nearly fell trying to retrace her steps back to the floor.

With the candle to light the small niches, Bahuraja finally found one that was not as deep as the others. There was a slab of rock covering it. He had missed this before. Carefully removing the slab, the light now revealed a faint handprint embedded in the wall. Placing his left hand over this imprint, Bahuraja was not too surprised to find it was a perfect match to his own. Where the three distinct lines of the palm were traced, the lifeline stood slightly raised. Making sure his matched, Bahuraja pressed. Nothing happened. He pressed a little harder.

Still nothing.

Words could not describe how his heart fell. They were so sure this was the clue to the discovery they were looking for.

Carefully climbing down, Bahuraja handed Sjhanara the candle and they looked at the wall again.

"I was so sure. There cannot be any other like it."

At that moment, the wall started to shudder. Stone grated against stone, wood against wood as the hinges creaked and groaned in ancient protest. Slowly, the edge curved inward and the room was filled with light from the area beyond.

Bahuraja didn't waste any time, he bolted through the break into the most brilliant light he had ever encountered. Sjhanara was right at his heels and had to cover her eyes at the sight.

There were crystals everywhere. Light shot forth from every one. It was the center of the room that commanded their attention, however. There, before their vision, was a tall dais. Lying atop of it was a crystal case of some length.

Stepping to the platform, they viewed the sword encased within. The crystal case appeared to have no hinges or clasps of any kind. It was as if the sword had been frozen within its depths.

What a sword it was! The vision had not begun to show its magnificence. Fiery gems sparkled from the hilt. Ancient symbols were engraved both on the hilt and the blade. The most impressive part was a huge fist-sized ball cradled in the very center of the hilt. It was held in place by braided gold strands wrapped around in a cross design. Yet the ball seemed to be suspended in the center of the strands and not really held at all.

The color was beyond description. It seemed to be alive with a myriad of hues with a bright dot of light at the center.

Bahuraja examined the crystal case further, but could find no way to open it. It was odd to him that if he had created this wonderful blade, that he did not remember how to free it from its entombment.

As if in a dream, Sjhanara stepped forward and gazed into the depths of the ball. She seemed mesmerized and unaware of the man who stood beside her. Bahuraja stepped aside keeping his mind open to any sign of danger to his beloved.

"Nam Myho Renge Kyo", she whispered. Her fingers caressed the case at the sides and over the top, all the while she chanted the words, over and over. Inside, the ball began to glow even brighter.

The other crystals in the room suddenly were silent. Their light dimmed. Finally the only light was from the dais. From the air, other voices from beyond the beyond joined Sjhanara's in the ancient chant.

Bahuraja stood and reveled in Sjhanara's beauty and the mystery of the scene before him. There was no fear, this was as he had ordained so long ago.

There had to be another to release the sword. He had not trusted himself in that other world, yet could only trust one other. His beloved.

The top of the case slowly lifted and rose to several feet above the dais. Sjhanara reached inside and placed her hands beneath the sword near the center. Even though it must have been quite heavy, she lifted the blade as if it had no weight. Turning, she stepped down from the dais and walked to where Bahuraja stood. Kneeling before him, she lifted the sword above her and bowed her head.

"My liege, your sword. The Sword of Sarach. Created by you, for this sphere, for this time. Your Destiny is forged."

Taking the sword from Sjhanara, he held it upward to the ceiling with his left hand and then lifted Sjhanara to stand beside him. As he spoke, his deep voiced words echoed throughout the halls.

"Bahuraja Muebin Sarach of old, your spirit comes forth in this sword to guide me Bahuraja Muebin Sarach of now in this, your created world. Let all know of your greatness and power and love."

The ground began to shudder and quake. Only the spot on which Bahuraja and Sjhanara stood remained solid. The crystals clanged in protest and fell to the floor and into cracks that began to form. The dais on which the couple stood began to rise.

Bahuraja still held the sword aloft. The ball gripped within his palm glowed and sent forth streaks of light in all directions. An envelope of light surrounded them and seemed to protect them from the crashing of the world around them.

Higher and higher they rose, ripping through the false sky beneath the earth; through this rose the tower ever changing - from crystal to black obsidian. The towers and parapets and ramparts forming and the gargoyles and dragons keeping sentinel on every corner seemed to come alive. Their eyes aglow, their teeth bared, their wings flapping. No longer held suspended in waiting, the land burst forth to welcome the coming of their creator.

The phasing that had divided this sphere merged into one and all creatures, both human and other, knew the prophesies of old were now come to pass. All rejoiced at the coming of age of their lord, Bahuraja Muebin Sarach, creator of Arcada, holder of the mighty Sword of Sarach.

THE BINDING

"**O**ld One, I am here", Hadjii's gravelly voice interrupted the loud snoring of the sage.

"Wha...? Oh, yes, yes, Hadjii. I am aware." The ancient mystic stirred in his furs and threw his skinny old legs off the pallet and to the floor. "Just thought I couldst get a few more winks, but I see it is time."

Gazing about the cluttered and blackened cave he had called home for so long, the Old One stood and stretched. "Art all things in order?"

It was barely a question, more like a statement. Nothing ever escaped the knowledge of the ancient.

"Yes, master, you know all." Hadjii sat on a small wooden stool near the fire. "Sjogai is winging his way here at this very moment. All creatures, including all human clans have been notified and travel to the Castle Sarach. Some, including Clan Hajatni, have already arrived."

"Good, good", nodding, the old sage seemed preoccupied. Picking up this vial, that pouch, placing herbs and whatall into his small leather traveling carpa, he began to hum an old tune. Occasionally a word came out. His raspy old voice was far from that of a true singer, but he found comfort in his song. No one but he knew the meaning of his singing, but it had an effect.

The cave room began to shimmer and swirl. The roof of the cave opened and the planets and stars beyond seemed to merge with that within. The doors of the ornate Butsudan near one wall opened and the aged parchment within lifted and emerged to hover before the old one's eyes.

Squinting in the faint light, he began to chant the words that seemed to lift from the page before him. With the sound of each, the words separated from the others and became worlds and galaxies, swirling before him. With the last word chanted, all merged and disappeared into the carpa. The scroll rolled up and without a hand touching it, also joined its predecessors.

Moving toward the stone on the floor that held the lift, Hadjii and the Old One gazed one last time at the cave-home in which they had lived for so long.

A small sigh from Hadjii was the only sound. The Old One never really called any one place home. One was as another to him.

As the stone descended to the ground level, all which had been above disintegrated. The molecular structure changed and dissipated into the atmosphere. By the time the pair emerged from the doorway below, there was only a large rock standing where once the cave-castle had stood.

Sjogai winged to earth as the Old One and Hadjii walked forward onto the grassy plain.

"Good Morrow, Old One. Fine day for a flight, is it not?" Sjogai knew the sage's dislike for flying and loved to tease.

"Humpff! I don't need thy wings to get where I'm going, thou scaly lizard! Watch thy forked tongue or I'll change thee into a thoad."

Sjogai laughed, his sides heaving and steam rising from his wide nostrils. His love for the ancient wizard was strong and this teasing was as much a part of the both of them as eating and sleeping.

Climbing Sjogai's snout to the saddle above his head, the wizard and Hadjii barely had time to settle when the dragon stretched out his wide wings and began to rise once more into the air. The old man and elven held on to the small horned thocks and closed their eyes. Neither wanted to look down at the rapidly disappearing earth below or to the swift passing of the countryside during their flight.

The next day dawned bright and beautiful. The rays from the sun gleamed on the black obsidian walls of the Castle Sarach. On the grounds below, travel tents dotted the area, colorful banners denoting the different clans flying in the breeze. There was a festive air all around. Both human and creature alike were anticipating the great event to take place this day.

The cooking fires emitted wonderful smells and all had donned their finest seshus, hauberks, vests, or whatever passed for native or clan dress. Only the finest materials were selected. All had brought gifts fit for a king and his lady. The whole world of Acarda celebrated the waited event.

A huge shadow temporarily cut out the light as it passed quickly overhead. The people and creatures below lifted their eyes to watch as a huge golden dragon descended to the ground before the doors of the castle.

To their astonishment, two personages climbed down and strode to the doors. Before they entered, however, the tallest of the pair turned and faced the crowd. Despite the distance where some were encamped, they all heard his voice.

"Rejoice! Prepare! This day the Prince becometh King and his destiny claimed. The creator cometh!"

Cheering, the peoples nearly deafened all else with their well wishes. Even the smallest child knew something very special was happening this day.

Entering the castle doors, the Ancient One and Hadjii were greeting by Bahuraja.

"Welcome, Old One, welcome!" Bahuraja embraced the wizard with a hug that nearly broke his old bones.

Hadjii stepped back a pace or two to try to escape his own crushing, but Bahuraja would not allow it. Grabbing the short elven under his arms, Hadjii was lifted up and swung around like a rag doll.

"Hadjii, you old sea dog! How glad I am to again see your ugly face!"

"Best put me down, Bahuraja, or I may not have the strength to stand at your side for the ceremonies." Hadjii's laughing eyes belied the stern face he tried to put forward.

Another figure entered the huge wooden doors to the castle at that moment. Sjogai,in man-form, strode toward Bahuraja and embraced him, placing a kiss on each cheek.

"Welcome to Castle Sarach, Sjogai", Bahuraja embraced his other self with gusto. "I take it the flight was pleasant?"

"You must know that to fly is never other than pleasant, my liege." Pausing slightly after the greeting, Sjogai looked around. "And where is the lovely Sjhanara?"

Bahuraja's face was alight with love at the sound of her name spoken. "She awaits us in her rooms. I have been told by Elvandora, who attends her, that I may not see her until the ceremony."

Turning to the Old One, his question was written on his face. "I assume you know the reasoning."

"But of course, Bahuraja, not only doest thou become king of this realm, but it is not the custom to see thy bride before she is given thee for wife on the day of thy binding."

The heart of the prince leaped within his breast. He knew the lovely Sjhanara and he would be married, but he had not known all would be accomplished on this day of days. He would become king of his own created domain and husband all in the same day. Was this not truly a day of greatness!

"I wouldst see thy intended for a moment, Bahuraja." The old sage began walking towards a large winding staircase. "I will only be a moment and will meet thee at the ceremonial platform without."

At a light tapping at her door, Sjhanara turned from her gazing out her window at the crowds below. Thinking it one of the many servants, she called the command to come in.

Elvandora was hurrying to open the door when in walked the tall impressive figure of the ancient sage.

"Oh!" was all that could escape the young girl's lips.

"You honor us, Ancient One", bowing, Elvandora exited as quickly as possible, knowing the audience with Sjhanara was to be without witness.

"I won't be long, Elvandora", the sage gave her a smile. "I only wish to counsel the future queen of Sarach for a moment."

What a vision stood before his old eyes. With the light of the sun shining through the windows, the woman before him was aglow with beauty; truly the mate for the king. Her regal demeanor was apparent.

"Sjhanara."

The young girl's eyes looked boldly into those of the Old One. She knew who he was and yet was not afraid.

"Yes, my lord."

"Thou knowest this is the day of thy Destiny, Sjhanara?"

"Yes."

"Thy beloved awaits his final Destiny below. Art thou prepared to give him thy life and be a helpmeet to him for time and all Eternity?"

"Yes, oh yes!"

"Then let us not keep Destiny waiting."

Sjhanara put her small soft hand upon the bony, wrinkled palm raised toward her. The vision and the sage exited the room together.

The ceremonial platform stood several feet before the front of the castle. The grounds were covered with beautiful flowering bushes and trees. Every type of flora was represented here. All those gathered for the ceremony could only cover a small part of the grounds, so huge and extensive they were.

Bahuraja, Sjogai and Hadjii arrived at the platform to the cheers of the people. Special places were reserved for the families of Clan Sarach and Clan Hajatni. Tables laden with food and delicacies were set to the left of the crowd. Servants were plying the crowd with large goblets of special wines.

The elven community was already well into their cups and could hardly wait for the ceremony to end so the dancing and selection of a beautiful partner could begin. Elvandora, along with her husband Dorsoro, had been given a special place of honor to observe the ceremonies.

Bahuraja was resplendent. He was clothed in a luxurious white robe, embroidered in red and golden threads. Ancient symbols of his former world were outlined in gold down the center. At his side, the Sword was held suspended from his waist by an intricately carved sheath of gold. The blade, exposed, gleamed. The stone within the hilt was alight with a life of its own; rays occasionally shooting out from it to disappear into the air. If the din of the crowd had not been so intense, one could have heard the Sword's song, a soft humming whose vibrations rose to the cosmos and blended with that of the symphony of the Universe itself.

The Prince, soon to become King, was fully a man now. His facial features were chiseled and strong. The ice-blue eyes emanated wisdom and strength. The body was muscular and tall. There was no doubt in the minds of all that Bahuraja was the long awaited one of the ancient tomes.

Sjogai, standing beside him, was almost a mirrored image of his prince. In facial features there was a striking resemblance, but Sjogai, accepted his place as being as a brother, in a sense. His destiny was that of man-dragon, not the creator. His was to serve his liege in whatever capacity allotted him.

He was resplendent in his own right, however. His garb was of golden hauberk, leggings of spun gold and soft leather foot coverings with hand-sewn beading. Jewels dotted his clothing and sparkled in the sunlight. If gold was to be his main color as a dragon, then gold would be his raiment as a man. He found no harm in assuming this as his proper position and due.

Hadjii, had changed into his finest leather jerkin and leggings. According to his elven clan, they were softened dragon skins of a pale earthen willow-green.

He had his jeweled ceremonial bhalok strapped to his side and his topknot had been braided with small tatha leaves.

A hush came over the crowd as the Ancient One emerged from the castle doors. By his side, the lovely Sjhanara glided toward the podium.

She was dressed in a pure white seshu, that swirled or clung about her breasts and thighs with each step. Tiny seed pearls were sewn around the hem and along the edges with threads of gold. It was a very simple gown, yet its very simplicity made it elegant beyond description. A small golden pin caught at the V where her seshu crossed just slightly below the beginning of her cleavage. A wedding gift from her beloved Bahuraja, it was the shape of his talisman, the Namu. Her hair had been carefully dressed by Elvandora. Braided and wound with more pearls and jewels, it gleamed with golden highlights.

Bahuraja felt his breath catch as he watched this vision move toward him. To become a king and take this woman for his wife the same day was truly from the gods.

The Ancient One raised his hands. The time had come. Beckoning Bahuraja to step forward, the old wizard motioned for him to kneel before him.

"To all Acardadom, witness thy creator! To all, pay homage for thy creation or existence in this world. May he rule with wisdom, kindness, and honor for all his days!"

Opening an ornately carved box the wizard drew forth the large gold chain with the Namu medallion suspended upon it. This he placed around Bahuraja's neck. "This, thy talisman, the Namu, was cherished by thy other self in thy old world. It stands for honor, strength, and sacrifice. Wear it in honor and pride, Bahuraja, for its very presence will bring forth power."

From within his robes, the Old One brought forth a crown. Wrought in gold, the crown resembled a Namu whose spreading wings circled round from front to back to form the headpiece. A large perfect diamond was the eye. As soon as the light from the sun shown upon it, the facets sent forth a blinding array of brilliant colors. The golden feathers of the band were carved with ancient symbols and design. Where the wings came together in the back, the tips held a large Amethyst.

Placing the crown on Bahuraja's head, he began chanting in a language known only to himself.

As the words were spoken, Time was suspended. All was wrapped in swirling threads of the stuff universes were made of. When the words ceased, no one doubted that this was more than the crowning of just any king. The medallion the other Bahuraja had fashioned and worn in his former world glowed in testimony.

Stepping to one side, the Old One motioned for the new king to rise. "Arise, Bahuraja Muebin Sarach, King of Acarda. Greet thy subjects!"

He presented Bahuraja to the crowd who cheered and waved banners. His parents, sitting just below him, were slightly in awe of their son, but proud. His mother, tears streaming down her still beautiful face, felt that all the mystery now had meaning. She had given birth to the creator - the King. Within her womb had grown the entity from another time. What blessings had been bestowed upon her to be given such an honor.

Bahuraja's father, could only be more proud of his son. All that had been given him he had tried to teach his son. He had always felt Bahuraja was special and now it was proven. What more could a man ask than to have been the father of such a son?

Again, the Old One raised his hand. "Praise be given to King Bahuraja, creator of Acarda and all within!"

The crowd filled the air with a deafening roar of cheers and their approval of the new king.

The Old One motioned the crowd to silence. Turning to Sjhanara, he motioned her to step to Bahuraja's side. Sjogai moved to the left of his brother. The Ancient One looked down to Sjhanara's father, who arose and approached the steps of the platform to climb to the right side of his daughter.

"As the father of Sjhanara Yagenta Hajatni, doest thou consent to the binding of thy daughter to that of the creator and king of Acarda, Bahuraja Muebin Sarach?"

"It is the honor of the Clan Hajatni that our fairest daughter who has proven herself worthy by the Test of the Zandorn to be chosen by our creator and king. With pride, her mother and I willingly give Sjhanara to be the bride of King Bahuraja Muebin Sarach!"

Taking her hand within his own, Janor gave it a squeeze. Looking into her eyes, he smiled, then kissed her cheek. "Daughter, you have given this old man much in this life. Go to your husband with all the Clan's blessings, but especially your mother's and mine." Placing her hand within Bahuraja's, Janor returned to sit beside his wife whose tears were begun anew.

"Bahuraja Muebin Sarach, doest thou take Sjhanara Yagenta Hajatni to be thy wife and queen for Time and all Eternity?

"I will."

"Wilt thou honor her in all things, provide for her and give your protection to her in times of need?"

"I will."

"Sjhanara Yagenta Hajatni, doest thou take the King, Bahuraja Muebin Sarach to be thy husband and king for Time and all Eternity?"

"I will."

"Wilt thou honor thy husband and king in all things and be a helpmate to him in times of need?"

"I will."

Taking a small blade from within the folds of his volumous robe, the Old One made a small slice to the palms of both man and woman before him. Placing their palms together, he wrapped a braided golden cord around their hands. Then, having the couple kneel and placing his right hand upon their heads, he canted an ancient blessing.

"As the blood flows and mingles with that of the other, thou becometh as one in the mind and the flesh. Merge thy minds as one. One thought, one flesh, one purpose."

Motioning them to rise, one more ceremony was performed. Another crown appeared in the Old One's hand, this one a smaller version of the one adorning the head of Bahuraja. The eye of Namu was a jewel of amethyst sparkling at its center.

Placing it upon Sjhanara's head, he spoke his final words. "With this crown I name thee Queen Sjhanara Yagenta Sarach, wife to King Bahuraja Muebin Sarach, of the Clan Sarach, Creator of Acarda, and all who dwell upon this planet. May thy loins bear many children and bless the house Sarach!"

Bahuraja looked deeply into the eyes of his wife. Without taking his eyes from hers, he reached his left hand to Sjogai, the man-dragon, who handed him a small band intricately carved with mystic symbols.

Taking her left hand, he placed the band on her fourth finger. Then he placed a long lingering kiss upon her lips. Two hearts beating in love and two minds blended in perfect harmony seemed to turn the universe upside down.

When he finally took his lips from those of his wife's, he whispered, "No turning back now, my lamaish".

"No desire to, my king, my husband."

Turning to the crowd he spoke his first words as king. "Behold thy King! Behold the King's wife Sjhanara! Long live the people and all who dwell in Acarda! Let the celebration begin!"

Any more words were drowned out by the cheers and well-wishes of the people. The wine began to flow, songsters sang newly created songs to record the great event, the flutes and stringed instruments were unsheathed and tuned for the dancing. Not one creature on the planet Acarda would escape the joy and happiness of this celebration.

Bahuraja led his beautiful Sjhanara to the center of the dancing ring. Taking her into his arms, he began the Dance of the Wedding. Looking only into her eyes, he boldly swung her up into the air, then crushed her to him as he kissed her soundly before continuing the steps to the dance.. As they twirled and stepped to the music, others joined them in the dance. Soon the ring was full of twirling, kissing, hugging, and more than slightly inebriated celebrants.

Occasionally a couple would suddenly dash from the circle of dancers to rush into the darkness. One sidelines guest made the observation that come nine-month, there would be a large crop of new babes born.

Long before the celebrating ended, but well into the night, the newly married couple stole away to their wedding chamber. King and Queen they might be, but for now, they just wanted to be alone together as man and wife. As Bahuraja slipped the soft fabric of her wedding seshu from his wife's shoulders, and she opened his ornate robe, the two who stood before each other and who walked toward the decorated wedding bed were just two people much in love.

The richly embroidered coverlet and finely woven sheets had been turned down. Crushed fresh and aromatic petals of red rosebells were sprinkled liberally between the sheets. This was the gift of an ancient tradition of the elvens which signified the blessing of children from the lovemaking.

As they confirmed their vows with their physical union, the symphony of the Universe regained even more of a melodious harmony.

The world of Acarda was now permanently set in the space of Time. No one really noticed the bent skinny form of the Old One as he left the podium and silently strode away from the celebration. He had given his final instructions to Hadjii and knew they would be carried out without question. He had other worlds to govern. Other galaxies to record. As he walked, a swirling mist formed and surrounded him. When it dissipated, the Old One was gone.

FINI